JUDGE DREDD

A novel by **NEAL BARRETT, JR.**
Based on the screenplay by
WILLIAM WISHER and **STEVEN E. DE SOUZA**

SMP

ST. MARTIN'S PAPERBACKS

NOTE: If you purchased this book without a cover you should be aware that this book is stolen property. It was reported as "unsold and destroyed" to the publisher, and neither the author nor the publisher has received any payment for this "stripped book."

Published by arrangement with Cinergi Pictures Entertainment Inc. and Cinergi Productions N.V. Inc.

First published in Great Britain in 1995 by Boxtree Ltd.

JUDGE DREDD

Distributed by Buena Vista Pictures Distribution, Inc.

Copyright © 1995 Cinergi Pictures Entertainment Inc. and Cinergi Productions N.V. Inc. All rights reserved.

Cover photograph by Terry O'Neill.

All rights reserved. No part of this book may be used or reproduced in any manner whatsoever without written permission except in the case of brief quotations embodied in critical articles or reviews. For information address St. Martin's Press, 175 Fifth Avenue, New York, N.Y. 10010.

ISBN: 0-312-95628-2

Printed in the United States of America

St. Martin's Paperbacks edition / June 1995

10 9 8 7 6 5 4 3 2 1

In the Third Millennium, the world changed. Climate . . . Nations . . . all were in upheaval. Humanity itself turned as violent as the planet. Civilization threatened to collapse.

And then, a solution was found. The crumbling legal system was merged with the overburdened police, creating a powerful and efficient force for the People. These new guardians of Society were given the power to dispense both justice and punishment. They were police, jury and executioner. They were . . .

. . . the Judges.

—History of the Mega-Cities
James Olmeyer, III
Chapter II: "Justice"
2191

ONE

YEAR 2139:
"JUDGE DREDD"

Herman Ferguson ran as fast as he could.

Fergie had been running all his life. Running from his father, from his brothers, from the law. From outraged victims of this scam or that. Now the streets were full of blood, and he was running again. He shut out the howls of the dying and the rattle of gunfire and didn't look back. Lead stitched the side of the building, pitting the grimy brick wall. Fergie wrapped his hands around his head as razor-sharp shards of stone stung his neck and sliced his cheek.

He ducked into the alcove and slammed his hands flat against the rusty metal door, praying it wasn't locked. The door issued one protesting squeal and gave way. The stink in the entry was strong enough to gag a goat. The floor was ankle-deep with garbage, broken bricks, old foodpods, and several items Fergie didn't care to think about.

The elevator shaft was a black and open wound. Fergie headed up the stairs. He glanced once more at the address on his card:

RED QUAD
BLOCK Y

HEAVENLY HAVEN
SUITE 666

The stairway was worse than the hall downstairs. He stepped on something that squealed. Something darted up the sooty wall.

Fergie gasped for breath as he passed the second floor. Aspen Prison offered cons athletics, but he didn't have the physical bearing or the right attitude to be a jock.

He rested on four. Took it easy up to five, and ran up to six. The hall was empty except for trash. The building was old as Time. The thick walls sucked up every sound. If gunfire still raked the streets, the noise couldn't reach him up here.

Garbage shifted down the hallway to his right. Fergie went flat against the wall. A battered foodkart rounded the corner and headed his way. Its wheels were out of line, and it wobbled like his father used to do when he tried to find his way back home.

"Delicious and healthful rationpaks,
piping hot and ready to eat . . .
delicious and healthful rationpaks,
piping hot and re——"

Fergie stepped out of its way. He passed number 662 . . . 664 . . .

Number 666 was a door smeared with the usual unintelligible graffiti, but Fergie didn't care about that. Instead, he felt a great sense of relief. He hadn't actually been *alone* for six months—no space, no privacy, just a couple of thousand mean, hairy sons of bitches who'd kick you to death for entertainment, or slide a rusty shiv into your heart.

"All *right,*" Fergie said. "The Fergie is *home,* the old Fergo is *by himself!*"

He turned the knob and stepped inside. A man with a

scar-covered face and purple ears jammed a pistol up
Fergie's nose.

"Hey-*hey*, what we gots here? You a Judge *spy*, little
man? 'Zat what you bes, you bes a muckin' *spy?*"

Fergie blinked and stepped back. There were two
other men in the room. They howled with laughter at
Purple Ears' remark. They'd never heard anything fun-
nier in their lives. They stood by an open window. They
gripped enormous weapons in their hands. Now Fergie
could hear the crowd below. Weapons. Window. Crowd.
Fergie felt the hair creep up his neck. All the slaughter
down there was coming from here. In 666. In *his* room,
which he didn't really want any more.

"All *right,*" Fergie said, "I'll tell you what, I can see
what's happening here. What it is, I got the wrong room.
Hell, I probably got the wrong *building,* you know? I am
always doing that." He grinned at the three maniacs. "So
I'll just run along, I'll leave you guys to your—"

"You *hold* it, droog." Purple Ears stepped in his path.
"You don't bes goin' anywheres, okay? You *hear* 'em
down there? It's a *block war,* man!"

Purple Ears' companions cheered. One had two rows
of shiny hyponeedle teeth. The other wore a metal jacket
he'd made from tin cans. A dead mouse hung from the
lobe of each ear.

"Yeah," said Needle Teeth, "if you l-live here, if you're
a R-R-Rezzie, you gotta stand up fer your block."

"You gotta," Metal Jacket added. "You don't and
you're a—"

"—a *neek,*" Purple Ears finished.

"Yeah, you don't, you're a n-neek."

"That sounds bad," Fergie said.

"It is, man."

Metal Jacket grinned and pointed a dirty finger at
Fergie's chest. "He don' look like no Judge spy to me. I
don' guess he bein' big enough for that."

"Or *smart* 'nough, neither," Purple Ears said. He

winked at Needle Teeth. Needle Teeth showed Fergie a hideous grin. Fergie noticed the deep scars that covered Purple Ears' face were actually words—two words carved over and over again, words that Fergie wouldn't want his mother or his sisters to see. He wondered if Purple Ears had any idea that both of the words were misspelled. Fergie had no intention of being the one to break the news.

"Let's go, Haven!" Metal Jacket shouted out the window. "Heaven-ly Ha-ven, all the *way!*"

Needle Teeth gave a blood-curdling cry and loosed a burst of automatic fire into the crowd down below. Smoke filled the room and empty cartridges rattled on the floor.

"Hey, you guys, stop that!" Fergie was appalled. "You're *killin'* people down there!"

"Yeah, you noticed, huh?" Purple Ears grinned and snapped off a dozen rounds with his automatic pistol. *"Block* war! *Block* war! Pour it on 'em, droogs!"

Metal Jacket joined in. The noise of his big black-and-copper weapon ripped through Fergie's head. It was loud —but not loud enough to drown out the screams from far below.

"Damn it, you got to stop this," Fergie cried out. "I'm on *parole.* They catch me with you morons my ass is back in Aspen again!"

No one could hear him. Fergie knew he had to do something. People were getting slaughtered down there, and though he didn't really know his new neighbors that well, blowing them all to hell was the wrong thing to do —especially if the Judges blamed him for having a bunch of crazies in his room, and with his luck, that's exactly what they'd do.

Fergie threw himself at Purple Ears and grabbed for his gun. A small voice told him it was a stupid thing to do. And, as it always seemed to happen, the small voice warned him half a second late. Purple Ears turned and looked at Fergie swinging on his arm, looked at him like he couldn't believe this stupid neek was there. Then he whipped the butt of his pistol around and whacked Fergie firmly on the jaw. . . .

TWO

It was close to sunset outside, but it was always high noon in the harshly-lit corridors of Mega-City's Hall of Justice. The building was a towering fortress made of rough black granite that seemed to eat the light. The familiar shield and eagle of the Judges was carved in massive relief above the outside entryway.

Few ordinary citizens ever passed through these doors. Fewer still got beyond the high-security area of the first floor. And *none* of them ever reached the heights of the Hall of Justice, or penetrated its depths, which plunged thirty stories below the street. At least, that was the number the Judges allowed to leak to the curious public. There were secrets in this building only a handful of people ever knew.

It was exactly 1847 hours when Judge Hershey left Locker Room G and walked down the narrow rampway to Level Seventeen, her black helmet tucked beneath her arm. Rookies stopped and saluted as she passed. Tekkies and office personnel nodded in respect and stepped out of her way. A few seasoned Street Judges looked her up and down, but only after she'd safely passed by.

Judge Hershey's eyes were dark and wide-set, her skin slick as satin and perfectly clear. Her black hair was cut

nearly as short as a man's. A curl formed a perfect half-
moon on either cheek, her only concession to fashion
and her sex.

Not that anyone had ever mistaken her for a man.
Though Hershey was dressed in the standard, beetle-
black armor, gauntlets, and boots of a Judge, no one with
normal vision would make a mistake like that. She was
trained, disciplined, and quick as death, or she would
never have earned the eagle-and-shield badge molded in
copper and chrome across her breast. Still, it was clear
there was more to Hershey than impact plastic and steel.
Every male Judge could see that, though no one among
them could truthfully say they knew she was a woman for
sure. A hopeful rumor was whispered now and then, but
none of them were true.

Armorglass doors slid aside with a sigh, and Hershey
walked into the vast, curved tunnel that was the heart of
the Street Judge's life. The thunder of engines echoed
off the concrete walls. The deep, throaty roar was more
than just a sound, it was a living force that rose up
through Hershey's boots, rippled through her belly, and
spread like a tremor of the earth into her arms and legs.

She had never discussed this effect with the other
Judges—it would have been a sign of emotional weak-
ness to do so—but she was certain hers was a feeling
shared by any man or woman who had ever walked into
Level Seventeen among a hundred gleaming Lawmasters
growling like metal beasts, crouched and waiting to come
alive at the hands of their keepers.

If there was a more powerful, awesome machine in the
world, Hershey couldn't imagine what it might be. A
lawman from the twentieth century would recognize the
basic motorcycle shape, but the resemblance ended
there. These squat, black monsters were incredibly dura-
ble, lightning-fast killing machines a hundred generations removed from their ancestors of the world of Way

Back When—and nearly as deadly as the peace officers who rode them through the streets of Mega-City now.

Hershey spotted Rookie Briscoe on the far end of the line of machines. It was 1852 hours, eight minutes until the shift change at 1900, and the tunnel was filled with armor-clad Judges and red-sleeved maintenance personnel. Hershey checked her helmet, saw all the points of light on her visor wink emerald-green, started for Briscoe, then stepped back to let a Lawmaster pass.

"Judge! Judge Hershey!"

Hershey recognized the voice, hurried her step, and pretended not to hear.

"Judge—ma'am . . ."

Hershey stopped abruptly and wheeled around.

"Olmeyer! If you have read *Manners and Conventions,* Article Seven, you will be aware of the fact that there is no such thing as a *ma'am.* Ma'am is a gender title, Cadet. All Judges are addressed as *Judge.* They are not, I repeat, *not* addressed as sir, ma'am, miss, it, or any other discriminatory word or phrase. Do you *read* me, Cadet?"

"Yes, ma—yes, *Judge!*"

"Fine. Now what do you want? I'm on duty in forty-two seconds."

Olmeyer backed off. His throat went suddenly dry. It always happened when he spoke to Judge Hershey. He couldn't look her straight in the eye. If he did, she took his breath away and scared him to death at the same time. So he did what he usually did, which was gaze at the tunnel ceiling, as if he were searching for flies.

"I was, uh, wondering if you'd had a chance to think about what I—"

"No. Forget it, Olmeyer." Hershey's eyes were black as winter ice. "I am *not* interested. You will not speak of this again."

"It's—it's for the yearbook, Judge. It's classic poses is all. It's not some Way Back When p-porno centerfold or anyth—"

"Olmeyer . . ."

Hershey leaned down, cocked one gloved finger and aimed it directly between his eyes. "Olmeyer, I *know* what it is. Don't *tell* me what it is. And if you mention this again I will fry your fat head and eat it. Am I getting *through* to you, Cadet?"

"Yes, Judge."

"I can't *hear* you."

"YES, JUDGE!"

Hershey glared at him hard enough to kill a house-plant, then turned and marched away. She felt the heat rise to her face and jammed the helmet on her head. The helmet offered more than protection from criminals on the street; no one could read you if they couldn't see your face.

Briscoe was standing by his Lawmaster. He'd seen the exchange between Judge Hershey and Olmeyer, but hadn't been close enough to guess what it had all been about. He didn't really care. Anything Judge Hershey did, thought, or said was fine with him. He had dreams about Hershey he wouldn't even tell his best friend Miguel. It frightened him to even think about things like that. If he ever had to do a Truth Session, he'd take the killpill before he let them know what was churning through his head.

"Nice evening, Judge," he said. "I hope that little droog didn't bother you any. Cadets are sure a pain in th—"

"Shut up, Briscoe." Hershey gave him a chilly look. "A Cadet is lower than a slug's belly, and a *Rookie* is a quarter inch higher than that. You read me clear?"

"Yes, Judge!"

"Good. Excellent, Briscoe. Now pay attention and get your act together. The citizens aren't paying you to look nice in your new black suit. Straddle that mother and find me some crime!"

THREE

*T*he bench was hard as stone and the sound of the shuttle droned in Fergie's head. The sound nearly put him to sleep, but Fergie knew better than that. A couple of cons had dozed off, then woke up yelling as the hot metal scorched their backs raw. The hull had been shielded when the craft was brand new, but it was far from new now.

Iron sweat dripped from the rusting pipes overhead. The air-recycler had blown on liftoff and the stench was unbearable in the hold. There were thirty-seven cons, cramped together on either side of the narrow aisle. No one was shackled. You could get up, move around, do whatever you wanted to.

"If you groons are crazy enough to kill each other on the way back home, then have at it, boys," the guard said.

The con on Fergie's left had a deep and deadly cough. The man on his right had a silver-plated leg. Fergie had heard of the guy but had never actually seen him before. His name was Jimmy Eyes, and he'd spent twenty years in Aspen Prison etching the leg with acid he'd stolen from the metalwork shop. He had done the whole thing with a magnifying glass. Unless you had a glass, all you could see on the leg were squiggly little lines. Strongly magnified, you could see the screaming faces of the 887 people Jimmy Eyes had killed. He had driven his airbus into a power pole at three hundred-plus. No one but Jimmy got out. Everyone else was squashed flat or burned alive. A drug test showed Jimmy Eyes was bombed out on Triple Zetamine at the time.

After Jimmy finished his art—which everyone said was real fine for a man with no training at all—Jimmy took his etching acid and poured it into his eyes.

Fergie felt like a real nobody with cons like Jimmy Eyes and some of the other hardguys around. He recognized the Butcher from the paper hat he never removed from his head. The Lizard himself was supposed to be aboard. Everyone said he was a small, ordinary man, the kind you'd never notice in a crowd. Fergie shuddered at the thought. There was nothing ordinary about the Lizard, or what the Lizard had done.

Fergie knew he was small time, and that was fine with him. He had always made a real good living with a scam, and they'd only caught him once. Six lousy, miserable months, but he'd made it to the end in one piece, and he sure as hell wouldn't let the Judges catch him cold like that again.

Fergie was certain he felt a change in the shuttle's engines again. Maybe they were finally coming down. Or maybe the ancient crate had simply given out and they were plummeting to the ground.

There was no way to tell, no way to look out. And even if you could, there was nothing there to see. Nothing but the Big CE, the Cursed Earth itself. Death and desolation where nothing ever grew, where no one but a scrawny Dusteater could live, if you called that being alive. There was nothing else down there but the dry, hot winds that swept across the continent for three-thousand terrible miles. The winds, and one thing worse than that: Giant tornadoes that stalked the arid plains and sucked the earth dry—black, roaring funnels older than any man alive. Some people said that they weren't simply weather anymore, like they were in the Way Back When. Now, they said, they were really alive, creatures as cunning as man himself.

That was just Dusteater talk, Fergie knew. Except he had seen one once from far away, on an Aspen Prison work detail. Now, he could no longer swear that the poor souls cast out upon the Cursed Earth weren't right.

The shuttle tilted on its side, squeezing the seatbelt hard against his belly as the big engine started whining down. Where? Fergie wondered. Mega-City, most likely. They hardly sent anyone down to Tex-City anymore, and they *never* sent you back to the place where you'd committed your crime.

Fergie had tried to put that thought out of his mind for six months. He would never see LA again. Maggie, Bix and Gant—as far as he was concerned, they might as well be on Mars.

Okay, that's that, put it out of your head. There are guys you can work with everywhere, and there's plenty of Maggies out there.

Bix and Gant, right. But another Maggie, she wouldn't be that easy to find . . .

No one was talking now. He knew what the other cons were thinking. That's what he was thinking, too. Maybe they'd change their minds. Maybe they'd send him back. Judges could do that. Every man who'd ever been caught knew the Judges could do whatever they wanted.

He could hear the massive lock-gate grind, then thunder shut again as the shuttle passed through. Metal squealed, and the giant craft settled to the ground. The portal hummed, then opened like a massive steel eye. Fresh air filled the hold. The afternoon light was harsh after hours in the gloomy bowels of the ship. The cons opened their mouths up wide and shut their eyes.

"The Aspen Prison Shuttle has docked. Commence anti-contamination procedures at once . . . Parol-

ees will disembark from Portal One-Niner now . . .
You will maintain a single line. You will proceed in an
orderly fashion to the assembly point outside . . ."

The voice grated from the antique speaker overhead.
It sounded like gravel in a can. The cons stood and did as
they were told. Fergie choked as he walked through the
disinfectant spray. Whatever it was, he was certain it
would kill anything inside a man or out.

When he blinked the sting away, he could see he'd
guessed right. It was Mega-City, there was no mistaking
that. The massive wall they'd just passed through was
easily half a mile high. Ahead, he saw the awesome city
itself, the silver-gray structures rising up abruptly, shut-
ting out the sun, the great spires lost in the clouds twenty
thousand feet above. Crowded skyways curled like graceful ribbons among the heights.

And, nearly out of sight, he could see the flying barges
and shuttles speeding people and goods to those rich
enough to live in the sparkling city towers. Fergie knew
the rules. It was the same in LA. The mighty live high,
and the droogs live low.

Videos didn't do the city justice. It was bigger,
grander, more terrifying than Fergie had ever imagined.
LA was big—but not big like *this*. He had a momentary
vision of a million iron swords, blades rising up north and
south as far as the eye could see. And to make the image
complete, the sun dipped beneath the city wall, turning
the sharp planes of the city blood red . . .

FOUR

*T*he thin blanket was spread in the corner on the hard plastic floor. The room was totally dark. He lay perfectly still, feet together and arms at his sides. The temperature was set at forty-four degrees. Though he wore no clothes, the cold didn't bother him at all. Heat and cold were subjects he never thought about.

He knew other people were concerned with such things—they liked to be comfortable, they liked to eat and sleep. He did not understand these feelings. Sleeping and eating were necessary for the continuance of life. Like breathing and pumping fresh blood from the heart. These were not pleasures, they were actions of the body. Some were automatic. Others were performed with intent.

He did not discuss these thoughts with the people he knew. He did not ask himself why he didn't feel like everyone else. What difference did it make? What people did was important. Not what they thought. People could think about anything they liked. There were *Laws* that governed what they did.

Drawing himself erect, he began the set of exercises he performed every day. It was a hard, rigid routine, one that pushed his body to its limits, took him to the fine, exquisite edge of pain, and sometimes far beyond.

When he was done, he walked across the small room in the dark and stepped into the shower stall. Needle sprays at thirty-four degrees assaulted him from the walls, the ceiling and the floor. The shower lasted exactly three minutes, then the fans clicked on and blew him dry.

Back in his room, he punched on the harsh ceiling light. His few possessions were in a drawer built in the wall. A food dispenser was just above the drawer. There was nothing else in the room. No table or chairs. No video screen, no music, no books. Nothing but the blanket on the floor. The room was eight by ten. His position entitled him to much better quarters. He didn't understand why anyone would need more than this. What for? No one ever came here but him. He didn't know why people went to other people's rooms, but they did.

He wasn't hungry, but he ate. He punched the green button that would send him the proper daily nourishment for his age, sex, and current health assessment. The food dispenser blinked, and his meal popped out. The pellets were compressed into the shape of a chocolate bar. The color keys were off, and the chocolate bar was blue. It didn't taste like anything at all.

He dressed quickly and quietly in skin-tight black underwear. There was a clock set in the wall but he never looked at that. He always knew what he had to do. He always knew when. His only regret in life was that his body required these minimal periods of rest, refueling, and care. It was four hours wasted every day. *They* were always out there, whether he was on the job or not. There were thousands of them—the killers, the rapers, the druggos-belly-gutters-head-hackers-sex-choppers, and the screaming maniacs.

In a rare display of emotion, he clenched his fists and let a cry of rage escape his lips. It wasn't anger at them—he had no feelings at all about the citizens of Mega-City who broke the Law. When they crossed that fine line, they were subject to arrest, judgement, imprisonment, or instant execution, depending on their crime. It was his job, his duty, his purpose in life to see that these actions were properly done.

The fury he felt was not for them but for himself—for the hours he was not allowed to do his job, for the crimes being committed *at that very moment* he didn't know about—and, though they were few—for the times he had pursued a lawbreaker and failed. Each day he promised himself he would push himself harder, that he would bring the cause of justice another step closer to the goal he knew was impossible to reach. Most of all, he promised himself that he would *never* fail again.

He drew the shutters back from the one narrow window in the room. The sun had disappeared behind the great wall in the west. The galaxy of Mega-City sparkled like a hundred-million stars. He turned away and faced the wall. He pressed his palm against the black plate of carbon and a panel slid away. The armored suit was black as space, so black it seemed to drink in all the light. The heavy gauntlets lay on a shelf. His boots were on the floor. Resting in its holster was the Lawgiver, the deadliest handgun in the world. In the left boot was a blue-steel knife. In the belt of the dark armored suit was a daystick and a cluster of studded mini-grenades. A visored helmet hung just above the collar of the suit.

On the left breast of the armor was a shield-and-eagle badge. Every Judge in Mega-City wore one, from the Street Judge to those trusted few who sat in the high, vaulted chambers of the Hall of Justice. Every badge was the same, and each was engraved with the name of the Judge who had earned it, and sworn to wear it proudly for life. The blood-bones, the clutchers, and the slicers feared every Judge in Mega-City, every chrome-and-copper badge. And every scummer who prowled the dark belly of the city prayed that *he* would be the one that fired the bullet that pierced the badge that bore the name of Dredd . . .

FIVE

"**M**ove along, damn you, I ain't got all day!"

Fergie took a short step. The line shuffled forward. Glancing over his shoulder, he could see the broad curve of the shuttle's hull. Like the cons it had carried, the shuttle had gotten its cleansing spray as well. Fingers of dirt dripped down its eroded sides. Nearly-faded letters on the side read:

MEGA-CITY JUDGE SYSTEM: ASPEN PRISON SHUTTLE # THREE

I hope to hell I never see your ugly self again, Fergie thought to himself.

"Next," the guard said.

He stuck his right hand into the blinking red slot. The robot sensor whirred, then winked at him in green.

"Ferguson, Herman, ASP-niner-zero-zero-seven-six-four . . . Sentence served: Six months, three days. Welcome back, Cit-i-zen . . ."

"Thanks," Fergie said.

The robot didn't answer back. It made a bleeting sound, and flipped him a blue plastic card. The card showed Fergie's face the day he'd entered prison. That was not a good day. He decided he looked better now.

He walked through a gate. He looked down at the

ground. He waited for someone to tell him what to do. It struck him, then, and the thought nearly brought him to his knees. There was no one watching, no one telling him where to go, no one telling him what to do. He was free. He didn't *feel* free, but he'd be damned if he let that hold him back.

The back of his card read:

LIVING ASSIGNMENT:
RED QUAD
BLOCK Y
"HEAVENLY HAVEN"
SUITE 666

"Sounds great," Fergie said aloud. "Better than where I've been."

A passerby saw him talking to himself. He glanced at Fergie's prison-issue clothes, gave him a sour look, and hurried on. The man's face was painted half cobalt-blue, half Chinese-red. His hair was coiled in a pile atop his head and tied with razor wire. It was impossible to guess the current fashion trend. Everyone he passed looked totally different from the person who'd passed before.

Poking his card in an infoslot led him to the Skycab station that would take him to the Red Quad sector, some sixty miles away. He hadn't seen a woman on the street—or if he had, he didn't recognize them as such. The Skycab ride made up for that. The great towers of Mega-City swept by below, but Fergie hardly noticed the sight. As the Skycab veered sharply to the left, he glanced down and saw a dazzling blue rooftop pool. Under a brightly-striped umbrella were three young women, standing and laughing by themselves. All of them were lean and impossibly tall. All of them had bright scarlet mouths and silver eyes. They wore their thick raven hair down to their thighs, and little else.

Fergie felt a knot in his stomach. He wanted to cry. He

wanted to follow the women wherever they planned to go. One of the cons in the electronics shop had patched together a VIRG program, a Virtual Reality Girl. It tended to overload. Several prisoners burned out their skulls before the guards found the thing and hauled it away.

The Skycab set him down on a pleasant street. Fergie stood and stared at the breathtaking sight before his eyes. There was a shady green path winding through a forest of thick-boled trees. Sunlight filtered through the branches to sparkle in a gentle waterfall. Couples strolled hand in hand. Children chased each other across the lush lawn.

The scene brought a smile to Fergie's face. *Man, can these frigs possibly be as dumb as they look?*

New variations on old schemes danced through his head. The platinum-brick routine, the antique-Coke bottle scam. These groons mooning in the park would buy a sackful of spiders if they thought they could get them half-price.

"Wonderful," Fergie said aloud. "Herman Ferguson loves Heavenly Haven. Herman Ferguson is going to fit right in!"

". . . coming soon, Citizens, the Heavenly Haven Pocket Park. Bringing fresh air and recreation to your lives. Another design for better living from the Mega-City Council . . ."

Fergie blinked, startled by the kindly, sonorous voice that seemed to come from everywhere. It was a warm, commanding voice, a voice you knew you could trust.

"—ming soon, Citizens, the Heavenly Haven Pocket Park. Bringing fresh air and . . ."

Heavenly Haven Pocket Park suddenly disappeared. Fergie stared at a dirty, graffiti-covered wall and felt the color rise to his face. Six months in Aspen and he'd let himself be conned by a damn holo poster!

"I gotta get with it," he said, shaking his head. "I got to get straight before some scammer starts sellin' *me* spiders . . ."

With the holo poster gone, Heavenly Haven didn't look all that terrific anymore. Dark, skeletal tenements formed brooding canyon walls on every side. Citizens scurried through the murky streets. This part of the city was obviously incredibly old. Reminders of the Way Back When were squeezed between the tenement walls. Fergie saw a row of marble columns that held up nothing at all. Something that might have been a twentieth-century church was imbedded in a bleak slab of stone. Swallowed by the years, its brick entry surfaced now and then like the bones of some long-dead creature buried in a geologic fault.

Just to his right, half-covered by a tenement that rose out of sight, Fergie made out the remains of a statue from the very distant past. The metal was eroded and green. Half the face of a woman was left, and one raised arm. Whatever it was, time and pollution had taken its toll, and it was nearly rotted out and gone.

Fergie checked his directions again. There were no street signs. Nothing that said Red Quad or anything else. He spotted a fly-specked window, half a block away. A faded sign read: NICKO'S. He decided it was better than nothing, crossed the street, and stepped inside. There was a bar and a dirty wooden floor. A flickering bulb hung from a frayed electrical cord. There was no one in the place except the man behind the bar.

"Ah, you got a beer?" Fergie said. "Okay if I come in?"

"You got a card?"

"Of course I got a card. Everybody's got a card."

Fergie slapped his card on the bar. The bartender had half a steel face and two ruby-cut eyes. A cheek tattoo said he was a veteran of some obscure war.

Fergie quickly downed his first beer in six months. He closed his eyes and let his taste buds come back to life.

"How long you been out?"

Fergie didn't bother to lie. "An hour and a half. Aspen Shuttle Three."

"You want another one of those?"

"What do you think?"

The bartender slid another beer Fergie's way and pushed his card into a slot. Fergie wondered how much they'd put in his account. You got some pitiful amount when they let you out of the joint. It couldn't be much. He figured he'd have to get a scam going pretty fast.

"Since you know where I come from, maybe you can tell me where I am," Fergie said. "I've got a room in Heavenly Haven. Where they're going to do the park—"

"You're in it, pal." The bartender jerked a dirty thumb straight up. "Heavenly Haven. Looks a lot like Celestial Heights and Paradise Woods, only it ain't." The bartender grinned, showing moldy teeth. "Nice, huh? Welcome to the neighborhood."

Fergie shrugged. "Beats hell out of Aspen Prison."

"Yeah? That's 'cause you just got here, friend."

The day was nearly gone. Old-fashioned lampposts shed amber pools of light on the pot-holed streets. Far above the dark walls, the heights of Mega-City shimmered bright as day.

As he stepped out of Nicko's, Fergie heard the sound. It was a deep, angry drone, and it echoed off the tenement walls. Fergie walked back the way he'd come. Turning the corner, he walked right into the crowd. They were boiling out of every building, shouting and waving their fists. He backed against a wall and let them by. He had seen one riot in Aspen Prison and he didn't want to see one again.

Everyone was running south. Fergie followed a comfortable distance behind the crowd. They were throwing rocks and bottles at the wall where the holo of Heavenly Haven Pocket Park had been. The holo was different now. It showed a great shining building, stretching to the skies. The golden shield and eagle of the Judges was superimposed on the image, glowing in a painted blue sky. He could hear the booming voice, even over the anger of the crowd:

". . . *Coming soon, the Heavenly Haven Law Enforcement Barracks,. bringing surveillance and security to your lives. Another design for better living from the Mega-City Council . . . Coming soon, the Heavenly Have—*"

A stone shattered a window past the holo. A woman beat at the image with the leg of a chair.

"They stole our park!"

"Damn them all!"

"Lying bastards!"

"*Stinkin' lying Judges!*"

The crowd swept forward in a wave, a dark and ugly beast with half a thousand heads. They tossed bricks and stones, and tore at the empty air with their hands. A lamppost snapped, and a bright electric arc crackled along the street. A Citizen jerked in a crazy dance and fell.

And that was the moment the weapons opened up on the crowded streets below. Men and women screamed. Lead ripped flesh and bone. Heads exploded and limbs tore away. A river of blood spattered the dark and grimy walls, and Herman Ferguson, ASP-niner-zero-zero-seven-six-four, peed in his prison-issue trousers and ran like hell . . .

It is difficult to imagine that even in the late twentieth century our nation was still paralyzed by a primitive, ineffective system of Justice. In those times, the trial of an accused criminal was often delayed for months, even years. In some cases, the accused was allowed to roam free prior to his trial, enabling him to commit further crimes before being judged for the first.

To add to this bizarre practice, the accused was allowed to hire a professional trained for the sole purpose of confusing the issue through any means possible, in order to set the accused free. This was not an overly difficult task, since accused persons were judged before a "jury of their peers"—that is, ordinary Citizens picked at random who had absolutely no knowledge of the legal system of the times.*

It is little wonder, then, that lawlessness was rampant in the land in those days, and no one was safe in the streets . . .

—History of the Mega-Cities
James Olmeyer, III
Chapter XIX: "The Way
Back When"
2191

*(Today, rituals involving "prosecutors" and "defenders" occur only when a Judge is accused by his or her peers, a decidedly rare occasion, indeed.)

SIX

Hershey leaned into the wind, taking the skyway curve at a non-regulation twenty-two degrees, the hard surface inches from her head. The Lawmaster screamed but the broad tires held to the road. She didn't dare look at her speed. A sensor would record all this somewhere; if she didn't squash herself like a bug, a sergeant would eventually give her hell.

She was vaguely aware that Briscoe was still behind her, still in one piece. Maybe the Rookie would make a Street Judge after all, if she didn't get him killed.

Mega-City rushed by in a blur of white light. A shuttle whined by overhead. Hershey wondered if Maintenance had checked the loose brake switch she'd red-lined the night before.

"Red Quad, Code Alpha-Two . . . Red Quad, Code Alpha Two . . ."

She flipped the signal off with a blink, slowed the Lawmaster for a second and a half, then squealed off the skyway onto Rampway Six. The rampway was for emergency traffic only. It circled down to the depths of the city, four thousand feet below. It was nearly pitch dark down there. Hershey punched on her brights. Code Alpha Two was Riot in Progress, and Red Quad was about as mean as you could get. The Rezzies who lived down there . . .

"Easy, Briscoe," she spoke into her comm. "Keep your eyes open. There's no one on the way yet but us."

"I'm right with you, Judge!"

Hershey caught the excitement in his voice. "Don't be so damn eager, *Rookie*. It's real bad country down here."

"I got you, Judge."

"Good. Just so you do." Hershey could hear the sound of automatic fire in the distance. She keyed the map on her dash. Red Quad. Left, then a minute and a half.

"We don't have time for a recon," she told Briscoe. "There are very likely people in danger right now. You take the street left, I'll take it right."

"I read you, Judge."

"And Briscoe—*watch* yourself, okay?"

"Hey, don't worry about me. Action is my middle— *yawwwk!*"

Yellow tracers stitched the street. Briscoe's Lawmaster veered dangerously to the right, then straightened and roared ahead.

"Take cover!" Hershey shouted, "Combat One!"

She threw the machine into a skid, drew her Lawgiver and loosed a stream of fire into the tenement above. In a single motion, she was on her knees crouched in the protection of the heavily-armored machine. A glance to the left told her Briscoe was safe.

"Hang in there," she said. "Keep cool."

"I'm doing great, Judge!"

She couldn't risk another look, but his voice said he still had that stupid Rookie grin on his face.

"What do you want me to do?" he said. "What are your orders, Judge?"

"Shut up," she said, "I'm thinking."

"Let's go get the lousy droogs. I'll lead off, you fol-low!"

"As you were!" Hershey ducked as a burst of fire

slammed into her machine. "You *see* that? This is *not* an Academy simulation, Briscoe, this is real! We will stand down and wait for backup!"

"Judge—"

Briscoe's words disappeared in a hail of fire that sent him reeling. When the acrid smoke cleared, a concrete gully a foot deep snaked across the street from one curb to the next. The line ran an inch from Briscoe's knee.

"That is mucking *heavy arms*. These guys aren't kidding!"

"What'd you expect," Hershey said, "spitballs? Comm-Delta, Comm-Delta, this is Jaybird-Fiver, in position outside Heavenly Haven, Red Quad. Under fire, I repeat, we are under fire. Request backup, nearest Judge. Nearest—"

A fireball suddenly erupted behind her. Flames licked the side of the building and glass exploded from the windows. A woman shrieked as oily smoke blackened the street. A second blast geysered beside the first and a wall of heat struck Hershey like a fist.

"Request backup *now,* damn it," Hershey shouted into her comm. "Now, or *forget it!*"

Briscoe raked the upper floors with his Lawgiver. A section of the wall collapsed and tumbled to the street.

"That is *fire-ammo*, Judge. Where'd they get their hands on that?"

"Where the hell do they get their hands on anything?" Hershey muttered. "They just do."

Hershey tried to give the shooters a blast but the withering fire drove her down. The street was a wall of flame and there was no place to go. She glanced at Briscoe. She was glad the Rookie couldn't see her face. It suddenly struck her that they'd stick a roach on her record for improper comm behavior. So what if they did? Who's going to chew out a barbecued Judge?

Where's the backup? What are you jerks doing out there!

"Judge, we could—I could lay down some fire. You could maybe get out of here, get us some help."

"Forget it," Hershey said, "no one's going anywhere."

Briscoe nodded. "Yes, Judge. I just thought . . ."

"I know what you thought. And thanks for the offer, all right? I won't forget you made it."

"Judge Hershey . . ."

"What, Briscoe?"

"If we don't get out of this, if anything should—"

Hershey's Lawmaster lifted into the air. Hershey screamed as the blast sent her rolling helplessly, head over heels along the street. Blood trickled from her ears. From the corner of her eye she could see the big machine against the sky. Time played tricks in her head and the Lawmaster seemed to float forever like a black steel balloon. It was spinning very slowly, directly overhead. Which meant, she decided, when it did come down it would flatten her into mush.

It didn't seem important at the moment, the Lawmaster didn't show any sign at all of coming down, and if it did, she would certainly have the sense to get out of the way, any droog could do that . . .

Briscoe scooped her up in his arms as Hershey's Lawmaster struck the ground like a bomb. He leaped for the cover of his machine, gunfire chewing up the street at his boots. The Lawmaster exploded in a burst of white flame. Briscoe sprawled on the ground and covered Hershey's head. He opened her visor and saw blood coming from her nose.

"Judge, you—you all right?"

Hershey blinked. "No, Briscoe, I'm *not* all right. Now get off of me."

"Judge—" Briscoe's eyes went wide. What if she thought that he . . . Oh, God, she couldn't think that!

"These machines are supposed to serve as a protective barrier under any adverse circumstances a Judge might

encounter in the line of duty," Hershey said. "I repeat,
any adverse circumstances."

"I guess they don't," Briscoe said.

"If you can't depend on your equipment, you are in
deep shit, Rookie."

"Judge. We can't stay here. We've got to get out of the
street."

Hershey snapped her visor shut. "We *can't* get out of
here, we're pinned down under overwhelming fire. Don't
you know that?"

Tracer bullets rained down on the street. Lead beat a
steady tattoo on the armor of Briscoe's machine.

"No, Judge, I don't know that. I know if we don't get
out of here we'll die and I definitely don't want to do
that."

"You're not going to die."

"Who says I'm not?"

"I do, Rookie. When our back-up comes—"

"Our *backup* isn't coming, Judge. Our backup is somewhere else, caught in another street fight."

Hershey raised her visor again and gave him a chilling
look. "You are *wrong,* Briscoe. Article Nineteen says a
Judge in pursuit of his or her duty is *never* abandoned.
When a Judge requires aid, aid will be rendered in suffi-
cient force to remedy the situation in question. Have you
read the Articles, Rookie?"

"Sure, but this time—"

"There is no '*this time.*' The Articles apply to every
time. Do you read me? Do you—"

Hershey jerked around as a deep roll of thunder
reached her ears. The thunder exploded and a black
Lawmaster burst through the curtain of flame. The rider
slammed a heavy boot on the brakes, spinning his machine in a circle, blasting the scent of rubber into the
smoky air. Gunfire ringed the man in a cage of hot steel.

Briscoe stared. "Who the . . . Who the hell's that?
He's a sitting duck out there!"

"Shut up and pay attention," Hershey said, "you might learn something."

Flames licked at the dark figure's heels. He stalked through the fire, ignoring the chatter of weapons from overhead. Lifting the speaker-mike from his Lawmaster, he turned and let his visored gaze sweep the tall buildings on every side.

"Drop your weapons. Everybody. This block is under arrest."

His voice filled the streets, echoing off the dark walls.

"Holy crud." Briscoe raised up and blinked. "It's him —it's Dredd!"

High-pitched laughter rang from the tenement overhead. "You want us, come up and get us, Dreddy!"

"Yeah, c-come up and get us, okay?"

Gunfire dug up chunks of pavement at Judge Dredd's feet.

"Judge Dredd, take cover!" Briscoe shouted.

Dredd ignored him. He walked over and looked down at Briscoe, then at Hershey.

"What are you doing down there, Judge Hershey?"

"Waiting for backup," Hershey said.

"Backup's here." He slapped the side of his Lawgiver. "Let's go. Keep it simple. Standard relay. Single file. I'm point."

Hershey nodded. Briscoe straightened eagerly, snapping to attention in front of Dredd. "Judge, I would consider it an honor if you allowed me to—"

"You . . ." Dredd raised a gloved hand and pointed past Hershey. "Back there. You're tail-end Charlie. *Go.*"

Dredd turned away. He looked at his weapon and spoke.

"Grenade!"

The door exploded and slammed against the far wall. Dredd stepped inside. He looked at the trash and the darkened elevator shaft.

"Upstairs. The perpetrators' fire comes from Six."

He kicked the door to the stairwell aside and started up. It was nearly pitch-dark and he didn't use a light. He kept up a hard and steady pace and didn't stop until they reached Six. Hershey was grateful she hadn't slacked off on her ASJEX routine—the Advanced Street Judge Exercise program. Briscoe was breathing hard behind her. She hoped Dredd didn't hear that.

Dredd paused in the stairwell, peered around the corner, then stepped into the hall, sweeping his weapon from left to right.

"Clear. Let's go."

Dredd started off, then abruptly raised his arm and stopped. The foodkart rounded the corner. It was moving slowly now, dragging a trail of garbage in its wheels. *". . . delicious and healthful rationpaks, piping hot and ready to eat . . ."*

Dredd glanced at the robot and shook his head. Bending at the knees, he made his way swiftly down the hallway, listening to the walls. At 666, he stopped and raised his hand. Motioned Hershey to the left, Briscoe to the right.

"Lawful entry," Dredd said aloud. "Suspicion of felons with illegal weapons inside." He drew back a lever on his Lawgiver and blew the door apart.

Metal Jacket and Needle Teeth turned from the window and stared.

"D-Dredd!" Metal Jacket went white and swept his automatic weapon toward the door.

"Armed. Resisting Arrest." The Lawgiver jerked in Dredd's hands. Metal Jacket and Needle Teeth splattered against the wall and exploded in flames. Smoking flesh slid to the floor.

"This room is pacified," said Dredd. "Hershey, stay with me. Briscoe, check the hall."

"Yes, *sir,* you got it, Judge!"

"I have told you people not to use a gender address for

a Judge," Hershey said. "Don't you ever listen, Roo— *Briscoe, look out!*"

Hershey saw the figure appear in the doorway. Briscoe was looking at Dredd. Purple Ears grinned, raised his pistol in a blur and shot Briscoe in the head. Hershey turned on the man but Judge Dredd was already there. He swept the Lawgiver in an arc and rammed the butt hard in Purple Ears' gut.

Purple Ears dropped his weapon, gagged, and grabbed his belly. Dredd hit him again on the jaw. Hershey went to Briscoe at once. She raised his visor, saw what was there and shut her eyes.

Dredd looked at Briscoe for a full ten seconds. Then he stepped over to the man on the floor and poked him with his boot.

"You have obscenities written all over your head. Are you aware that's a violation of the Law?"

Purple Ears looked up at Dredd. He spat a mouthful of blood on the floor and laughed.

"Hey. Are yous kiddin' me or whats? You goin' 'rest me or something, then do it, man!"

"Mega-City Municipal Code Three-Three-Four-Dash-Eight," Dredd said. "Willful destruction of property. Two years."

"Listen, pal—"

"Code Eleven-Dash-Fiver. Illegal possession of weapons. Five years. Code Thirty-Four-Dash-A. Resisting arrest. Twenty years . . ."

"All *right!*" Purple Ears raised his hands. "I gives up. You bes takin' me in!"

"Niner-Eight-Zero-Four. Assault on a Judge with a deadly weapon . . ."

Purple Ears forced a weak grin through bloody teeth. "Don't tell me. Life, right?"

"No," Dredd said. "Death."

He squeezed the trigger of his weapon. Squeezed it and didn't stop. Purple Ears began to sizzle like bacon in a pan. Putrid steam rose up to the ceiling and the floor turned black.

Hershey swallowed hard but she wouldn't look away. A Street Judge didn't betray her feelings. She didn't throw up. She maintained her cool at all times.

Dredd released the trigger.

"Court is adjourned," he said.

SEVEN

Black-clad Judges, Mediks and Tekkies crowded the sixth-floor hallway of Heavenly Haven. Helmet spots bobbed in the grim surroundings, bringing more light to the murky walls and trashed-out floors than they'd seen in fifty years.

Briscoe's body was the first one into the hall. The Mediks had scraped the remains of the three lawbreakers into one plastic bag, but Briscoe was one of their own. As the stretcher passed Hershey and Dredd, a gloved hand dropped from the blanket and swung limply above the floor. Hershey wanted to look away, but she forced herself to watch.

"He was a Rookie," she said. "He was *my* Rookie. I was supposed to watch out for him, damn it!"

Judge Dredd shook his head. "Don't blame yourself. He made the mistake, not you. His reactions were slow, judgement faulty. Didn't concentrate on his work."

Hershey turned on him and glared. "Well, that's just great. I feel a lot better now. My God, Dredd, is that all you have to say? He got his *face* blown off his first week on the job!"

"He beat the odds, then. Mort-stats say five-point-seven days. If a Rookie gets past that, he's got a four-in-seven chance of making it through the month. If he makes it past that—"

Dredd stopped. He raised a warning hand and cocked his head. Hershey followed his glance and saw a blur of motion down the hallway to their right. A quick snap of her chin brought the helmet spot to full, filling the corridor with harsh white light.

Hershey touched the butt of her weapon, then relaxed. The battered foodkart was rolling toward them again, wobbling drunkenly on its broken wheel.

". . . *ummm, ummmm, yumm! Healthful and nutritious rationpaks, ready to eat . . .*"

"Somebody ought to turn that thing off," Hershey said, "before it drives everyb—"

Dredd suddenly pushed her aside, stepped in the robot's path, gripped his Lawgiver in both hands, and aimed it at the robot's shiny dome.

"Halt! You have ten seconds to surrender. Ten . . . nine . . ."

"Dredd, take it easy," Hershey said, "it's a *servo-droid.*"

". . . *Make your selection, please. Insert your card in the slot . . .*"

Dredd took one step forward and shoved the barrel of his weapon half a foot into the slot.

". . . Make your select—*oh, shit!*"

The front of the robot came totally unhinged. Boxy foodpaks in drab shades of gray, brown, and mildew-green spilled onto the floor. Half a second later, Fergie tumbled out of the back. He blinked in the unfamiliar light, staring at Hershey and Dredd like an animal caught in the woods.

"Listen," he said, "I know what you guys are thinking,

but that's the way it looks . . . I mean, that's the way it
is but it's not the way it looks—"

Dredd grabbed Fergie by the collar, lifted him straight
off the floor and slammed him hard against the wall.

"Wuuuuh, listen a minute, okay?" Fergie's teeth rattled. He kicked his feet and grabbed at empty air.

"Mega-City Municipal Code One-Deuce-Niner-Six.
Willful sabotage of a public droid. That's six months,
Citizen. Let's see your card."

"Come on, give me a break, Judge—Judge—" Fergie
stared at the eagle and shield an inch before his eyes.
"Judge—*Dredd?* Oh, my God . . ."

Fergie's card fluttered out of his hand. Hershey
snatched it out of the air. Snapping a scanner off of her
weapons belt, she slipped Fergie's card through the narrow slot once. A holo cube blossomed into life. Magenta
words crawled across its face:

FERGUSON, HERMAN D.

MEGA-CITY 2, L.A.

SENTENCE: ASPEN PRISON

TIME SERVED: SIX MONTHS, THREE DAYS

PRISONER NUMBER: ASP-900764

CHARGES: TAMPERING OF CITY DROIDS . . .

COMPUTERS . . . CASH MACHINES . . . ROBO-TAXIS

RELEASED: MEGA-CITY 1, SENTENCE COMPLETED

Dredd scanned the rest of the message, and shook his
head in disgust. "You got off of the shuttle this afternoon. You haven't been out of jail five hours, Ferguson."
He turned to Hershey. "He's a habitual. Automatic five-
year sentence."

"What!" Fergie turned white. "Five *years?* No, no *way.*
Look, I didn't have any choice. Those droogs were in my
room. They hit me on the head. Come on, look at my
head. Will you *look* at my head, just look at it, okay?

What was I supposed to do, jump out the damn window!"

"It's legal," Dredd said.

"It's suicide," Fergie shouted. "It's six floors down!"

"Case closed. Five years."

"*Wait* a minute!"

"I've got a question," Hershey said. "How did you do that?"

"How did I do what?"

"Work that food droid. That's a highly complex electronic device. Only a trained, skilled professional could possibly do that."

"Yeah? You're kidding." Fergie grinned. "What you do is you cross the yellow wire with the blue wire. Unless you got a Model E, then you gotta—*uuuk!*"

Dredd let go and Fergie dropped to the ground. "You have just made a confession, Citizen. Duly dated and recorded." He nodded at a Street Judge standing in the hall. "Take this person away. Next shuttle back to Aspen Prison."

The Street Judge walked up to Fergie. Snake-locks whipped around his wrists.

"I am telling you, I didn't have any choice. I didn't *do* anything!"

Fergie's voice echoed down the hall. He dragged his heels, plowing two clean furrows on the floor.

"You think that's good, the foodkart stuff?" he called out to Hershey. "You ought to see me with a Poker-droid!"

"Gambling devices are illegal," Dredd said.

Hershey wiped her hands along the sides of her uniform. "The guy's scared to death, you know? He might've been telling the truth. He's just a scam artist. He's not going to be hanging around with crazies, Dredd."

Dredd shook his head. "I've heard every sad story in Mega-City, Hershey. What did you expect him to say?

Lawbreakers are liars. Liars are criminals. Criminals must be punished to the full extent of the Law."

Dredd gave Hershey a curious look. "These are all things you know as well as I do. Why do I get the feeling you do not clearly understand what I'm saying? You are familiar with the Articles. You know the Legal Code."

"I am completely familiar with *every* aspect of my work, Judge Dredd." She snapped down her visor to mask her eyes. "I do not need you or anyone else to tell me how to perform my duty!"

"I'm pleased to hear that, Judge Hershey. Thank you for clarifying the matter."

"You're welcome, *Judge!*"

Hershey stalked off, taking careful measured steps, keeping her back straight. She was determined not to betray her feelings in front of Dredd again. *Damn the man,* she thought, *is there anything inside him, any soul, anything behind those armor-plated eyes?*

There had to be. Every person had something in his heart—some small light of understanding, some connection to the rest of humanity. Even the filth who'd slaughtered those people in the street and murdered Briscoe. It was hard to imagine them as members of the human race, but they were. And Dredd, as far above their kind as the towers of Mega-City were above Heavenly Haven . . . Dredd was human, too.

Downstairs, Hershey stood in the night and looked out over the ruined neighborhood. The street was a combat zone. Broken glass littered the ground, and the tenement walls were blackened by fire. The bodies of the victims had been hastily removed, and maintenance trucks were spraying down the street. By first light, the place would probably look better than it had in years.

She could hear the wail of sirens in the night. There were fifty million people in Mega-City One. Fifty million packed into three hundred twenty square miles. A hundred and twenty years before, a city with another name had stood here. That city had held *eight*-million people, and in the same three hundred twenty square miles!

Crime had nearly overwhelmed the city then, and there had been no Judges to keep the vast and lawless population under control.

If we ever lost the upper hand here . . .

Hershey shuddered at the thought. Maybe she was wrong and Dredd was right. Maybe they couldn't afford to understand . . . maybe there was *no* way to let their guard down. Article One, carved on the high wall at the entry to the Hall of Justice read:

FIRST THERE IS THE LAW.

It was something Dredd understood. That there was no other way. No other means to assure that civilization survived.

Maybe I'd better think about that instead of feeling sorry for some miserable little groon in a foodkart. Maybe I'd better think about how to stay alive . . .

She walked out into the street and studied the burned and twisted mass of metal that had been her Lawmaster half an hour before.

That's another thing I'd better do. I'd better start thinking how I'm going to write this sucker up.

She kicked a piece of blackened chrome and sent it clanging along the street.

"It better be one hell of a report," she said aloud. "Some jerko at the Hall has a real bad day, I'll be *buying* this wreck for the rest of my natural life . . ."

If the Hall of Justice is the heart of Mega-City, the Chamber of the High Council of Judges is its soul. It has been said that if a priest (formerly, a religious practitioner) from the fourteenth century were suddenly transported to this great chamber, he would be struck by the majesty, the size, the stark and unworldly beauty of the place. He would gaze in disbelief at the vaulted ceiling sweeping nearly four hundred feet overhead, its graceful span of arches broken only by shimmering planes of cobalt-blue, lit by artificial suns.

This priest would likely fall to his knees and clasp his hands in prayer, certain that here was the Cathedral of Heaven, that he was, indeed, in the presence of his mythical Creator. He would soon learn he was wrong. He would find neither "love" nor "forgiveness," or the debilitating emotions of compassion and understanding, so often associated with the "tragedy of the misguided lawbreaker." He would learn that these false values which weakened society for centuries have been cast aside in favor of the more practical and realistic standards of our time. He would learn that our world has its own definition of Judgement Day. That we have given new meaning to the ancient concept of "the quick and the dead." He would learn that the god worshipped here is named Law . . .

—*History of the Mega-Cities*
James Olmeyer, III
Chapter VII: "The Chamber"
2191

EIGHT

*T*he room was small.

The walls were painted a rich shade of blue. There were three comfortable chairs, an antique glass table and a video screen mounted on the wall. The room was just off the hallway leading to the Chamber of the Council of Judges. It was used as a waiting room for those occasions when the Council allowed officials, high administrators, and prominent Citizens to bring their business before them.

This was not such an occasion. The session that was about to begin was closed to all but the Council members themselves. And, though no one would admit where they'd heard such information, it was said that this meeting was an emergency session of the gravest order. Even those who had no reliable source in high places had reason to believe this was so. There was only one topic of note in Mega-City at the moment, the only subject covered on the video news: Terror was loose in the streets, and the city was caught in a web of fear.

"This is Vardis Hammond, and I'm standing in front of the ruins of Heavenly Haven Block. As you can see behind me, city workers are still busy sifting through the burned and twisted debris from the savage battle that took place earlier

*this evening. Fifty-three Citizens have been hospitalized
. . . five of them children. The death count is nineteen so
far, and many victims are still on the critical list. The perpetrators themselves are among the dead. They have tenta-
tively been identified as 'crazed squatters' who were
allegedly killed in Summary Execution by Judge Dredd himself. The number of squatters involved has yet to be determined, due to the difficulty in separating the individual
bodies . . ."*

Judge Dredd looked at the video screen, but paid little
attention to what he saw. He stood in the center of the
room, his helmet under his arm. He did not consider
sitting in one of the chairs. It made him uncomfortable to
place his body in a position where precious seconds
might be lost if he were called upon to act quickly. This
was how Judges lost their lives, by letting their guards
down for that one single instant when they should have
been fully alert. This was why Rookie Briscoe was dead.
He had taken his mind off his business for the blink of an
eye. It seldom took longer than that.

Dredd turned as the door to the hallway slid aside. He
came to attention and nodded his head in respect as
Chief Justice Fargo walked into the room.

"Joseph, Joseph, no formalities, please." He smiled
warmly at Dredd. "You make me feel like an old man.
Which is precisely what I am, by the way."

"If we had a hundred men like you, sir, we could clean
up Mega-City by morning."

Fargo shook his head. "I'd call that blatant flattery if it
came from any other man. Coming from you, I take it as
a sincere compliment. A great exaggeration, but a compliment all the same."

The Chief Justice sighed and lowered himself into a
chair. "Sit down, Joseph, please. I appreciate you coming." He glanced at his watch. "This won't take long. I
have to be in session in a few minutes."

Dredd knew better than anyone else how serious the

situation was becoming in the streets. He had been there and seen it, and he had an idea what this session was all about. Even if he hadn't been aware of the meeting, he could not have missed the lines of fatigue around Fargo's eyes, the deep sense of concern that seemed to slow his steps and weigh him down.

For the first time in a lifelong association with Fargo, Dredd saw past his image of a man who was indestructable, as strong and enduring as Mega-City itself. Now he saw a man who seemed even older than his seventy years, a man dragged down by the hounds of adversity that forever snapped at his heels.

Dredd had trained himself to bury those feelings that might intrude upon the task he had set himself to do. He did not want to experience love or hate. He did not wish to want or need anyone or anything. Yet, when he saw what was happening to Fargo, how the man was disintegrating before his eyes, Dredd felt a mix of sorrow, rage, and despair that he couldn't cast aside.

"I think you know I have always taken a special interest in your career, Joseph. I also know there are certain others who—very much resent the fact. I do not regret my actions, and I do not apologize. I have always tried to do what is best for the cause that I serve."

Dredd sat on the edge of the chair, his back straight. "I know what you've done for me, and I greatly appreciate it, sir."

Fargo looked intently at Dredd. His body might be aging, but his eyes still mirrored the strength and power that had inspired two generations of Judges.

"Tell me, Joseph. The . . . Summary Executions at Heavenly Haven. Were they . . . absolutely necessary?"

"Unavoidable, sir."

"Unavoidable . . ." Fargo glanced away, lost in thought for a moment. "We make our own reality, don't we Joseph? The severity of those executions. Were they unavoidable, too?"

Dredd felt the color rise to his face. "With all due respect, sir, a Rookie Judge died out there today, too. Times have changed in the city. Life doesn't mean much to some people anymore. You'd be able to see that if you weren't—"

Fargo raised an eyebrow. "If I weren't what, Joseph?"

"Always at the—Academy, sir."

Fargo allowed the beginning of a smile to crease his features. "Don't you mean at the Academy *wiping Cadets' asses?* That's what they say in the squad room, isn't it?"

Dredd cleared his throat. "That's irrelevant, sir. You set the standards, Chief Justice Fargo."

"No, that's not true." Fargo wet his lips. "Now, *you* do . . . to the young Cadets you're a legend."

"I don't feel much like a legend, sir."

"We don't decide what we are. *They* do . . . Do you remember your time at the Academy, Joseph?"

"I remember what you taught me, sir."

Fargo studied the ceiling. "And I remember a Cadet who embraced Justice. The *ideals* as well as the lessons. My finest student—out of all the thousands I have been privileged to congratulate as a newly-appointed Judge . . . you are the best, Judge Dredd."

"Thank you, sir. The compliment is undeserved, but I am grateful for your words."

"Fine, fine." Fargo pulled himself erect and glanced at his watch. He seemed to have regained his powers, called upon a new reserve of strength.

"I'm going to give you a chance to pay some of your debts to the Academy that made you what you are. I have found the experience most satisfying, and I'm sure you will as well." He rested a hand on Dredd's shoulder. "I have drawn a new assignment for you. Starting tomorrow morning, you'll be spending two days a week at the Academy."

"I would be honored, sir. Unarmed combat or marksmanship?"

Fargo grinned. "Ethics, Joseph. The moral code of the Judges, Article Twenty-two. I'll drop by and see how you're doing."

Fargo placed his helmet on his head and lowered the visor. "Tradition has its purpose, Joseph. There are some of those old buzzards in the Council I cannot stand to look at anymore. And I'm certain many of them feel the same about me."

Dredd didn't move for several minutes after Chief Justice Fargo left the room. He had known and revered the man all his life. He thought he knew him as well as any man could know another who was much older in years, and held such an exalted position in the profession they had both chosen for themselves.

Yet, he had no idea why Fargo had given him Academy duties—especially at this time, when every experienced Judge was needed on the streets.

Even if he could make a wild guess at the Chief Justice's reasons, Dredd knew he'd probably be wrong. Fargo's mind was like one of those antique boxes. The secret in the first box was another box. And within that box . . .

Dredd thrust the thought aside. It was a waste of time to try to get one step ahead of Fargo. His friends and enemies—within and without the Judges—had tried it for years. Most of them were dead or defeated. And the Chief Justice himself was still there.

Dredd was aware that Vardis Hammond was still on the video behind him, still doing his best to look grave, intense, intelligent, and informed in the ruined street before Heavenly Haven:

". . . *Some say that working these mean streets day after day is bound to have a dehumanizing effect on the Judges.*

But is it the streets or the Judges themselves that have created this atmosphere of savagery.

"As my special undercover report continues tomorrow night, I'll take you behind the walls of the Hall of Justice for a disturbing probe into these recent riots and block wars. Coincidence or deliberate provocation? That's tomorrow with Vardis Hammond . . ."

Dredd glared at the screen. "What the hell do you know?" he said aloud. "You want to see a disturbing probe? Give me a call, I'll show you a disturbing probe, pal!"

NINE

THE SETTING:

With a scarcely-perceptible sigh, a massive stone eagle and shield rise up from the floor of the Council Chamber. This symbol of Mega-City Justice was carved from a single slab of black marble thirty-seven meters high and twenty-eight meters wide. Its weight and dimensions were calculated to a fine tolerance by the architects to achieve the perfect spatial ratio of the Chamber itself.

Seconds after the great stone is in place, a table of carved ebony, a wood now worth its weight in gold, rises up before the high symbol. There are five chairs behind the table. On the high, ornate backrest of each chair is a carved replica of the eagle and shield, and below each emblem is the name of the High Judge who is privileged to sit on the Council.

On the wall opposite the Judges, a large holo flickers into life. The holo is a map of New North America.

There are three pulsing blue stars on the map: Mega-City One, which rests on the twentieth

century foundations of New York City; Mega-
City Two, a massive extension of the old city of
Los Angeles, and Mega-City Three, Tex-City,
which was once called Houston. All else on this
map is a dull and coppery hue, the color of the
sun-baked ground, the color of the land of
Cursed Earth, the no-color of Death.

Finally, the members of the High Council file
into the Chamber and take their places. Their
uniforms are black, with scarcely any hint of
their rank. They do not wear the traditional hel-
met of the Judges when the High Council is in
session. Here, their heads are bare, their faces
open to one another.

[Judge Griffin rises slowly from his chair. He is a man
of sixty years, with silver hair and eyes the color of
Arctic ice. Still, he is a solid, broad-shouldered man
with the strength and passions of a man half his age.
When he stands, he presses strong fingers against the
black surface of the table and addresses his fellow
Judges . . .]

JUDGE GRIFFIN

My fellow Judges, can it be true that we have forgotten
the lessons of History? Can we not see that establishing a
system of Justice is not enough—that we must constantly
maintain that system with whatever action, whatever
force becomes necessary?

It is quite clear that these block wars that erupt across
the city are becoming an epidemic—an epidemic that
must be dealt with immediately. The measures we are
taking now can only contain this sickness that threatens
our Society. Containment is *not* the answer. The only
solution to our problem is a tougher Criminal Code—a

code designed to show this filth they cannot run amok in
Mega-City!

JUDGE SILVER
[Stands, and enthusiastically pounds the table.]
The situation gets worse every day—seventy-three Citizen riots in two months in, what? Sixteen different sectors.

JUDGE McGRUDER
Violent crime is rising fifteen percent every quarter. If
we don't *increase* our resources they will be inadequate
in under three years.

JUDGE ESPOSITO
Three years? They are totally inadequate now!

[The Council is in an uproar. A gavel strikes the
table, a sound that echoes like thunder off the high
Chamber walls. Chief Justice Fargo rises from his
chair. While Judge Griffin never fails to stir the
Council, it is Fargo, with his dignity and iron will
who brings instant silence to the room.]

JUDGE FARGO
My friends, my fellow Council members . . . As a
city, we continue to grow. And growth is painful. Over
fifty million people live in an area that was originally
built for under twenty. It is not enough that they rely on
us for clothing, food, water, and clean air . . .

[Judge Griffin comes to his feet. He spreads his
hands in exasperation.]

JUDGE GRIFFIN
Chief Justice, with all due respect, this city is in *chaos!*
Grand oratory—even yours—can't help us now. Main-

taining the social order calls for tighter reins. My curfew proposal should be implemented *immediately!*

[Chief Justice Fargo turns to Griffin.]

JUDGE FARGO
Treat men like animals and they will act like them, sir.

JUDGE GRIFFIN
Perhaps you'd prefer we strip the Judges of their current powers and return to the antiquated system of trial and jury? No, I am certain you do not. But I tell you this, Judge: Incarceration has not worked as a deterrent. It did not work in the past and it does not work now. We can lock them up by the thousands and there will *still* be enough of them out there to destroy us all. There is only one answer: *We must expand execution to include lesser crimes!*

[Judge Fargo cannot see the faces of his fellow Judges, but he knows them all too well. He knows that there is enough truth in Griffin's words to sway them.]

JUDGE FARGO
This body is not the first assembly to think that more laws and fewer choices will bring peace and order. That delusion has been tried and has failed before. I was hardly in my teens when I put on this badge. When the time comes for me to take it off . . . let me do it knowing that it stood for freedom . . . and not for repression.

[Chief Justice Fargo takes his seat. The room is silent. It is clear that his words have hit home, that the awe and respect that elevated him to his position have once more turned the tide in his favor.

No one is more aware of this than Judge Griffin himself.]

JUDGE GRIFFIN
Once more, sir, you have served as a moral compass for us all. I . . . I wish to withdraw my proposal. I hope my action is one for the good.

JUDGE FARGO
Thank you, my friend. Your strength and wisdom are always an asset to this table. Now . . . let us all work together to continue the task we have sworn to perform, to protect and serve the citizens of Mega-City . . .

[The Judges file out of the room. The lights in the Chamber dim.]

CURTAIN

TEN

*I*t was the first winter storm of the season and the worst in twenty-three years. It began as a silent snowfall, a thickening curtain of white that masked the dark peaks, the grim and barren plains. For half a day, this small section of Cursed Earth looked like an ancient Christmas card. Then, the blizzard struck in full force, bringing howling winds and numbing cold.

The guard towers of Aspen Prison rose like skeletal fingers behind the white veil. A chill wind moaned through the razor wire atop the granite walls. And, though there were thousands of men behind these dark battlements, not a single light was visible through the storm. Anyone who has ever been to this tomb of the living knows it is a place of darkness, not a place of light. If the Cursed Earth is Hell, then Aspen Prison is the stairway that leads to the underworld below . . .

They made their way down the narrow maze of granite stairs, their shadows bent and warped, dark and mis-shapen on the cold stone walls. The public was familiar with Aspen Prison from the countless videos, grim and deliberate reminders of the fate of those who broke the Law. This was a part of that prison they had never seen, and never would—unless they became one of the two hundred nine incarcerated here, the elite, the monsters, the terrors, the men who had committed such unspeakable crimes they were sentenced to live instead of die. The Judges had decreed that every effort would be made to keep these men alive, that they could never deserve the merciful release of execution.

Warden-Judge William Otis Miller followed the two guards down the wet and treacherous stairs. He did not glance to the left or to the right, at the cells descending on either side. This is what they were called, but they were not cells at all. Each was a three-foot circle in stone laced with flat strips of tightly-woven steel bars. They looked for all the world like the overflow gates of city sewers. The small rooms behind these bars were seven feet square. Every other day, a jet of frigid water sluiced the prisoners' waste away. Every morning at four, waterpaks and food-pods were automatically dropped in each cell. The water contained a drug that would prevent a man from killing himself, or escaping into any degree of madness that would let him forget about his punishment or his crime. The drugs didn't make a man *feel* any better, they just made him do his forever-after time.

The stairs continued to wind into the bowels of the earth. Warden-Judge Miller was numb to the bone. He sighed with relief when the stairs came to an end at a massive steel door. The door was nine inches thick and incredibly old. The small computer lock inset in its center was relatively new.

Miller nodded to the guards. They took a step to either side of the door. Miller laid his right palm on the center plate of the lock. A winking red light turned green. The door slid open without a sound, and Miller stepped inside.

A dim light glowed from a slot in the ceiling. A pair of Autoguns wheezed from the wall.

"Identi-fy yourself," a metalic voice said.

"Miller. Warden-Judge."

"Voice sam-ple recognized. Pro-ceed, Warden-Judge Miller."

The walls of the small room were steel instead of stone. The blind muzzles of the Autoguns swung toward a circular platform against the far wall of the room. A pale blue light, a cobalt haze, surrounded the platform from the ceiling to the floor. A figure stood and moved about beyond the haze.

"Well, Warden . . . back for another chat, are we?"

The voice behind the barrier of light was cold as glacier ice.

"A very short chat," Miller said. "I have a good deal to do."

"Of course you do. You're a *very* important man, Miller."

"Warden Miller," Miller corrected. "Warden-*Judge* Miller. Don't forget that again."

"Of course. No disrespect intended, sir."

The voice behind the blue veil was different now. Considerate. Warm and soft-spoken. Obsequious almost to the point where Miller could call it insolence.

"I know it must be a strain, sir. Yours is a thankless job, feeding and caring for all these parasites who have sucked the living blood from Society." The man laughed lightly. "I don't speak of myself, of course. I'm a ghost. I don't exist."

The man stepped to the edge of the platform. The air around him sizzled as he approached the blue light. He was tall, well-built. Flesh pale as raw milk, flesh that had long forgotten the warmth of the sun, stretched over classically-handsome features.

The man looked at Miller, and Miller instantly looked away. He felt the heat rise to his face. He could never look directly into the man's eyes. His eyes were too bright, too intense. The color of mercury floating on polished blue steel.

"We are both prisoners here, Warden-Judge Miller.

You behind a desk. Me behind . . . this. The good
Judge Fargo's reward for our . . . *services.*"

"You killed innocent people. You went far beyond service!"

"Innocent?" The man spread his hands in a helpless
gesture. "The innocent exist only until they are perpetrators themselves. You are as good an example as any, sir.
You became a perpetrator when you conspired to keep
me alive, when you began to accept the generous bribes
to make certain I retained a healthier and more positive
outlook on life than those poor devils in their pestholes
out there."

Miller shifted his weight. He did not like to be in the
same room with this man. Even with the force field and
the Autoguns, he felt vulnerable and alone.

"I can't stand here listening to your ravings all day," he
said. "I came here because your—because our benefac-
tor has sent a package for you."

"A package, is it?" The man showed Miller a terrible
smile. "How delightful, I'm sure. No one sends me pack-
ages any more."

"Computer. Deactivate shield," Miller said. "Autoguns only."

The blue light flickered and faded, melting into a
warm amber glow. The Autoguns in the wall whirred
toward the man.

Miller waited until the weapons were in place, then
stepped up on the platform and handed the package to
the man. It was small, square, wrapped in the standard
shell designed for AO, Addressee Only.

"I'm awfully excited," the man said. He cocked his
head quizzically to one side. "I wonder if it's my birthday
today? I simply can't remember all the special days any
more."

"Get on with it," Miller said irritably.

The man pressed his thumb on the smooth surface.
The package opened like a flower. The man held it close

to his chest, his very own treasure that no one else could see. Finally, he reached in and drew out a plastic ellipse, no longer than his thumb. Bright bands of yellow, blue, red, and green circled the object in complex geometrical patterns.

Miller frowned. "What the hell is that?"

"I do believe it's a puzzle," the man said. He began to turn the bands of color in different directions. Red on red. Blue on blue.

Miller cursed under his breath. "I wasted my time bringing you that? Damn those people."

"Your time, perhaps," the man smiled. "Not mine. I simply love puzzles. I remember this one. It's from India, I believe. A place that isn't there any more. It's supposed to contain the meaning of life."

The warden laughed. He made a show of looking around the small room. "You think that's what it is, huh?"

"Yes, I do think so, sir."

"Good. I'm real happy for you. I've got maybe a minute. Why don't you enlighten me some. Tell me what's the meaning of life."

The man gave him a weary, almost sorrowful look. "It ends," he said.

"What?"

The puzzle made a quick, sibilant sound, like the hiss of a snake. Miller felt a jolt of pain in his throat. For an instant, he had the irrational thought that someone had shot him with a miniature sun. The pain was unbearable, intense, the nuclear heat of a star concentrated in one tiny spot. He gasped and fell to his knees, one hand clawing at his throat.

"Computer . . . acti—activaaa—alarm!"

"Voice is not rec-ognized. Repeat: your voice command is not rec-ognized. Please remain still . . ."

"D-damn you!" Miller choked on the words, felt the

terror grip his heart. "I—am—Warthejud—Warga-Jushh —M-M-M—"

"Security Break . . . Security Break. Autoguns targeting . . ."

"N-N-Noooo!"

The guns came alive, catching Miller in a precise crossfire, cutting him in half before he could take a single step toward the door.

In the corridor outside, the two guards jacketed Buklead shells into their riot guns. One slammed the override button with his fist. They both stepped back, guns at the ready. The door slid open. The top half of Miller's body lay sprawled on the floor. The first guard gagged and stumbled back. A shadow came out of greater shadow, twisted the guard's neck, jerked the weapon from his grasp in a blur and squeezed the trigger once. The second guard slammed against the wall. The top of his head disappeared.

The man slid another shell into his gun. He reached into the open package and retrieved two items Miller hadn't been close enough to see. One was a small photograph of Mega-City newscaster Vardis Hammond. The other was a pocket-sized badge embossed with a familiar eagle and shield. A name was engraved on the badge. The name read RICO.

Rico looked at the two dead guards then dismissed them from his mind. He took three steps to Miller's body and kicked the corpse soundly in the head.

"Keep it to yourself," he said softly. "I'm back . . ."

NOTE: While every reader will be familiar with the life and legend of Judge Dredd, there are few historically authentic records of his actual words. The following is transcribed from a partial audiotape of a lecture given by Judge Dredd at the Academy of Justice. No date is given, but from the equipment described, it would seem this event took place circa 2139.

JUDGE DREDD

This is the Lawgiver Two. Twenty-five round sidearm with mission-variable voice-programmed ammunition. Pay attention. *Signal Flare!*

[A flare explodes in the target area.]

JUDGE DREDD

Yours, Cadets, when you graduate . . . if you graduate. Now, I don't have to tell any of you what this is. But I will, because you are Cadets and you don't know from nothing even if you think you do.

[Nervous laughter.]

JUDGE DREDD

This is the Mark IV Lawmaster, improved model. With onboard dual laser cannons, vertical take-off and landing flight capacity and five hundred kilometer range.

[NOTE: An evaluation of the background sound at this point would indicate that maintenance personnel have set the machine in motion at this time. Apparently, the Lawmaster then rises in a hovering mode for five-point-seven seconds. At that time, the drive unit fails and the Lawmaster drops heavily to the floor.]

JUDGE DREDD

Yours . . . if they ever get it to work.

[Judge Dredd walks to another location in the classroom. A Cadet coughs in the background.]

JUDGE DREDD

All of these things are nothing, Cadets. Nothing but toys. End of the day, you're alone out there in the dark, all that counts—is this.

[The sound of a book dropping heavily on a table.]

JUDGE DREDD

This is the book. This is the Law. And you *will* be alone when you swear to uphold these ideals . . . For most of us there is only death on the streets . . . or, for those few of us who survive to old age, the prouder loneliness of the Long Walk into the unknown of the Cursed Earth, to spend your last days taking the Law into the Outlands . . .

There are medically-disabled Judges and there are dead Judges. There are retired Judges who have taken the Long Walk. Do not ever forget, Cadets, that there is no such thing as a Judge who has set aside those vows you will take . . . Class dismissed.

[Except for background noise, the tape ends here.]

> —*History of the Mega-Cities*
> James Olmeyer, III
> Chapter XXI: "Judge Dredd,
> the Man and the Myth"
> 2191

ELEVEN

*T*he barge wasn't made for beauty. It was three blocks long, solid and black, and built like a slag-iron whale. The Mega-City wall-lock opened like a dark and empty eye; the barge shuddered down through the night and poked its pitted nose inside.

In the amber light of the lock, the rusty hide of the barge seemed afflicted by ugly metal warts. The drive-rings in its belly pulsed in alarming shades of blue. The docking engineer frowned at the rings, glanced at his watch and cursed beneath his breath. It was 0610 and Clydo, his morning relief, was late. If the barge's rings went totally out of sync—which they very well might, from the way they looked now—a white ball of fire would appear in the wall. He'd be a vapor, and Clydo would get another roach in his record for being late.

The barge finally whined into silence and the lock took hold. The massive craft creaked and moaned. A portal came open with a hiss of dirty steam. A crewman stepped out, rubbed a sleeve across his face, and nodded at the guard.

"Two loads from the prison factory in Hold Number Nine. One from the mines in Six. Prisoner mail in Two."

The guard looked up from his computer tablet. "No prisoners comin' back?"

"Just dead ones." He nodded back into the dark. "Families probably glad to get rid of 'em, now they gotta bury the bastards."

The crewman stalked off. The guard stepped past him into the dimly-lit hold. Fifteen body bags were strapped to the deck. Each had a yellow plastic tag stapled to his chest. Each bag was stenciled: ASP.

The guard leaned down to check the names. When he first got the docking assignment, it bothered him to get near the bodies. Like he told his wife, it was spooky as hell in there, like a Saturday holo show where the zombies and stuff came to life. He had been on the job eight months now, and the bodies didn't bother him any more. They didn't look like zombies, they looked like black bags with dead guys inside. Which proved you could get used to anything if y—

He heard the slight crinkle of plastic and jerked around. One of the body bags sat up, and the hair stood up on the back of the guard's neck. He reached for his weapon, then stopped, and threw back his head and laughed. He knew what had happened and he knew who it was that'd pull a crazy stunt like this.

"Okay, I'm *scared,* all right? Get the hell out of there, Jak!"

A pinhole slit appeared in the black body bag. A laser beam thin as a needle touched the guard between the eyes. The guard looked surprised. There might be a punch line to this, but he was too dead to wait around and see.

Rico stepped out of the body bag and smiled at the guard.

"Home, sweet home," he said.

The lights were always on. The streets were always wet. Everything in Mega-City was above Redtown, and everything above dripped down.

Rico ignored the hungry eyes, the men and women

who offered him a peek at their sorrow and their souls. He walked past the crowded taverns, past the holo-kill parlors where every kiss and cut was good as life, and every crime was real.

On a video screen, he saw Vardis Hammond silently mouthing a replay of the city's block wars. Rico winked at the image and rolled his eyes.

The sign outside said: GEIGER'S BAZAAR. The jittery neon offered SURPLUS PAWN FAXO TOOLS VOUCHERS CASHED.

Everything nobody wanted hung from the ceiling and the walls. Rico made his way through the maze. In the rear of the store a fence guarded better merchandise.

Geiger himself looked up and blinked. A cigar dangled from the side of his mouth. His face was long and narrow, his eyes bright gold, like a predatory bird that only hunts at night.

"We're closed," he said.

"No you're not," Rico said. "You've got a package for me. Codename Lazarus."

The pupils in Geiger's eyes shrank to tiny points. "Gimme a second," he muttered, and disappeared.

Rico waited. He timed Geiger. He was back in twenty-nine seconds. Not too long.

"Nice place," he said.

"It might look like junk to most people, but there's stuff in here that's real antiques. *Valuable* stuff, man."

Rico nodded at a row of metal men in shadow behind the security fence. The tall figures looked hollow, like toy soldiers some giant had cast aside.

"Odd to run into something like that," Rico said. "I thought they slagged all the ABC warriors after the last wars."

Geiger shrugged. "DeWats. People collect 'em, got nothing else to do. They're fifty, sixty years old. Nonfunctional, of course." Geiger showed yellow teeth. "Like my old lady, you know?" He handed Rico a long box. "Here you go. Says 'Hold for Lazarus' on top."

Rico swept a pile of surplus breathers aside, set the box on the table, and thumbed the lock. Geiger pretended not to look, but when the lid slid back he could easily see what was inside.

"Holy . . . !" Geiger stood back. "Man, is that what I think it is?"

A black, perfectly pressed uniform was laid neatly in the box. On top of the uniform was an item any Citizen of Mega-City would recognize at once: The personal weapon of a Judge, the Lawgiver.

Rico reached for the weapon. Geiger sucked in a breath and grabbed Rico's wrist.

"Wait a second, don't *touch* it! Whoever sent you this is no friend of yours!"

"No? And why is that?"

Geiger shook his head. "Where you been, pal? That's a *Lawgiver.* Don't you know that? They're programmed, like they only recognize a Judge's hand, the one the weapon was *made* for. I can get you somethin' nice, but you touch that and the sucker'll take your arm off."

Rico smiled. "Really?"

"Yeah, *really.* You think I'd kid about a thing like—"

Rico gripped the Lawgiver in both hands. Geiger stared, waiting for the weapon to explode.

"That—that don't make any sense!"

"No?"

Rico squeezed the trigger. Everything above Geiger's shoulders moved six feet back. It looked as if someone had slammed a dozen pizzas against the wall.

Rico frowned at the mess. "I must be a Judge, pal. What do you think?"

Rico retrieved Geiger's keys from his pocket, took two of his cigars, unlocked the security fence, and stepped inside. He studied the battered robots, one by one. Finally, he stopped before a tall combat warrior, its metal hide dented in a dozen forgotten wars.

"You'll do just fine," he said.

Stepping up on a plastic box, he studied the robot a moment, then removed a narrow panel on the side of its head. A nest of thin cables spilled out, dangling like silver dreadlocks. Rico patiently sorted them with practiced fingers, matching one slender tendon here, twisting another into place. Finally, a golden spark hissed, lighting Rico's face and eyes. A faint sound began to whir in the warrior's head. The powerful torso jerked. A spasm shot through its right arm. Steam covered the monster in a mist, and its eyes glowed like rubies in its head. The eyes blinked once, and turned on Rico.

"Status . . . Commander . . . Mission . . ."

The computer voice was old and it rustled like a snake.

"Status is Personal Bodyguard," Rico said. He struck a match on the robot's chin and lit one of Geiger's cigars. "Commander is *me*. Mission is, we're going to war again. Geronimo, pal . . ."

Lily Hammond had taken care of herself. Her husband's status as Mega-City's top broadcaster enabled her to make regular appointments at Lovely-U. Her breasts were always firm, her skin always clear, and though she hadn't been born that way, her legs were slender and long. She was forty-seven and looked twenty-two. Vardis Hammond was fifty-five, and looked thirty-eight. No one at the studio dreamed that he spent his annual vacation getting re-studded at Handsome-Him.

"My God, Vardis . . ."

Lily looked up from the paper in her hand and stared at her husband. "A—a conspiracy in the Justice system? Radical elements on the City Council? Where did you *get* this stuff?"

Hammond didn't look up. He sat at his desk in the corner, under his favorite antique light, tapping on his lap computer.

"What do you mean, where did I *get* it? That's my job, Lily. I followed up some grumblings I found in some low level Council papers. They confirm what I've known all along. The shadow of oppression goes deeper than the Street Judges. *Much* deeper."

Lily frowned. "Please, dear. Don't say things like 'shadow of oppression.' You're home, you are not on the video." Lily paused, then studied her husband again. "Vardis, are you going to use that? Are you going to say that on the *air?*"

Vardis gave her a chilly look. "Well, it's the truth. Why shouldn't I say it?"

"I think you're out of your mind, you want to know what I think."

"I'm a reporter. I am a reputable journalist and I have an obligation to the Citizens of—"

"That doesn't mean you have to go and get yourself killed."

Hammond laughed. He set his keyboard aside and stood. "The Judges don't kill reporters. Not yet, anyway."

Lily watched him as he crossed the room to the bar. "Vardis, I'm serious. They'll never let you put this on the air. Something like this could . . . it could bring down the Council!"

Vardis poured a generous glass of clear liquid from the bottle.

"Maybe it should, Lily. I know a lot more than I did when I started poking into this business. I wasted a lot of time investigating individual Judges. The problem is the entire system, not just . . . *maniacs* like Judge Dredd who—what the hell's that?"

Hammond turned as the door chimes sounded gently in the hall. He walked to the door, the irritation clear in his dark eyes, the tension around his mouth. Lily didn't have any idea what was really going on out there. She didn't have to go out on the street where you could smell the burning victims of the block wars, try to get a visor-head to tell you something besides the official line.

"What is it?" Hammond said, jerking open the door. "What do you—"

Hammond had nearly a quarter of a second to look at the black silhouette, the helmet without a face. The Lawgiver coughed once. The Judge stepped over Hammond's corpse and walked into the room.

TWELVE

She knew it didn't make any sense, that it wasn't like her at all. She simply didn't *do* things like this. She disciplined herself, kept her emotions totally under control. *And if you were going to let yourself get out of hand, why spend your feelings on Dredd!*

She stood in the shadows by her locker. There was a textbook on arrest procedures on the shelf, half a box of practice ammo that she should have turned in. A good thing Briscoe didn't see that. She was supposed to set a good example.

Hershey caught herself, closed her eyes and drew in a breath. *Easy, lady, don't lose it. Remember what they taught you . . . one day at a time in the streets. Yesterday was bad but you don't have to go through that one again . . .*

"And neither does Briscoe," she said aloud. "Briscoe doesn't have to do anything anymore."

She heard the hiss of the shower and smelled the scent of steam and soap. Someone slammed a locker, the sound bouncing off the tile walls like a shot.

She glanced at her watch. Time to grab a cup of something hot before her shift. Check out the new Lawmaster, see if the tekkies had found any slips. She turned and started for the door, took four determined steps then stopped, turned on her heels and walked back the other way.

"You aren't losing it, Hershey," she muttered under her breath, "you have flat *lost* it, girl."

He was changing his shirt, peeling it over his head. His back, his shoulders, and his arms were tight with cords of muscle, the perfect symmetry of his upper body marred only by the harsh, pink ridges of tissue, scars earned in combat on the streets. A Judge emblem was tattooed on his left shoulder. Hershey had one like it herself—only hers wasn't blurred where a killer's bullet had plowed an ugly groove.

Dredd turned as he heard her behind him, paused and drew his shirt down over the flat plane of his belly.

"You on today, Hershey?"

"I'm on. They gave me an option day after—after that Red Quad fracas . . ."

"And you didn't take it." Dredd's expression didn't change, but he nodded his approval.

"I think it's better if you just keep doing what you do," she said.

"You thought right."

He picked up his helmet and closed his locker. They walked together out of the room. Cadet Olmeyer had one foot up on a bench, polishing his boot. He stared at the pair, wondering if he ought to come to attention, say something, keep his mouth shut or what. By the time he decided, Dredd and Hershey were gone.

"I caught your lecture today," Hershey said.

"Good."

"You, uh, laid it on pretty thick, Judge."

"Thank you. I appreciate that."

Hershey let out a breath. *He's impossible. He thinks it's a compliment!*

"What I'm saying is, I wonder . . . do you really think that's what the Cadets need to hear?"

Dredd glanced at her. "I told the truth. What do you think I should tell them?"

"The truth is fine, I'm not arguing that. It's just . . . you made it sound as if their lives are practically *over*, and these people haven't even started."

Dredd looked straight ahead. They were walking down the rampway toward the Lawmaster tunnel.

"The life they came from *is* over. They're Judge Cadets."

"Which means what? You toss everything out but that? I'm a Judge, and I think I'm a good one. But I still have a personal life, too. I have things I like to do. I have friends . . ."

"When did you see them last?"

"What?"

Dredd stopped. His dark eyes seemed to look right through her. "These *friends*, Hershey. When did you see them? What did you do?"

Hershey felt the color rise to her face. "Okay, it's *been* awhile. My shifts keep changing a lot. It's hard to stay in touch, but that doesn't mean I don't *want* to see anybody. And I will, when things settle down."

"Things won't," Dredd said.

"Maybe not for you. I don't think you *want* things to slow down . . ."

She was sorry as soon as she said it. If he heard her, though, if he cared, he didn't let it show.

"You've only been on the street a year," he told her. "You're still a Citz-head. You'll get over it. You'll be a Judge."

"I *am* a Judge, damn it!" Hershey turned on him. "I'm a Judge right now. And I don't care for that name, either."

"What name is that?"

"You know exactly what I mean. Citz-head. The word makes it sound like Citizens are in a . . . a different class, or something. They're the people we're supposed to protect, Dredd."

"Exactly. We have to protect them because they won't take the responsibility for themselves. They don't *have* to do anything. They can be as ignorant and as irrational as they want. They can make mistakes because we're there to look after them. We can't let what we *might* want to do interfere with what we *have* to do, Hershey. Anyone who doesn't understand that doesn't have what it takes to be a Judge."

Hershey reached out and stopped him, touched his arm and turned him around.

"Is that really how you feel—it's just you out there, you against them? Don't you ever feel like . . . haven't you ever had someone you felt close to? Have you ever had anyone you could call a *friend?*"

"Yes. Once."

"What happened?"

She saw it, then, just for an instant, a shadow of pain across his features and then it was gone. Dredd turned quickly and walked away. She felt it, knew it at once, as if he'd spoken the words aloud. That's how it had happened. He'd had a friend, and he'd had to decide between friendship and the vow he'd taken to uphold the Law. It had been an agonizing decision, even for a man as dedicated as Dredd. In the end, he had judged his friend. Kept his vow and lost his soul. Shut it all out and left himself hollow inside.

Why did I have to ask, Hershey thought, *why the hell couldn't I leave him alone!*

"Dredd, wait a minute, please!" She ran to catch up with him. He stalked through the doorway into the tunnel, into the thunder of a hundred growling machines.

"I'm sorry," she said, reaching his side. "I didn't have any business asking you something like that. Your life is your own, and I had no right to—"

"Forget it, Judge Hershey. It is not important."

"It is to me," she said. "I opened my big mouth and I'm sorry. I apologize."

Dredd looked her with no expression at all. "Do whatever you want. I have work to do. So do you."

Dredd set his helmet on his head, flipped down the visor and walked away. Hershey wished she could rewind the morning, run it over again. Try not to screw it up, try to get it right.

She wondered which of the many Lawmasters was hers, tried to remember the number the maintenance sergeant had given her and couldn't make a guess. Completely irritated with herself, she turned and started back inside. It was bad enough totalling a Lawmaster, even in the line of duty. But then you had to listen to everyone make the same, tired jokes about—

Hershey stopped. They walked out of the semi-darkness at the curve of the tunnel, four of them, visors down. They were dressed in combat armor, like every other Street Judge there, only it was not the same at all. Their stance, their manner, marked them as a breed apart— Judge Hunters, the men who watched the watchers, the Law within the Law.

As Hershey watched, too stunned to move, they drew their Lawmasters, made a tight left turn in perfect step. Everyone in the tunnel stood still. The Hunters walked past Hershey, past the other Judges—and stopped in front of Dredd.

No! Hershey tried to breathe, but her throat went tight.

"Judge Joseph Dredd?"

Dredd was the only Judge in the tunnel who had completely ignored the group. He turned and gave them a curious stare.

The Hunters took a step back. "Don't move, Dredd." The leader held his weapon to Dredd's chest. Another stuck a paper in Dredd's face.

"You are under arrest, Joseph Dredd. We have the

right to confiscate your weapon. We have the right to remove your badge. Should you choose to resist, we have the right to—"

"I know your rights," Dredd told him. "What is this, what's the charge?"

"Murder."

"What? Who did I kill?"

"We have the right to remain silent, we have the right to subdue you in any manner we may choose, including Greengas, Skidders or electronic restraint. Do you have any comments to make at this time, Joseph Dredd?"

"Yes," Dredd said, "just one. You groons can go straight to hell."

THIRTEEN

*F*ergie couldn't think of any painless way to die. There were a lot of ways to do it. People did it all the time. There were illegal shops in LA if you knew where to go. If you had enough bucks, they'd fix you up fine. If you had a whole *lot*, you'd leave your miserable life feeling like a thirty-ton orgasm blasting off for outer space.

The only thing wrong was, he wasn't in LA any more and he didn't have a Reagan dollar to his name. That, and the fact that he was down in a concrete pit somewhere, waiting for the shuttle to whisk him off to Aspen again. Other than that . . .

Someone threw up nearby. That inspired somebody else. Fergie didn't care. There were sixty-two men in the pit and they'd been there crowded up together for twenty-nine hours or more. He'd done his throwing up the first three. He couldn't get sick anymore, and there was nothing on earth he hadn't smelled by now.

Fergie spent most of his time thinking up tortures for the guy with purple ears. He knew the droog was dead, but he was very much alive in Fergie's head. Alive and in excruciating pain. Every time he died, Fergie brought him back again. Sometimes he thought about Dredd, and the good-looking Judge who's name he couldn't recall. He didn't have any quarrel with them. Judges were simply a fact of life. You don't look where you're going, a truck'll squash you flat. You stay in a cheap hotel, a rat's going to bite you on the ass. When you're in the law-breaking trade, you're going to get caught now and then.

What drove Fergie nuts was the fact that he hadn't done anything at all. That wasn't right. Fate didn't have any business pulling such a lousy trick when he just got out. If you steal you get caught, but they shouldn't ought to cheat you like that.

When he got tired of thinking so hard he closed his eyes and slept. Sometimes the dreams were awful, sometimes they weren't bad at all. One was a real good dream about him and Maggie. It was a real lazy day and they'd paid to ride up the Electric to the top of the LA Wall. They had a big railing up there but it was still real scary if you stood and looked down. The sign said the Wall was two thousand twenty-seven feet high. Who could get over that? Fergie wondered. Who the hell was dumb enough to try?

It was hot on the Wall, but Maggie leaned in close and trembled against his shoulder. Fergie didn't blame her. It was an awesome thing to see. Cursed Earth stretched out to the east, the land disappearing in a wavy mirage that looked like a pig-iron sea. The sky in that direction was always brick-red from the dust storms that howled day and night across the Cursed Earth.

There were telescopes on the railing. You could put in a token and look out over the wasteland and bring everything up close. Hardly anyone did. And no one ever did it twice. There was always a chance that you'd see something more out there, something worse than the parched red earth. Something you didn't want to see like a Krazy or a Cull. A Booter hopping on a single leather foot, or a Dusteater with skin the color of clay. Outcasters came up to the LA Wall all the time, especially at night. You weren't supposed to feed them, but sometimes a guard would toss something off the Wall. Sometimes something would fall off a shuttle or a barge. A lot of the time, Fergie knew, an Outcaster came out of the wild just to look at the Wall, to see where he couldn't be.

Fergie dreamed Maggie was beside him. He dreamed she touched his leg and slid her hand up his thigh. Fergie opened his eyes and saw the skinny con squatting over him, grinning with rotten teeth.

"You son of a *bitch,*" Fergie yelled, "get *out* of here!"

He knocked the man's hand away, raised his foot and kicked him in the chest.

The con coughed, spat on the bare ground, and pulled himself up. He wiped a ragged sleeve across his face.

"You don' have to get all heated up," he said. "I wasn't doin' what you thought it was I did."

"Yeah? What are you, then, the local massage parlor, or what? I'm going to get a free rub?"

The man smelled like he'd just won the hundred-meter cesspool event. Fergie wondered if he smelled as bad, and decided he didn't want to know.

"I'm Dix," the guy said. "Donnie Dix."

"I'm not," Fergie said. "Beat it, pal."

"Listen, ol' Donnie ain't offended. I got a real thick skin. Don't anything much bother me. Say whatever you want, it don't mean anything to me."

Fergie gave the con a curious look. "Nothing, huh?"

"Not a thing, friend."

"If I was to maybe hit on something, you'd tell me, okay?"

Donnie grinned, showing jagged rows of green teeth. "I don't just side up to anyone, mister. I been around the track once or twice an' I can pick the right feller out ever' time. I got an insight into people won't quit."

"And you picked me."

"Right off. Minute I spotted you sittin' over here."

"What for?"

"What for what?"

"What did you pick me out *for?* What did I win, a free trip to Hell?"

Donnie looked puzzled, then his eyes lit up. "Well, say, I might've got you wrong, friend. It sure ain't likely, but I won't say I didn't or I did. This *is* your first time goin' up, ain't it? I got to figure it is."

"Yeah, first time up," Fergie lied. "How can you tell?"

"Like I say, it's a gift." Donnie raised a dirty finger. "You got to look real good, is all. There's a first-timer look and that's what you got."

He glanced over his shoulder to make sure no one was close.

"You'll learn about that once you get up there. I'm not supposed to say anything an' I'd get in a whole lot of trouble if anybody found out I did."

"Did what?"

"Told you about the ERP. That's the Extra Ration Plan. Prisoners get extra rations on Sundays and holidays. The thing is, a new guy like you, a *fish,* the old cons, they'll take away your ERP. Unless you join up with one of the guilds. You do that, you got *protection,* see? Nobody's going to screw with you, you're in a good guild. Am I coming through okay? You got any questions, you let me know."

"No, I think it's pretty clear."

Fergie had figured the scam about the first two seconds the droog started talking, he just didn't know the wrap-up, the end.

"So what do I do when I get to Aspen, I join one of the guilds, right?"

Donnie looked pained. "No, man, you get it up there, it's going to cost you a mucking arm and a leg. What you want to do, you want to join *before,* you want to join *now* and save half of what you'd have to pay."

"Half sounds good," Fergie said.

"Sure it does. Now you're talking, man."

"No I'm not," Fergie said. "I haven't got any bucks

and neither do you. Neither does anyone else in this hole because the Judges took everything away."

"Don't I know that? Don't Donnie Dix know that?" Dix looked irritated. "The guild don't expect you to have any cash. They know how it plays here, man. That's why I'm authorized to take goods instead of dough."

"Goods." Fergie looked at him. "Like, what kind of goods?"

Donnie tried not to let it show, but Fergie caught the look, caught the hunger and the need.

"You got stuff, man. Like boots, okay? You got real boots and good socks."

Fergie didn't blink. "You want my boots? I'm going to freezing-ass Aspen Prison, you want me to give you my boots?"

Donnie waved him off. "Don't matter. You can get some more when you get there. They got boots, warm clothes, anything you want. I mean, Aspen isn't no vacation spot, I'm not about to tell you that, but it's not as bad as everyone thinks. You keep your cool, they'll treat you okay."

"Forget it," Fergie said.

"What?"

"I said forget it. Get your sorry ass out of here. Now."

A vein began to throb on the side of Donnie's head. "You don't want to mess with me, pal. You don't want to mess with me at all. You screw around with me, word gets back to the guild, and they ain't going to be happy at all."

Donnie scooted in closer, and Fergie smelled the fury and the fear, saw the light of the wolf in Donnie's eyes.

"I work for people up there you don't want to piss off. Guys that can do stuff to you you don't even want to think about." Donnie paused to let that sink in. "You ever heard of Jimmy Eyes? You ever heard of him?"

"I heard of him," Fergie said.

Donnie showed him a nasty grin. "Yeah, I thought you maybe did."

"What I heard is he's *out,* he's not in. He got in off the shuttle a couple of days back."

Donnie blinked. "Where the hell you hear that?"

"Dinner last night. Before the Judges picked me up. It was a setup is what it was, I wasn't doing anything at all. All I was doing was coming out of Jimmy's house."

"You was—huh?"

"Coming out of Jimmy's house." Fergie grinned. "You don't get it, do you? You stupid groon, I'm Jimmy's *brother.* I'm Fergie Eyes."

Donnie went white. "No, you ain't either."

"You want Fergie Eyes' boots? You want his mucking *socks?*"

"Hey, forget it, okay?" Donnie shook his head and scuttled off like a crab who wasn't wearing shoes or socks. "I don't want *nothing,* man!"

"Right," Fergie said. "Go straight to hell, *man.*"

FOURTEEN

"When the Judge Hunters came for you, Joseph. What did you say to them?"

"I think they probably told you what I said to them, sir."

"I'm not asking *them*, Judge Dredd. I'm asking you."

"I told them to go straight to hell, sir."

"Joseph, Joseph . . ." Chief Justice Fargo ran a hand across his face, as if the gesture might relieve the great weight that seemed forever to drag him down.

The cell was scarcely large enough for one man. Dredd sat straight on the edge of the steel shelf that served prisoners for a bed. Manacles bound his hands behind his back, and another set held his legs.

The sight of this sent a jolt straight to Fargo's heart. Even in his worst nightmares, he had never imagined something like this. Anyone else, perhaps—things could happen, things could go wrong—even among a body of men and women like the Judges. But not Dredd, not Joseph Dredd.

"I have to ask you this," Fargo said. "I ask it as Chief Justice, not as a friend."

"And I'll be glad to answer it, sir. I'm innocent. I have not committed any crime."

Fargo looked at his hands. "I have to tell you this. The

Council is said to have irrefutable proof against you. That's the reason this is not merely an inquiry. This is a full Tribunal, Joseph. I don't have to tell you what that means."

"No, sir. I understand. And with all due respect, sir, you shouldn't be here. You're a member of the Court. The Articles—"

"Damn the Articles, Joseph! If I choose to come here as your friend, then I will!"

Dredd was startled by the fury, the sorrow in Fargo's eyes. He wanted to look away, but he couldn't do that. He could not dishonor the man like that.

"I'm sorry," Fargo said, "I had to ask. I don't *believe* the evidence, whatever it is, but I had to face you myself."

"Yes, sir. I know that. And I'm grateful to you, sir."

"Is there . . . anything you need, Joseph? Anything I can do?"

Dredd shook his head. "How could this happen, Judge? Something like this. I don't understand."

"I don't know. I've thought of nothing else since they informed me. I'll use every resource at my command to find out, and get to the truth of this. You know I'll do that. I will fight for you, Joseph."

"I know that, sir."

Chief Justice Fargo stepped to Dredd's side and squeezed his shoulder. "We'll see this through. We'll get it over and done."

"Yes, sir. We'll do that, sir."

Dredd stood when Fargo left the cell. He looked at the bare, white walls. Something was growing at the edge of his mind and he couldn't say what it might be. It was something *different*, something he had never felt before. Whatever it was, he didn't like it at all. He didn't want it in his head anymore.

When it finally broke through, it came in upon him like a rush of cold, dark water. He closed his eyes and a cry stuck in his throat. He saw the unfamiliar feeling for what it was. He was alone. He had experienced that terrible emotion once before, when he had to weigh friendship against his vow to uphold the Law. He had tried to sweep that from his mind, to put it aside as best he could. And now it was happening once more. Now he knew the awful feeling of loneliness again.

The screen flickered, brightened. The video suddenly focused on a hallway, a closed door. Digital numbers raced across the bottom of the image, blinking the time and the day. For a few seconds there was nothing. Then, a dark figure appeared, a figure in the unmistakable black armor of a Judge. The Judge drew his Lawgiver and pressed the button inset in the door. The door opened. Light from the room flooded the hall.

"What is it? What do you—"

Vardis Hammond's face was stricken with fear.

"Dredd! No, please—!"

A quick flare of light in the Judge's hand, a nearly-imperceptible sound. Hammond doubled over and fell. The Judge stepped over his body, walked into the room and closed the door behind him.

Judge Hershey drew in a breath and held it. Beside her, Dredd stared at the screen, unable to believe what he was seeing.

A low murmur swept through the Council Chamber. A full Tribunal was a rare occasion, and seating had been brought in to accommodate the crowd. Every off-duty Judge in Mega-City was on hand, and every Cadet from the Academy. Members of the media, who were seldom allowed in the Hall of Justice itself, let alone this chamber, had been alloted a special section today.

Judge Dredd stood on a raised dias before the table of Judges. Chief Justice Fargo sat in the center chair. Beside him were Judges Esposito, Silver, and Griffin. Judge McGruder, acting as Prosecutor, stood to Dredd's left.

Judge Hershey stood to his right. Fargo had expressed his concern when Dredd announced that he had chosen a Street Judge as his Counsel for Defense.

"I trust her," Dredd had said simply, and that was that.

"Before we continue, I would like to make a personal statement," McGruder said. "I have observed your career from the outset, Judge Dredd, and I have the highest regard for you. Nevertheless, you understand that it is my duty to prosecute this case to the best of my ability."

"I would expect no less, sir," Dredd said.

Fargo leaned forward. "The Court shares Judge McGruder's sentiments. Proceed, please."

McGruder nodded and faced the table of Judges. "The video you have just seen is *prima facie* evidence that the Defendant is guilty as charged. Mark it People's Exhibit number—"

"Objection, Your Honor!" Hershey boldly stepped forward. "The video we have just seen is inadmissable as evidence. I ask that it be rejected as People's Evidence."

McGruder stared. "What? It is perfectly clear that—"

"If I may be allowed to explain, Your Honor?"

Judge Fargo nodded. "Please do, Counselor."

Hershey gave Dredd a furtive glance. She had known McGruder had strong evidence, but she hadn't seen the video before. The sight of that dark figure gunning Hammond down in cold blood, then watching a Judge walk into the apartment to murder Hammond's wife . . . She hoped her emotions wouldn't betray her, that none of the Judges had been watching her at that particular moment.

Taking a deep breath, she brought all her will to bear to keep from shaking as she drew a document from the thin case she held at her side.

"Your Honor, I have here an affidavit from Cadet Olmeyer, who is currently attending the Academy."

From the muttering behind her, she guessed that everyone in the room was craning their necks to find one

Cadet Olmeyer. Olmeyer would love that. He had an ego that was bigger than his over-educated head.

"By way of credentials, Cadet Olmeyer is acknowledged by all of his instructors to be an expert in the field of still and video graphics. He has been at the top of his class five years running in Computer Programming and Manipulation. He helped create and develop Central's video analysis system. His affidavit states that the surveillance video in question is of such low definition that even after *all known* enhancements have been utilized, no possible identification can be made of the alleged killer shown in this presentation. Cadet Olmeyer, who is also experienced in micro-analysis of—"

"Prosecution will accept the Cadet's credentials," McGruder said wearily. "With the qualification that we *are* talking about a Cadet, here, a *student,* and not an experienced professional in the field."

"Thank you," Hershey said. She let her gaze touch each of the Judges in turn.

"Since the uniform of a Judge could easily be counterfeited, since the badge and every other accessory can be duplicated, and since neither video nor audio in Prosecution's clip can identify positively the accused *in any way* —or anyone *else,* for that matter—I repeat my objection to this video being entered as evidence in this case!"

She turned to McGruder, then to the table of Judges. "I am asking for a ruling, Your Honor!"

No one in the great Chamber moved. Behind the Judges' table, Judge Esposito leaned to his left to whisper to Judge Silver. Silver looked thoughtful, then shook his head. Judge Griffin looked right at Dredd, his eyes unwavering, as if he might somehow draw Dredd's thoughts from his head.

Chief Justice Fargo folded his hands on the table before him. He looked at himself in the dark, polished surface of the wood. It was a ritual he had practiced from the first day he had presided over the Council. The answer was always there. It was always the truth, it was always the Law, for the two were one and the same. Sometimes, the answer didn't match his deep, personal feelings, the wisdom and insight he had gained from a lifetime of serving the Citizens of Mega-City. Still, it was the right decision, and he took great comfort in that. It was the one thing he could count on, the one thing he could trust in a dangerous and rapidly changing world.

Fargo slowly raised his head. He looked past the defendant and Hershey, past Judge McGruder and the media and the black-clad Judges. His gaze came to rest on the Cadets, the young men and women who held the future of the city in their hands. The Truth, the Law, his decision, was for them.

"Objection . . . sustained. I find the Prosecution's video evidence inadmissable in this Tribunal."

For a moment, the crowd seemed to hold its collective breath. Then the Chamber exploded in a burst of sound. Fargo's gavel struck again and again, but no one seemed to hear. The cheers went on unabated, and the most raucous yells of all came from the Cadets.

Hershey leaned close to Dredd so he could hear her above the sound.

"Go ahead, tell me. I don't mind."

"Tell you what?"

"Admit it. You're impressed."

"Thanks. I'm impressed," Dredd said.

"Hey. Unbound enthusiasm. I can hardly stand it, Dredd."

Dredd looked straight ahead. "You think he's through? You think that's it?"

"No, I don't think he's *through,* I didn't say that. Nevertheless—"

"Thanks, Hershey."

"You already said that."

"Now I've said it again."

"What for?"

"In casé you do something else."

Hershey gave him a curious look. Did he mean that? Was he serious? *Of course he is,* she told herself, *he's Judge Dredd.* Either that, or Dredd had made a *joke.* That, of course, was unthinkable, and she dismissed it from her mind at once.

FIFTEEN

Judge Dredd was right. The Prosecution wasn't finished. McGruder was just getting started.

Chief Justice Fargo called a brief recess, and McGruder quickly went into a huddle with her staff. Hershey watched from the dias. She didn't have any aids; there was no one to talk to but Dredd, and Dredd was stiff as a statue, looking straight ahead. She wondered what he was thinking. There had to be *something* going on in his head . . .

The sound of Fargo's gavel echoed through the Chamber. The room went silent at once. McGruder stepped back up on the dias. She glanced calmly at Hershey, then faced the Judges' table.

"Your Honor, in light of your ruling regarding evidence presented in this Tribunal, I am forced to move to *technical* evidence which I believe is of a most critical nature. I will need the Court's permission to access documentation marked 'Judge Secret' from the Central Computer."

Hershey felt something cold at the back of her neck. Dredd didn't move. At the Judges' table, Griffin leaned over to speak to Fargo. Fargo listened, then turned to Silver and Esposito. Finally, he spoke to McGruder and Hershey.

"The request is granted. You may proceed, Prosecutor."

A slight, almost imperceptible shadow crossed McGruder's face. Hershey caught it, and knew it for what it was at once.

She doesn't want to do this. She doesn't, but she can't back away from what she's found . . .

"Central, are you on-line?" McGruder said.

"On-line, Judge McGruder."

The voice was feminine; it was a calm, reasonable, and soothing voice, that instilled both confidence and authority.

"I want you to access weapons schematics," McGruder said. "Please describe the working of the standard Judge's firearm, the Lawgiver Two, and especially its improvements over the earlier Lawgiver One."

A rotating schematic of the Lawgiver, stark white on blue, appeared on the big screen at once.

"Seven years ago, the Lawgiver Model Two replaced the Model One. The difference between these models lies in two areas: The computer chip and the ammunition coding. Like the Model One, the computer chip in the Model Two recognizes the palmprint of its owner. An imposter's hand will activate the weapon's alarm . . ."

The schematic dissolved into an animated figure. The figure pressed the trigger of a Lawgiver and was promptly blown to bits in a clean, computer-generated explosion.

". . . Model Two is somewhat different. It is coded to the personal DNA of the Judge using the weapon, via the skin's contact with the grip. A failsafe security precaution . . ."

Hershey turned to Dredd. "Did you know about this?"

"No."

"Neither did I. I don't think *any*body did."

". . . The DNA is obtained from my medical files and upgraded automatically every time the weapon is reloaded.

Each time a round is chambered and fired, the projectile is tagged with that relevant DNA . . ."

No, no! Hershey could see the whole thing now, see it all coming together.

"Chief Justice," she said suddenly, "the Defense was unaware of this information. I'm sure everybody else here is unaware of it, too."

"Let the Prosecution finish, Judge Hershey," Fargo said calmly. "I'll hear from you later if you so desire."

Hershey's shoulders fell. McGruder nodded her thanks. "Were the bullets recovered from the bodies of Vardis and Lily Hammond so DNA-coded, Central?"

"Yes, Judge McGruder."

"And what was the result of the computer check of the DNA coding of those bullets?"

"The DNA is a perfect match for Judge Joseph Dredd."

"That's a lie! This is a setup! *I did not kill those people!"*

Dredd dug his fists into his palms, drawing blood. The cords stood out in his neck. He stared at Chief Justice Fargo. Fargo met his eyes, hesitated, and looked away.

A terrible cry started deep in Dredd's throat. He didn't care about the rest of them, they could believe him or go to hell. But Fargo, if Fargo doubted him, if he thought for an instant that he had done such a thing . . .

He turned on Hershey, gripping her shoulders hard. "I wasn't there. I didn't do this."

"I know that. I know you didn't, Dredd." His fingers dug into her arms but she didn't complain. "I believe you, but I don't know what to *do* for you. The DNA evidence . . . it's *irrefutable.* He's left us without any case at all."

Dredd dropped his hands. "Everything he's saying is a lie. I'm telling the *truth.* What kind of case is that?"

"It's the Law," Hershey said. "McGruder may be

wrong, but the Law is right, Dredd. You, of all people, know that."

Dredd didn't answer. He looked at Hershey but didn't see her. He couldn't see anything at all.

"Your Honor, the Prosecution rests," McGruder said.

Under the judicial system of the Way Back When, crime not only took its toll on the individual Citizen, it also created an enormous financial burden on the community as a whole. Though it is difficult to imagine, it was the Citizen himself, through the payment of taxes, who supported lawbreakers when they were apprehended and sent to prison. Thus, food, housing, health care, and even entertainment were provided by the very people the criminals had victimized.

Under the modern penal system of the Judges, it is the inmates who bear the cost of their incarceration. If a prison is to be constructed, it is built by prison labor. Only the cost of the materials is borne by the Mega-Cities. Much of this cost is recovered through COPP—Confiscation of Prisoners' Property. When a prisoner is committed, all material goods such as real estate, vehicles, credit accounts, etc., are forfeited and cannot be recovered, even after the prisoner's sentence has been served.

Further costs of incarceration are borne by the prisoner during his sentence. Prison industries manufacture goods which are sold at a profit on open market. All food consumed in prison is grown by the inmates themselves. Clothing is manufactured within the system. Power and sanitation services are purchased from prison industry profits. A small percentage of those profits is allocated to prison "entertainment," which is restricted to health-related activities such as rigorous exercise that would aid the inmate in maintaining the proper conditioning for performing his duties.

Prisoners do not receive wages for their work, as they did in the distant past. Upon release, each man is given the equivalent of one month's income based on current minimum wage standards. A man who has served six months, or thirty years, receives the same amount upon his release. He is expected to use these funds wisely and sparingly, to rehabilitate himself at once, and obtain gainful employment.

It is unfortunate that approximately seventy-eight percent of prisoners released eventually commit the same crimes they committed before, and find themselves sentenced once again. However, it should be noted that this figure does not accurately represent those lawbreakers reincarcerated. Under the Judges, sixty-three percent of prisoners convicted receive sentences calling for execution arrest—either for the severity of the crime, or under the "Second Offense" rule. This relatively low rate of imprisonment results in a penal population that remains at a controllable level.

—History of the Mega-Cities
  James Olmeyer, III
  Chapter XXII: "The Modern Penal System"
  2191

SIXTEEN

THE SETTING:

This is Chief Justice Fargo's private study, just off the Great Council Chamber. Fargo's quarters reflect less of the man's lofty position than of the man himself. Instead of the dark, heavy furniture, thick carpets, and rare objets d'art other high officials might demand, Fargo's quarters are almost Spartan. There is a bookcase against one wall. On a simple table is a pitcher of water and two glasses. There is an ordinary plastic desk stacked with papers, and two relatively comfortable chairs.

The plastered, white-washed walls contain no pictures, certificates, holos, or awards. The one feature of Fargo's quarters which sets them apart is something few might notice at all, unless they were familiar with the architecture of the Council Chamber. The immense marble shield and eagle is, of course, the focal point of the chamber. The back of this enormous stone forms one inner wall of the Chief Justice's study. It is hard to miss the symbolism here: Here is the emblem of power, and the man at its foundation who makes that power real. This interesting bit of mythos and wisdom is pointed out to each new class of Cadets. For most of them, this place will remain a mystery throughout their careers as Judges. The chance of actually seeing the Chief Justice's quarters is something on the order of none.

[Chief Justice Fargo stares out a small window overlooking the sprawling order and chaos of Mega-City. At this moment in his life, he would gladly trade places with the most ordinary Citizen below.]

CHIEF JUSTICE FARGO
What have I done? How could I have been so wrong? Dredd, Rico—*both* of them homicidal. Only this time it will be impossible to cover up. Damn it all, this simply couldn't happen!

[Fargo buries his face in his hands. Judge Griffin walks up behind him to lay a comforting hand on his shoulder.]

JUDGE GRIFFIN
Chief Justice, it *did* happen. We can't know how or why, so there's no use whipping ourselves over that. The point is, it's not too late to pull our boots out of the fire. We carefully buried the Janus Project nine years ago, along with Rico and all his victims. No one will ever learn of your involvement. Nothing that happened leads back to you.

[Fargo shakes his head. Griffin makes it sound easy to forget about the past. Fargo knows that yesterday is always there, dogging the heels of the present.]

CHIEF JUSTICE FARGO

No, we can't hold it back this time, my friend. The media know how close I am to Dredd. They've got connections, they always do. They'll dig until the whole mess comes out. And they'll love it, too. It's the perfect excuse to *ruin* what little government, what little control we have left.

JUDGE GRIFFIN

Your motives were pure, untainted, Chief Justice. You thought Dredd was—different, or you would never have spared him.

CHIEF JUSTICE FARGO

And that little *mistake* may just bring down our whole judicial system. All of us. It won't just be *me,* you know. Once they get the taste of blood they'll go after everyone who wears the badge.

JUDGE GRIFFIN

You can't look at it that way. We are all Judges, all responsible for the acts of one another. And if they bring us down, then . . . Sir, you and I have not always agreed in judicial matters, but I shall be proud to stand beside you, Chief Justice Fargo.

[Fargo looks at Griffin a long moment, then abruptly turns away to hide his emotions.]

CHIEF JUSTICE FARGO

I am grateful for what you have said. Your words mean much to me. And you have done me a greater favor than you know, my friend. So much greater than you can know!

JUDGE GRIFFIN

Chief Justice—

[Fargo turns and faces Griffin again. Griffin knows this man well, but he is startled by the strength, the will, the terrible sense of anguish he sees in Fargo's eyes.]

CHIEF JUSTICE FARGO

There is another way to resolve this problem. It is the rational way, and, more important, it is the *responsible* way. Responsibility is the brother of privilege—we must never forget the truth of that.

JUDGE GRIFFIN

What are you saying, Chief Justice? I don't understand . . .

CHIEF JUSTICE FARGO

I think you do. I think you must know exactly what I am saying. I have the option, and I have the desire to exercise that option, Judge Griffin. I will retire. I will take the Long Walk . . .

[Judge Griffin stares, then violently shakes his head, as if this gesture might deny Fargo's words, his intentions.]

JUDGE GRIFFIN

You cannot. You *will* not, Chief Justice. The Long Walk is a death sentence and you know it!

CHIEF JUSTICE FARGO

Then it is my death sentence, is it not? It is my choice.

JUDGE GRIFFIN
Your . . . choice grants you certain rights, of course.

CHIEF JUSTICE FARGO
I am quite aware of those rights, Judge Griffin . . .

JUDGE GRIFFIN
Sir, I did not mean to imply—

CHIEF JUSTICE FARGO
It does not truly matter at this point what you may or may not imply, my friend. I hold you blameless. And yes, I *will* use the power of my retirement to save Dredd's life. This *was* on your mind, I believe? Fine. If everyone sees this as my motive, so much the better. They will not bother to look for any other . . . benefits of my decision. I believe the media will be so ecstatic at the chance to innundate Mega-City with countless holos, videos, broadcasts of my actions, they will have neither the time nor the inclination to turn over any other rocks searching for dirty laundry.

[Chief Justice Fargo pauses to pour himself a glass of water. Griffin's mouth is parched as well, but he finds he cannot bring himself to break the spell Fargo has cast upon this room.]

CHIEF JUSTICE FARGO
The judicial system we have worked these many years to establish will remain intact. And the secret of the Janus Project will be secure. That should be . . . *adequate* work for one day, don't you think?

JUDGE GRIFFIN
What you do is . . . more than anyone could ask of you. Your action shames us all, sir.

CHIEF JUSTICE FARGO
We shamed *ourselves,* Judge Griffin, when we allowed ourselves to become involved in Janus. There is no need for all of us to pay for that foolish mistake, but I cannot say that it is asking too much for one of us to bear that burden.

JUDGE GRIFFIN
I wish it were someone else, Chief Justice. I would—I would take your place if I could, sir, and consider it an honor.

CHIEF JUSTICE FARGO
I appreciate the thought, Judge Griffin. But do not be in such a great hurry to give yourself to the cause. It is not necessary. Someone will make the decision for you one day—long before you're ready to be so noble yourself . . .

SEVENTEEN

This is a dream.
I have never had a dream, but I am certain I am
having one now. Other people talk about dreams, so I
looked it up to see what a dream might be. A dream is a
thought in your head when you're asleep. You do not con-
trol what you dream; it's simply there. A dream is either
good or bad. This dream is bad. It doesn't matter though,
because a dream isn't real. When you wake up everything is
fine. Everything is like it was before . . .

The Council Chamber was hushed. The Judges filed into
the room. There was no way anyone could tell from the
expressions on their faces what they intended to do.
Some enterprising members of the media tried to read
the verdict from the way the Judges walked, from the
way they held their shoulders, from the way their arms
moved. Were Fargo's shoulders bowed? Did Esposito
stand as straight as usual? Didn't Griffin usually come in
before Judge Silver, instead of just behind?

The reporter looked up past the Judges at the cobalt
light that shimmered from the high, vaulted panes. One
beam of light streaked down upon the massive granite
shaft. The beam seemed to race across the shield, trace

the eagle's wing, and settle on the razored talons of its leg.

The reporter drew in a breath. It had to be a sign. The light wouldn't strike the claw at that moment if there wasn't meaning there.

He hastily scribbled a note on his pad: *In the old days, in the Way Back When, superstitious men and women believed they saw signs from their Maker everywhere* . . .

It would do just fine. He would describe the beam of light as a sign of Dredd's conviction or acquittal. It didn't matter which. That was the thing about signs: They worked any way that you wanted them to.

Chief Justice Fargo struck the table with his gavel. Council Judge Esposito stood to speak for the Tribunal.

"In the charge of premeditated murder against Citizens Vardis Hammond and Lily Hammond, we find the Defendant Joseph Dredd . . . guilty."

Everyone in the room seemed to draw a breath at once. One of the Cadets lost control and cried out, shaking his fist in a fury of protest. A veteran Street Judge rushed the young man outside. Ordinarily, he would have punished the Cadet severely. Today, he would forget what he had seen.

Chief Justice Fargo looked down at Dredd, determined to face him squarely, to do his duty and not turn away.

"Joseph Dredd, you are aware the Law allows only one punishment for your crime. That punishment is death. However, it has long been our custom to carry out the last order of a retiring Judge . . ."

Fargo gripped the arm of his chair. His body felt massive, heavy with the weight of his years, with the sorrow of this terrible thing that was happening to him, to Dredd, to them all. He felt an instant of sheer panic when he was certain he could not bring himself to stand. Then, the strength that had always carried him through the worst of times came to his aid again. Gazing out over the crowd, he bowed his head, then lifted his face to the high ceiling, to the graceful arches of stone, to the fierce blue light.

"And so I now step down. And as I do so, I exercise my right. As I leave to take my Long Walk into the Cursed Earth, I ask this Court for leniency in its verdict against Judge Dredd, in gratitude for his years of dedicated service . . ."

Hershey was numb. Her heart pounded against her chest. She risked a look at Dredd, standing close beside her. What she saw sent a chill up her spine. Dredd's eyes were dead. As dead as frosted glass. His mentor, the man who had been his father in nearly every respect, had just saved Dredd and sentenced *himself* to die. And Joseph Dredd hadn't blinked an eye!

At that moment, Hershey didn't know whether to hate Dredd or pity him. The man was made of ice, an iceman with a chunk of iron for a heart!

Chief Justice Fargo closed his eyes for a moment, then stood aside and formally relinquished his seat to Judge Griffin. Griffin picked up the gavel of the Chief Justice, his new badge of office, then set it down again.

"We will honor your order, Judge Fargo. The sentence of death is revoked. Joseph Dredd is hereby sentenced to life in Aspen Prison."

His first act as Chief Justice completed, Griffin struck the table with his gavel. The Court erupted into chaos. Griffin pounded the table again and again, his face growing, dark with anger.

"Sentence to be carried out immediately," he shouted above the crowd. "This Court is adjourned!"

"Judge Griffin, this trial is a farce!" Hershey stepped off the dias and glared at the new Chief Justice. "I *demand* an appeal. You cannot simply—"

"Enough, Judge Hershey!" He picked up the Book of the Law and pointed it at her like a weapon. "You will

accept the Council's decision, and you will accept it without question."

He turned away from Hershey, and pointed at Dredd. "Remove this prisoner. Immediately. Get him out of here!"

The Judge Hunters appeared at Griffin's command, six of them, two marching swiftly down each aisle. A Cadet, in his excitement, made the mistake of getting in the way of one of the Hunters. The Judge Hunter swept him aside without breaking his stride.

"Let the Betrayer of the Law be taken from our Courts!" Griffin read from the Book of Law, his voice resounding through the great hall.

Hershey gasped and stepped aside. The Judge Hunters clamped manacles on Dredd's wrists. Dredd stared straight ahead. He didn't seem to notice the Judge Hunters were there.

"Let the Freedom he stole from others be stolen from himself!"

One of the Judge Hunters pushed Dredd roughly in the back. Dredd tripped and sprawled on the floor. Two Hunters jerked him to his feet. Another tore off his armor and threw it aside. Still another clutched Dredd's black uniform at his throat, and ripped it across his chest. Dredd didn't move. He stood perfectly still, solid as stone, while the Hunters tore at his body, stripping him naked of his clothing, his honor, and his life.

"Let his armor be taken from him, and all his garb of Justice . . . Let his name be stricken from our rolls. Let his memory be erased from our minds . . . Let him live his life in dishonor and shame, and let him remember every day that he has not only betrayed himself, he has brought that shame and dishonor upon us. It is our regret that Judge Dredd cannot live a thousand lives in contemplation of his crime . . ."

* * *

Hershey was uncertain how long she had been standing there, alone. The Judges' table was empty. The audience was gone as well—the Judges, the Cadets. The section reserved for the media was empty. The vultures had fed well; they had gotten even more than they'd bargained for today.

She wondered what had happened to Fargo. She didn't remember seeing him after Griffin took his place as Chief Justice. A strong, commanding presence one moment, and the next a shadow, no one at all.

Hershey started down the aisle, hesitated, then stopped, and turned toward the side door that led to the small room off the Council Chamber. There would be people in the hallway, people she knew. Street Judges, maybe members of the news media. Cadet Olmeyer, probably. She couldn't see Olmeyer now. He'd be mooning over her, offering his sympathy, unintentionally doing everything to make her feel worse.

The anteroom was empty. For a long moment, she stood there in the silence. It seemed a lifetime instead of only moments before since she and Dredd had waited there for the Council to consider its verdict. She couldn't recall what they'd said to each other. Probably nothing at all. At that point, there was little they could say. Both of them knew that miracles only happened in legend, in the Way Back When. Not in Mega-City, not now.

She glanced at the two glasses on the table. A Cadet steward had brought them water while they waited. Dredd had taken one swallow. Hershey had finished hers.

She picked up Dredd's glass. She was bone-tired, aching all over from the tension of the trial. The tissues in her mouth were parched. She raised Dredd's glass, held it just below her lips. The faint, pleasant scent of lemon rose from the clear liquid, and she was struck by the sudden memory of dark, brown eyes and a soothing smile, a summer afternoon. Her mother had liked the taste of lemon, and often added it to the water at meal-time. Hershey hadn't thought of that in years, and now her mother was—

Hershey stopped, stared at the glass and brought it closer to her nose. She set down Dredd's glass and picked up her own. It was nearly empty, but there was enough there to smell. Nothing. No scent at all.

Judge Hershey's hand shook as she set the glass down. The rage began to spread throughout her body, burning like a fire she could scarcely control. She clenched her fists in frustration, then grabbed up Dredd's glass and threw it against the wall.

Hexxadol Nine! It wasn't the scent of lemon, it was a powerful tranquilizer drug. They had passed around samples of dozens of dangerous chemical compositions at the Academy. She had been proud of herself because she was extremely sensitive to smells. Most of the other Cadets hadn't detected a thing when Hexxadol Nine had come around.

And Dredd hadn't either . . .

The rigid stance, the frozen stare. It didn't take much of the stuff to numb him to anything that was happening around him. They could have started a war right there and Dredd wouldn't have noticed. There was enough of the drug in his glass . . .

Who? Hershey wondered. *Why* wasn't the question, why was perfectly clear. Dredd would accept his own sentence, but he would go berserk when he learned of Fargo's sacrifice.

Hershey's rage turned to sorrow and she let it all out, didn't try to hold it back. The scalding tears were for Dredd, but they were for Chief Justice Fargo as well. He had traded his own life for Dredd's, but it seemed he had done more than that. He had made certain Dredd didn't have to share his pain. He would, but not in the Council Chamber. Not in front of the others. Dredd and Fargo had both been spared that.

EIGHTEEN

"*T*his is Duncan Harrow with the news . . .

"I feel a little out of place, a bit uncomfortable, ladies and gentlemen, sitting behind the news desk today. In my mind, this desk will always belong to a man who was revered and respected by the journalistic community, and the Citizens of Mega-City, for a number of years.

"This is Vardis Hammond's desk. And the tragic story unfolding before us today began with the brutal, senseless slaying of Vardis Hammond, and his wife, Lily.

"Why did the popular—the legendary—Judge Dredd slaughter two innocent people in the sanctity of their home? Some say Judge Dredd suffered from a serious mental disorder, a condition kept under wraps by Dredd's powerful friend and long-time mentor, the former Chief Justice Fargo. One informed source reports that the Hammonds were killed because of Hammond's continued criticism of the Judges, and Judge Dredd in particular. As our regular viewers will recall, Hammond long claimed that there was corruption within the judicial system, and that the increase in rioting and crime in our city could be traced to the moral decay within the hierarchy of the Judges.

"It's a question that may never be answered, but the

murder of the Hammonds, and the conviction of Judge Dredd for that crime, has led to another bizarre and startling development—the retirement of Chief Justice Fargo himself, and the commutation of Dredd's death sentence to life in Aspen Prison.

"As I announced previously, the news media is not allowed to bring you live video coverage of the Ceremony of Retirement. We apologize for this, of course, but we must comply with the decision of the Judges. In lieu of live coverage, I will read you the text of the ceremony, as given to us by a media spokesman of the Judges.

" 'At sunrise this morning, retiring Judge Fargo was escorted by an Honor Guard of Street Judges to the City Gate in the Wall of Mega-City. Judge Fargo wore the traditional tan duster, traditional lawmen's wear from a period dating to the Way Back When. A young Cadet, first in her class this year, read from the Book of Law, and a chorus of Cadets sang the solemn Judges' Anthem.

" 'The cadet read: "Let him who has been written in our hearts and memories be struck from our hearts and memories forever . . ."

" 'At this point, retiring Judge Fargo hands a bundle containing his uniform, Lawgiver, and badge to the presiding Cadet. The Cadet hands Fargo the Book of Law, and the weapon he will carry to the Cursed Earth, a black-burnished Judges' Remington pump. The Cadet salutes smartly. Judge Fargo returns the salute for the last time. The Cadet does an about face, turns her back on Judge Fargo, marches back to her post before the gathered command, and speaks again: "Let him go from us, from our city, from our protection, from our presence forever . . ."

" 'The city gates open, revealing the parched, empty land beyond. Judge Fargo walks through the gate, and into the Cursed Earth.

" 'He has gone from our midst, he has left us forever.

May he continue his pursuit of the Right throughout his life. May he bring Law to the lawless, Justice to the unjust . . . as he leaves our sight forever . . .'

"At this point, ladies and gentlemen, the great city gate closes behind Judge Fargo. The Cadets and the honor guard of Street Judges come to attention, and the Judges' Anthem reaches its stirring climax.

"This concludes our report on the Retirement Ceremony of Judge Fargo, former Chief Justice of Mega-City.

"As an ironic sidenote to this story, I can report to you that at virtually the same instant this ceremony was taking place, another, somewhat less *formal* event occurred at the Northwest Shuttle-gate of our city. Here, sixty-three men in chains and gray prison garb walked up the rampway to the Aspen Prison Shuttle Number Eleven. Some will be incarcerated for only a short time, some for many years. At least one among them will spend the rest of his life behind those forbidding walls for the crime of double murder. A prisoner named Joseph Dredd.

"Duncan Harrow here. Good night . . ."

The small craft whined above the city, catching the light of the sun on its crystal bow. It circled a tower that touched the morning clouds, hovered an instant, then settled gently into the magnetic lock that held it steady against the high structure.

A circular iris whispered open, and Chief Justice Griffin walked quickly out of the craft. The pilot saluted, but Griffin didn't bother to respond.

The walls of his apartment were simulated oak, a perfectly polished imitation of a material that had long since vanished from the earth. The furniture was stark black and white, the pictures on the walls abstract slices of silver and blue. Replicated logs burned in the large fireplace at the far end of the room. The light flickered off the rich, golden walls, lending the stark decor a warm and comforting glow.

Griffin walked straight to the bar beside a heavy glass table. He reached for the familiar crystal container, changed his mind, and bent behind the bar. In a corner near the back was a bottle with a faded gold label, the printing nearly indistinct. He brought the bottle out and held it to the light. The liquid inside was the dark and smoky hue of old gold.

"Real Scotch whisky," Griffin said aloud. "No simulations, not today."

He reached for a glass. He heard the soft laughter behind him, jerked around and nearly dropped the precious bottle on the floor.

"Damn you," he said, "what do you think you—"

Griffin stopped and sucked in a breath. The man stood in the center of the room, light from the fireplace glancing off the sharp planes of his face. But there was someone, something else—a darkness, a shadow that seemed to lift itself out of the substance of the floor behind the man, swell and grow until it nearly touched the high ceiling itself. It hissed and groaned, and steam rose from its dented metal joints.

Griffin recognized the monster at once. An ABC robot, a relic of some ancient war. A thing like that, here, in his *home* . . .

"Are you out of your mind!" Griffin stared at the man in anger. "Why did you bring that . . . that *thing* in here? I want it out of here at once!"

Rico smiled. "The Scotch is good. I tried it before you arrived."

"Anything else I can get you?" Griffin said darkly. "Anything you see, don't hesitate to ask."

Rico leaned against the fireplace and crossed his arms. "Chief Justice Griffin. It has a . . . pleasant ring to it."

"Yes, that's all very well and good, but we—"

Griffin stepped toward Rico. The massive robot creaked and slammed a heavy foot in his path. The room shook. Glass trembled in a cabinet on the wall.

"I don't like this," Griffin said. "You and that antique killer coming here. I said we'd meet somewhere safe. My home is supposed to be secure, but there aren't many secrets in Mega-City anymore."

"I prefer to choose my own meeting places, Mr. Chief Justice." Rico swept his arm in a casual gesture. "What are you worried about? That fool reporter is dead. The beloved Judge Fargo has taken the Long Walk, and Judge Dredd is on his way to Aspen Prison. I do hope he gets my old cell. It's quite special. So . . . *isolated,* so quiet . . ."

Rico looked into the fire. "Fargo was no trouble, I assume? Such a fine and noble man."

Griffin made a noise in his throat. "With Dredd convicted his back was to the wall. He didn't have any choice. He thought the Long Walk was all his idea. Dredd was the only one who could raise hell during the proceedings, and I made sure he kept quiet."

Griffin shook his head. "I'm not happy with the disposition of Dredd. He's an extraordinary man. I could've used him in this . . ."

"No. You could *not* have *used* him in this!" Rico swept Griffin's words aside. "Dredd *worships* the Law, and he would have blown you away the moment he found out how much you're pissing on it. Let him freeze his ass off in Aspen. Let him see what it's like to be *me!* After all, he and I have *so* much in common, don't we?"

Griffin looked at Rico. Rico's eyes seemed to glow with a light far greater than the reflection from the fire. They were a deeper, more molten red, like the unblinking eyes of the robot that stood silently over Rico's shoulder.

"I'm . . . sure you're right," Griffin said. "No use wasting time on Joseph Dredd. There's a great deal of work to be done."

Rico nodded. "Janus. Yes . . ."

"You'll see it soon enough. In the meantime, I want

chaos, Rico. The block wars were just the beginning. Now I want fear racing through every street." He slammed his fist against the wall. "Then the Council will *have* to turn to me. And when they do, I'll give them Janus!"

Rico rubbed a hand across his chin. "Fear, terror, panic in the streets. I think I can handle that . . ."

NINETEEN

*T*he air in the hold was thick and foul. The odor was of flatulence and fear, fury and the sour smell of sweat. The prisoners were chained to the hard metal benches. The guards stalked up and down the narrow aisle between them, mean-eyed men with big necks and arms like slabs of iron. They held their riot guns close to their chests, like lovers who might run away. They prayed to dark gods that they'd get a chance to kill someone today. Maybe a con would go mental and howl like a dog. Maybe a man would try to strangle his buddy with his chains. Maybe one or two men would try to escape.

No more than two. They never prayed for more than that. A shuttle guard's worst nightmare was a hold full of desperate men, all coming at them at once. The guards never told each other, but they knew what they would do. They wouldn't take a chance. They'd turn their weapons on themselves, blow off their heads in one clean and decent shot.

Fergie knew who the guy was. He knew, but he knew he wasn't right. He wasn't right because it didn't make sense. There wasn't a chance in hell that the man who had put him in this stinkhole was sitting next to him on the bench. Okay, it *looked* like the guy. A lot of people looked like someone, but that didn't mean they were them.

He held his hands up and brought them close together. He peeked through the gap until all he could see were the guy's dark eyes, a little piece of nose. He closed the gap, opened it, closed it shut again.

"*Dredd?*" Fergie couldn't believe it, but now he knew it was true. "Holy sh—Dredd, it's *you!*"

"So what?" Dredd didn't look up.

"Wha-what are you doing here? You can't be here you're a—I mean you're not a—Hey, you're undercover, right? On the job. Watchin' someone. Keeping your eyes open. Following a clue. I'm deaf and dumb, okay? My lips are sealed, I will not say a thing."

Dredd looked up. Fergie felt the man's eyes drill halfway through his head. "I was convicted of a crime. Wrongly convicted. That's what happened. That's why I'm here. I don't want to talk to you. Leave me alone."

"You, too?" Fergie slapped his head. "Hey, no kidding? That makes two of us. How about that?"

"No. That makes one of us." Dredd shook his head. "I remember you. Ferguson, Herman. Interference with public droids. Unlawful use of—"

"Five *years?* For saving my own miserable ass? You got an innocent man in here. It was big mistake, Dredd!"

"The Law doesn't make mistakes."

"Yeah? So what happened to you? How do you explain that?"

Dredd looked at his hands. "I can't. I don't know."

"Oh, right." Fergie made a face. "But the *Law* doesn't make mistakes. So what do you call this? A computer glitch, what? What did they get you for, jaywalking, spitting in the stree—"

"Hey, groon . . ."

A heavy finger poked Fergie in the ribs. Fergie turned. The con on his right had barbed wire tattooed in horizontal stripes across his face. Now and then, the artist had added tattooed drops of blood.

"You illiterate, or what? You don't keep up with current events, you goin' to look stupid, man. You goin' to be ill-informed."

"I've been busy," Fergie said. Wire-face had breath like a sewer. "I'm a big-time crime lord. I've got a lot of things to do."

Wire-face grinned. "What he done, man, is he hit two Citizens: that guy on the video an' his old lady, too."

Fergie frowned at Dredd. "What'd the droog do, spell your name wrong, what?"

"Hey, you slobs, listen up!" Wire-face strained against his chain and jabbed a finger at Dredd. "Look who we got with us. We got a muckin' *celebrity* on board. *We got us Judge Dredd!*"

The word went up and down the hold, spreading like an angry ripple from one con to the next.

"Dredd."

"Dredd."

"Dredd's here . . ."

"Dredd!"

"Dredd!"

"DREDD!"

The drone of voices swelled into a roar. The guards sat up straight, looked at each other, flicked off safeties, and stroked the triggers of their weapons.

"All right, cool it off down there. I ain't askin' you again!"

"DREDD . . . DREDD . . . DREDD!"

Someone snapped a chain. Someone found a plastic blade strapped to his leg, a weapon the detectors didn't find. Someone spit a shard of broken glass from his mouth and slipped it between the knuckles of a scarred left hand.

A man nearly seven feet tall came to his feet behind Dredd. He howled and rolled his eyes, spitting Dredd's

name, a broken chain whipping about his head. He came
at Dredd fast. Dredd kicked him in the gut, slamming
him back into a benchful of men. The men yelled and
shook their fists, straining at their chains. A burly arm
came out of nowhere, crooking around Dredd's neck.
Dredd drove his elbow straight back. The man grunted in
pain, but he wouldn't let go.

A riot gun exploded twice, breaking eardrums and
lighting up the hold. A scream pierced the air.

Fergie saw the man scooting on his arms across the
surface of the deck. Long arms, long legs, hairy as a
spider. Dredd roared in Fergie's ears, and pounded on
the enormous arm around his neck. Fergie didn't think
Dredd looked good at all. His face looked red. Then it
looked purple, then it looked blue.

If I get out of this alive, I won't have to do any time,
Fergie thought. *Dredd'll kill me and I won't have to do five
years—five minutes maybe, sure as hell not five years* . . .

Reverend Billy Joe Angel fought the urge to reach beneath his robe and scratch his crotch. That was wrong,
that was sin. God wouldn't care for that. There was
something crawling around down there—maybe a centipede, it felt kind of long. 'Course it might be a bunch of
red ants. There were lots of red ants in the gully, and if
you stayed on your knees long enough in holy prayer
they'd find you out.

Whatever it was, it stung bad. It was stinging parts that
hurt worse than anything at all. The Reverend rejoiced in
God's blessing, in the joy of the pain.

"Gwowy do Goht," he cried out, "gwowy do hids
nabe!"

He drew the hood tighter about his head, and raised
his face to the skies. He was blind, but he could feel the
terrible wrath of the sun. It burned through ragged cloth,
blistered his flesh and seared him to the bone.

Thou art good, oh Lord, he prayed in his head. *Thou*

*hast sent me bountiful suffering and near-unbearable pain.
I thank thee for this empty and worthless land, for the
merciless ball of fire thou hast placed overhead, for the tiny
creatures of the earth that do constantly sting and bite this
worthless body, which is unclean and eternally damned.
Bring forth festering sores upon me, and upon my wicked
sons, the filthy spawn of my loins, the—*

"Shuttle coming, Pa! Link-Link's got us a ETA of
three minutes flat!"

The Reverend felt a rush of glorious pain, a thrill of
agony more intense than the nest of scorpions he'd sat in
last spring.

"Praish the Lort who breegs us thish boundy!" Reverend Billy Joe Angel cried. "Praish hids nabe!"

He reached for his staff, found it, and pulled himself
shakily to his feet. The ants were angry at his movements
and swarmed up both his legs. He plodded up the gully,
dizzy with a hundred stabs of venom in his veins. He
avoided rocks and holes, for though he was blind, he
knew this piece of hell as well as he knew the welts and
bites that covered his scrawny form.

"Coe, coe my suds," he shouted, shaking his shaft
above his head. "Coe forth and gedder in the Harbest!"

Mean Machine jumped up and down with delight. He
covered one eye and squinted through one side of the
antique binoculars, the side that wasn't filled up with
dirt. He couldn't see a thing, but he knew it was coming,
knew it was there. He hadn't seen a shuttle or heard a
thing at all but he *knew*. The same way he knew a lot of
things, since Pa had put the little tick-thing in the hole
upside his head. Pa said the tick-thing was a blessed
curse of God. Pa was annointified and sorely ordained,
and Pa ought to know.

Junior Head-Dead scrambled up the pathway, making
pig-noises with his mouth. He dragged the big Boomer
along behind him, stumbling and falling and picking himself up again.

"You break that and Pa won't hit you fer a week," Mean Machine warned him. "And I ain't kidding, neither!"

"Snuk-Snuk-snuk!" Junior Head-Dead dropped the handle of the boomer, scattering parts on the ground. Snapped the shaky tripod in place. Lifted the clumsy weapon and set it on the stand, bolted it into place. Junior Head-Dead had no idea what it was. He knew it worked good and that was all he cared. It was a long, dented tube, still flecked with olive-drab paint. In an ancient incarnation in the Way Back When, it might have blown the treads off of a tank. It was hard to tell what it was then. Now, a missile that looked like a gas pipe protruded out the front. The missile had flat round magnets soldered to its snout. They looked like a plague of metal warts.

"Go-go-go!" cried Junior Head-Dead. "Going to catch me some citified boys!"

"Shut up," Mean Machine said. He looked at Link-Link. Link-Link squatted like a sausage as he always did. His rat-nose twitched at the sky. Mean Machine had the Numbers of the Beast in his head. He could see things before they happened, but Link-Link could see them when they did.

"Give me a range-oh," Mean Machine said. "Give me an Eee-Tee-Ay, gimme a G, gimme a O . . ."

"Sixty-Mixty-Levendy-Three," Link said. "A four and a two and a thing with two heads . . ."

"That's an *eight,* shit-brain," Mean Machine said. "You gettin' this, Junior?"

"Snuka-Snuk!" Junior said. "Goin' to whup 'em right out of the sky!"

"You jus' hold it," Mean Machine said. "There's nothing to shoot at yet, groon."

"Don't you—*snuk!*—go callin' me that!"

"Lo," said the Reverend Billy Joe Angel, "Lo, I am an

ins-drew-ment of the Lort. He shall blesh me with hids abomonashuns!"

Mean Machine saw it in his head, the way it would happen, the way it would be. The flash of light, thunder, and the roar.

"Fire One!" he yelled as loudly as he could, though he didn't know why because there wasn't any Two . . .

"F-F-Fire One!" Junior Head-Dead said. He pulled the trigger and closed his eyes. Fire blasted out of the rear end of the weapon. It seared all the hair off Junior's head. Junior hit the ground and rolled twice. The missile whined and wobbled drunkenly into the air. Mean Machine marveled at the white tail of smoke fading into the colorless sky. Reverend Billy Joe Angel prayed for God to send vipers and maggots to his bed.

Then, an instant before he heard the great din of retribution, the joyous sound of death, he felt the heat of the explosion on his face, felt the mighty flame of God's breath.

"Got the sinners, Pa!" Mean Machine shouted. "Got 'em real good!"

"Hagga-lulla!" the Reverend Angel said.

TWENTY

Dredd decided he was dead.

The big con had squeezed the life out of his lungs, pounded his head against the shuttle's iron floor. Blood filled his eyes. He couldn't feel his legs anymore. He beat at the man's ugly face until his fists went raw and the bastard wouldn't budge.

He had never thought about death. Death was just there. Death was what you did when you didn't do life anymore.

Then, in an instant, the world ripped apart in a ball of blinding light. Dredd and the con weren't fighting on the floor; they were spinning through the air, locked together like two angry cats. The walls of the shuttle went by in a blur. Dredd flailed out and missed, turned end over end and tried again. His fingers found steel; the con's grip tore free. He stared at Dredd and opened his mouth in a scream. The sound was lost in the howl of escaping air. The con seemed to shrink and disappear.

Dredd saw a ragged slice of blue sky and realized half the shuttle was gone. Something hit him solidly in the back and bounced off into the light, something without a head or legs. Dredd gripped the wall and held on.

Explosion, he thought. *Something hit us . . . not in the shuttle . . . something outside.*

The earth and the sky flashed by in a blur of blue and brown. Not too fast, Dredd noticed, gradually slowing down, spinning, but still slowing down. The front of the shuttle, half of the craft or more, ripped itself apart. The broken shell that was still intact was trying to stabilize itself, bring itself down in one piece. Dredd couldn't see them, but he knew micro-computers in the molecular structure of the hull were patiently firing thruster rockets to bring them out of the spin. The computers didn't know that there wasn't a ship anymore, just a twisted piece of scrap. It was a valiant attempt to put a scrambled egg back together and cram it in the shell.

"Dreeeeedd!"

Dredd heard his name shrieking in the wind. With an effort that strained the tendons in his neck, he turned and spotted Fergie a dozen feet away. He was still strapped down, his fingers clutched tightly around the bottom of the bench.

"Dredd, *do* something," he shouted. "Get me out of here!"

"Hold on," Dredd told him. "We're going down."

"No kidding? See, I didn't know that, I thought everything was fine. Now you tell me we're going down, you've got me all upset again."

Someone screamed. Fergie decided a lot of people were dead somewhere. A few were still alive and wishing to hell their luck would run out.

"This is all *your* fault," Fergie said. "You did this to me. I wouldn't be here if it wasn't for you!"

"You broke the Law, Ferguson. You do the crime, you serve the time."

"What time?" Fergie stared. "I haven't *got* any time!"

"Thirty seconds," Dredd said. "Maybe forty-five."

"Shiiiiiiiit!" Fergie said.

The corridors were dark. Even when Griffin thumbed his flash up to high the beam seemed to fade out and die.

The cold steel walls were always thirsty down here. They always drank the light. Griffin had supervised the construction of the tunnel that led to the project, but he was never comfortable in the place. The bowels of Mega-City burrowed deep into the earth, but the tunnel was farther down than that.

Too deep, too cold, Griffin thought. *Even too cold for a secret like this.*

He was aware of Rico beside him, Rico's silver eyes and chilling smile. Griffin knew Rico was aware of the fact that he feared the ancient robot, that its presence over his shoulder brought the memories of terrible wars to mind, horrors that Griffin had tried to forget. It filled him with rage that Rico could do this to him, that he couldn't control these emotions in himself. That Rico knew, that he could smell and taste a man's fear.

The corridor ended abruptly with a blank steel wall. Judge Griffin placed his left palm against a surface as cold as glacial ice. There was no marking there, no indication that this particular point was any different from the rest.

A sound almost too low to hear throbbed within the metal wall. The warrior robot shifted its massive weight. Its armored head extended from its neck; red eyes whirred from side to side.

"Oh, dear. Fido doesn't like what's inside," Rico said.

"Good. He can wait out here," Griffin said.

"Couldn't do that. He wants to be close to me."

Griffin didn't answer. The wall seemed to slip into itself, as if the metal had melted away. The scent of dust and ozone filled the air. The room was dimly lit, a large half-sphere. Black, opaque plastic covered the large, geometric structures scattered about the floor.

Rico stood perfectly still, his eyes taking in every inch of the room.

"I can't understand why Fido doesn't like this place," he said. "I simply love it here."

"I'm not surprised," Griffin said. "Welcome to Janus. You've been so anxious to see it, now you're here."

"There is a feeling in here. A sense of . . . a beginning." Rico closed his eyes. "Can you smell that, Griffin? Yes, of course you can. It's an *awakening*, a dawning. The light says that. It's always dawn down here . . ."

Rico opened his eyes, suddenly alert. The robot hummed and moved its bulk in Rico's path.

Rico glared at Griffin. "Who's in here? Someone is in here."

"We're not in combat," Griffin said irritably. "Tell that toy of yours to stand down!"

Rico looked past Griffin. His pupils swelled and turned gold. The woman stepped out of shadow into sight. She was tall, dressed in something blue that captured a million shards of light. Her mouth was wide and red, her eyes slightly tilted where the dark hair tumbled past her cheeks to her breasts.

"I know you," Rico whispered. "I remember you . . ."

"Yes, you do," the woman said. "You remember me." Her voice was a breath of chilly air. She rewarded Rico with a smile.

"You're Ilsa Hayden. The bitch who testified before the Council. You told the Judges I was insane."

"And therefore innocent of your crimes," Griffin added.

"I was simply trying to help," Ilsa said.

Rico's eyes burned. "You *insulted* me. You made me look like a—a mental degenerate. I knew exactly what I was doing. I did then, and I do now."

"Really?" Ilsa took a step toward him. One small motion with more silent meaning, more blatant sensuality than Rico had ever seen.

"You might want to reconsider your . . . state of mind, friend. You might need to call on my help again."

Griffin watched them. They stood well apart, but he

could feel the struggle between them, the invisible lines of tension, the hunger and the need. He forced himself to repress a smile. Ilsa was the gift he had hoped for, the control he needed to keep Rico stable, to use him, to keep the howling psychopath inside this creature from emerging and destroying them all. Ilsa could do that. The raw, animal smell of this woman could bind him tighter than the strongest chain.

"Miss Hayden has been a loyal supporter of this project for some time," Griffin said. "She has watched over it, kept it alive for me. I'm certain you'll find her experience . . . invaluable, Rico."

Rico didn't blink. "I'm most grateful. I'm sure I can use all the help I can get."

"We have our work cut out for us." Ilsa swept one hand about the room. "The equipment's been dormant for some time. It won't be up and running without a complete retrofit. I've made some notations for you. This should give you some idea."

Ilsa handed him a thin computerpad. Rico nodded, studied the figures quickly. He frowned, then looked up in alarm.

"Are you certain this is entirely correct? Yes, of course you are." He turned on Griffin like a snake. "Inducers, nitrogen coils, nano-pumps . . . Hell, is there anything you *don't* need? Why don't we just nuke the place and start over again!"

He looked at Ilsa. "You've kept the project alive, have you? With what, glue and tape?"

"With what I had to work with, Rico." If his words had offended, she didn't let it show. "There was never any intention of bringing the project up to working status until we were ready. We saw no point in that." She raised an eyebrow at Griffin. "Perhaps you should explain."

Griffin nodded. "Ilsa has kept me apprised of her needs all along, Rico. I've had the necessary equipment marked for our use. From hospitals, government facilities, research laboratories . . . everything slated for different destinations, different names. It's all there, all ready." He smiled at the two. "If I set things in motion, when can you be on line?"

"If you can really deliver all this," Rico said, "tomorrow I'll have the place working."

"We can begin to *think* about bringing the project on-line in a week. No less," Ilsa broke in.

They looked at each other, neither willing to waver. Griffin read challenge, resentment—and curiosity as well. Together they could do it. Working with each other, in spite of each other. The attraction between them was the heat that would light a fiercely burning fire, a fire that would change the world, mold it the way Griffin knew it had to be.

"On-line won't mean a damn thing if you can't get into Central's Janus files," Rico said. He flexed his fingers and ran one hand across his jaw. "They're still security-locked. If we can't pry the data out of there . . ."

"Leave Central to me," Griffin told him. "You have plenty to do until then. None of this, down here, will be effective if you don't stir up the Citizens in the street. Ilsa has some good suggestions in that area, too. I'm sure she can help."

"That won't be necessary," Rico said. "I don't need any help."

"Oh, I see." Ilsa shook her head, a gesture that tossed a wave of dark hair over one eye. "I thought you said he was the best, Griffin. I'm afraid I overlooked that evaluation somewhere. All I see is a petulant child."

"Look, you—" Rico's eyes flashed.

"Please . . ." Griffin raised a palm in peace. "Let's not bicker now, all right? We are all committed to the same goal, ending the squalor, the inefficiency of our world. Replacing it with a new, ordered society."

Rico's frown faded. He looked at Griffin and laughed.

It was a sudden, abrupt sound that shattered the silence of the room.

"You'll get your *New Order,* Griffin. We'll take care of that, won't we, sweets?" He winked at Ilsa, then turned and whistled at the robot warrior looming dark at his back. "Let's go, Fido. Daddy's going to find you something to bite."

TWENTY-ONE

It sounded like a wind-up bee, a tiny *clut-clut-bzzzt!* in his ear. Griffin stopped dead, jerked around and stared back down the tunnel. The shadows were empty, no one was there.

Of course there's no one there, you damn fool. No one but you!

Nerves, he told himself. That maniac and his antique killing machine were enough to give anyone the jumps. Ilsa Hayden was no paragon of mental health, as far as that was concerned, but compared to Rico . . .

"Yes, Griffin here. What is it?"

He spoke softly, almost a whisper. The micro-circuit in the silver threads of his collar scrambled his words, then released them in the clear, at any destination in the world.

"Captain Aachen, sir. Judge Hunter Search and Abort, Squad Seven. Sir, we're at a wreck site. Old Ohio Sector—"

"What!" Griffin felt a cold blade twist in his gut. He knew the answer, knew he had to ask. "What *wreck* are we talking about, Captain? Don't waste my time, damn you!"

A half-second pause. A little less confidence in the veteran officer's voice.

"Aspen Shuttle, sir. The one with—"

"—with Judge Dredd aboard," Griffin finished. His voice was deadly calm, assured. "Is he dead or alive? I want positive ID either way. No guesswork, Captain."

"Nothing yet, sir. We're going through the wreckage now. I'm getting a picture on-line for you, Chief Justice."

"About time, too," Griffin said. The officer was doing his job, but it never hurt to shake a man up when you could.

A holo sphere blinked into life at Griffin's eye level. It rotated slowly, giving him a complete view of the area. The wreck was a black, twisted metal shell. It had scooped out a shallow groove in the parched earth, plowed a hundred meters and stopped.

He's dead, Griffin told himself. *No one could live through that.*

The Judge Hunter Squad was going about its work with practiced care. Men moved through the smoking debris, using barcode scanners to check the ID tags of the dead. Griffin wrinkled his nose. He could almost smell the oppressive heat of the Cursed Earth, the unforgetable odor of burning flesh.

"Sir . . ." Captain Aachen stepped into sight, his visor raised to show a man with scarred features, a broken nose, gray eyes squinting against the harsh light. "The shuttle was struck by an unidentified weapon from ground level. Two-thirds of the craft exploded at once. We've spotted some pieces twenty, thirty clicks out. There are sixteen casualties here but no sign of Dredd. Two men alive. One guard and a prisoner. We are presently—"

The officer turned away for a moment, frowned, and looked at Griffin. "Chief Justice, we've found tracks leading away from the wreck site. At least . . . half a dozen men. I am assuming Dredd was one of the survivors, sir."

"No."

"Sir?"

"No, Captain, he was not. You are clearly in error."

Captain Aachen nodded. "Yes, sir."

"I repeat. Joseph Dredd did not survive the shuttle crash. *No* one survived the wreck. Is that clear, Captain?"

"Yes, sir. Perfectly clear, sir. Will there be any further—"

"Griffin out."

The tin bee in his ear pinged once. The bright holo winked like a bubble in the sun and disappeared. Griffin quickened his steps. His throat was dry as the Cursed Earth itself, and he felt the sting of sweat on his chest.

"Damn you, Dredd," he said to the dark tunnel walls. "You'd better be dead. You'd better be in *Hell!*"

Captain Aachen made his way back into the wreckage. The odor was strong enough to gag a hooker-droid, but he'd smelled the dead before. The prisoner who'd survived was nearly dead. A minute, maybe two, he'd be gone. A Medik was squatting over the guard. Aachen waved him away. He looked down at the man. The Medik had cleaned his face and set a compress against the ugly cut on his head.

"Thanks," the guard said. He showed Aachen a weary grin. "I'm grateful for your help. Glad you guys showed up."

Aachen brought the blunt-nosed pistol from behind his back.

"No problem," he said.

You have got to be out of your mind, Hershey. Plain stupid —totally out of your mind . . .

She stood in the shadows of the lockers, held her breath and listened to the sounds of the dead half of the night. How could the silence make so much noise? She could hear the sigh of air in ventilator shafts, the hum of the elevators in the walls. A drip in the shower was a full-blown waterfall.

Hershey looked at her watch. 0210. Two minutes and a life-time since she'd stolen a look before.

A voice at the far end of the room. Another, and a laugh. A locker slammed, shattering the quiet of the room.

"Go home," Hershey whispered. "Your shift's over, guys, get out of here."

Footsteps echoed down the corridor. A door whispered shut. The locker room was silent again. She closed her eyes and took a deep breath. Dredd's locker was 30914, two aisles down. She was grateful for the synthetic flooring that dampened her steps. You could stomp on the stuff and never make a sound.

So why didn't they put it on the ceiling and the walls? Why didn't someone think of that?

The lock was a simple magnetic, easy enough to open if you knew how, and every Cadet who'd gone through the Academy did. It was something you learned about the second day of Break & Enter, Basic B & E. The locks on the individual lockers were a courtesy, not a security measure. No Judge would even dream of violating the privacy of another Judge's space.

Yeah, right. No one but you, Hershey . . .

Towels. A spare helmet with an awesome dent on the side. She knew where Dredd had gotten that. Brass polish. Boot polish. *Really,* Dredd. She couldn't resist a smile. Still a Cadet at heart.

Something swung on a gold chain at the rear of the locker. Any Judge would know it on sight. A valor award. For outstanding heroism. And what did *that* get you, Dredd? What does it mean to anyone now?

Her eyes blurred and she wiped her sleeve across her face. *Damn it, no time for that. It isn't going to help . . .*

She spotted it on the floor of the locker, behind a

combat issue boot. A bullet had taken a bite out of the heel. A half-inch higher and Dredd would have a limp.

It was a black slipcase, half an inch thick, with something inside. She drew it out and held it to the light. A cheap viewie, from the quality of the picture, probably a frame from a home video. A young couple. The woman was holding a baby.

"*Baby* Dredd?" Hershey shook her head. "Didn't think you were *ever* a baby, pal."

She looked at the viewie a moment longer, held it, reluctant to put it down. A little too . . . what? Not too thick, too *heavy* by an ounce or two.

Turning the picture over, she slid her thumb along the rim. The frame popped open. Another image inside. Two men, mid-twenties, in Cadet blues. Graduation day at the Academy, couldn't be anything else. One of the men obviously a younger Dredd. The other . . . who? Enough like Dredd to be related somehow.

Hershey frowned, studying the picture again. Not a relative, that couldn't be. Joseph Dredd didn't have anyone, any life at all outside of the Judges. And even *that* family had finally rejected him, tossed him aside. Now he didn't have anyone at all.

TWENTY-TWO

Fergie knew he was alive. Everything hurt too much to be dead. His mother had been a closet Churcher. She told him when you died all you did was go to sleep for a while. When you woke up again, you were somewhere real nice. This wasn't it. This wasn't nice at all. This was like really, *really* bad and bound to get worse. You could tell by the ugly-looking goons who were squatting by the fire. Fergie didn't think they looked right. People you wouldn't want to know. That, and the hoods. The other thing his mother had told him was don't ever talk to a man who wears a hood.

What the hell were they doing over there? Snorting and sniffing, rooting through the junk they'd salvaged from the shuttle. Whatever *that* might be—whatever had come down in one piece.

His hands and arms were numb. They were up above his shoulders somewhere but he didn't look to see. If he didn't move—ever—the groons might think he was asleep or maybe dead. Dead would be good. You're not going to kill a guy, you think he's maybe already dead.

"Herman Ferguson . . ."

It was only a whisper, but Fergie nearly jumped out of his skin.

"Don't talk to me, Dredd. I'm not here. You want to talk, talk to somebody else."

"You're not making sense, Ferguson. There isn't anybody else. Get control of yourself."

Fergie risked a look without moving his head. Dredd was half a meter to his right, hanging from his hands, his legs dangling free. Glancing up a little farther, he could see the crossbar where their hands were tied. The building around them was a ruin, incredibly old. The ceiling above was caved in. The night was unbelievably dark. The stars were colder and brighter than Fergie had ever imagined they could be. You didn't see a black sky and stars in the Mega-Cities. In the Cities, it was never really night.

"Listen," Fergie whispered, "don't you tell me to get control of myself, Dredd. Don't you tell me a *thing*. It's your fault I'm in this mess. If I ever get out of here—"

"You won't."

"What?"

"It's against my nature to give up, Ferguson. Understand that. Given the chance, I will give a good accounting of myself. If at all possible, I will take several of these lawbreakers with me. Aside from that, it's pretty reasonable to assume we have little or no chance of escape. Especially if they are who I think they are."

Fergie felt his throat go dry. "And who—who would that be?"

"Angels," Dredd said.

"Angels? Like in—"

"No. Like in Angels of Death. God's Maggots. Painers. Dirt Chokers."

"God's *Maggots?*" Fergie looked at the fire. "What the hell is this, Dredd—no, don't tell me. I don't want to know, I don't want to hear this. I don't want to—"

Someone screamed. It was a high-pitched, terrible sound that echoed through the ruins and seemed to last forever.

"Oh shit, oh shit," Fergie moaned.

"They've got somebody else," Dredd said. "There were other survivors of the crash."

"I don't *care* about anyone else. Screw 'em. I care about me."

"That's a bad attitude. That's a typical lawbreaker outlook on life, Ferguson."

"Yeah? Well, that's *normal,* see? I'm a career criminal, Dredd. Not a really big-time criminal, but that's what I do. I wire robots, I rob public droids. I can get inside nearly any electronic device. I *did* time for that, okay? I am not supposed to be here now. *You* got me into this mess!"

"You said that."

"I said it again. What are you going to do about that? Arrest me? Good. Please do."

The scream cut through the night again, then abruptly stopped. Fergie closed his eyes.

"Hey, Pa! We got wakies over here!"

Someone else laughed. "We b-b-better. Pa's flat runnin' out of sinners."

Fergie opened his eyes, sucked in a breath and didn't let it out. There were three of them. Ugly. Tall. Short. Skinny. Fat. Their hoods were thrown back across their crooked shoulders. One had a face like a toad. His nose was sewn shut with leather thread. He was scarcely wider than a stick. He had enormous green eyes. The hair on his face and head was scorched black and his skin was burned raw. This one still had a nose, but his ears were sewn shut.

It was the third one that made Fergie want to throw up his lunch. If he'd had any lunch that's exactly what he'd have done. The groon had a patchwork face, alternating squares of copper and flesh like a nightmare checkerboard. One arm was real. The other was a dull metal stub. There was something mechanical protruding from his head, but Fergie couldn't make it out.

"Hey, how 'bout *you?*" The creature caught Fergie looking and grinned. "I kinda like you, man. I surely do." Something blurred, something hummed, something silver and gold sprang out of the metal stub. Something long and sharp touched Fergie's crotch. It trailed up to Fergie's belly and traced a narrow line. Fergie had to look. *Why did I do that,* he thought, *why did I have to look?* It was the longest blade Fergie had ever seen. They didn't *make* any blades longer than that.

"I think I'm going to like you *good,*" the man with yellow eyes said. "Real, real good. What you think of that?"

"Whatever you do, don't show them fear," Dredd said.

"Yeah, right." Fergie felt something roll over and die in his belly. "Thanks, I'll remember that, Dredd."

"Dredd. Did you say *Dredd?*"

Yellow Eyes cocked his head and studied Dredd. His eyes went bright when he spotted the Judge tattoo.

"Blessed be, Pa!" He turned and called into the shadows. "We got us Judge Dredd *hisself!*"

The two other freakos jumped up and down. Something walked out of the dark. Something tall and gaunt in bug-eaten rags, something that smelled before it even got near. It shuffled past the fire, tapping its stick on the ground. The others stepped out of his way. He stopped, sniffed the air, then turned his head up to Dredd. His features were masked by the filth-encrusted hood.

"Id id twoo? We gaht uds duh gwead bed up the log hidseph?"

Yellow Eyes winked at Dredd. "Pa wants to know it it's true we got us the great man of the Law himself. Well, is it, Dredd? That be who you are?"

"I'm Dredd."

"Hagga-lulla!" the man in the hood said.

"I know who you are," Dredd said. "You're the self-styled Reverend Billy Joe Angel. Wanted on a Six-Oh-Three, Crimes Against Humanity. A Five-Two-Niner,

Murder in Every Degree. You and your offspring are under arrest."

Pa Angel howled. "Oh, be are plessid, Lort! All we brayed vor was vood and sus-nance. Bud thou has delivert our gweat enemee undo our hans!"

"Pa says—"

"I heard him," Dredd said. "You're still all under arrest."

"Dredd . . ." Fergie shook his head. "You keep saying that, you're going to piss this guy off." He looked at the hooded horror. "Listen, friend, there's been a little mistake. Him and me, we're not together. I mean, *I* was in the shuttle, *he* was in the shuttle. You're in the same place with somebody, that doesn't mean you know each other, you're even acquainted, you know? Doesn't mean you've even *seen* each other before, you—*yahh!*"

Yellow Eyes poked Fergie sharply in the ribs. "Told you I liked you, man. I didn't mean I liked you *talking*. I like you when you don't."

"Hey, I can live without the—"

"Shut up!"

Yellow Eyes squinted at Dredd and Fergie, then nodded at the horror in the hood. "That's Pa. You already know that. You better be real nice. He's a au-thentic babbatized avenger of the Lord." He stabbed the air with his knife. "You mess with him, you messin' with the fiery hand of God himself!"

"Amen!"

"Amen!"

Yellow Eyes grinned. "They call me Mean Machine. That's 'cause I am." He pointed a dirty finger at his head. "Pa's got me set on *One.* I had a kinda accident when I was a'born. Shit. Bein' *alive's* a pure accident out here. Pa fixed me up best he could. He can turn me all the way up to *Four.* That's ber-serkin' dog-frothin' psycho-maniac is what it is. You don't want to never see that.

"The dumb-lookin' one's Junior Head-Dead. You can

likely figure why. The other one's Link-Link. He ain't as dumb, but he can't get his bodily functions workin' right. If the wind was right you could tell."

Mean Machine stepped up closer to Fergie. He pricked Fergie's foot with his blade, turned the edge around and around in the light of the flame. When he looked at Dredd, his half-smile faded away.

"We are mighty proud to have *you* here, Dredd. Mighty proud, indeed." His blade swept out faster than any eye could see. A thin line of red appeared on Dredd's chest. "You're hard to hurt, I bet. Pa's going to like that."

"Let me—*snuk-snuk!*—kill it, Pa!"

"Huh-uh!" Link-Link's face screwed up in a mask. "You said *I* could have one, Pa!"

"Hallelujah, brother!" Fergie cried out. "Right on. Glory to the Lord! May His mighty sword smite sinners from the face of the earth! May His wrath stomp down on the unbeliever, may He damn the rich and raise up the poor!"

Mean Machine's eyes went wide. He gave Fergie a puzzled look.

"What you doing? Why you sayin' stuff like that?"

"Lo, the wicked shall eat the dust of thy path, O Lord. E-ternal damnation to him who follows the false law of the Cities and curses the one true Lord of this dry and forgotten land!"

Pa Angel took a step forward. He turned his shrouded face up to Fergie. "Cud id be? Frum duh Cidy ub duh fallen, a fate-ful wud has a-beered?"

"Amen," Fergie shouted. "The sheep's come home, man, that's me!"

"Ferguson . . ." Dredd shook his head in disgust. "You don't want to do this. Believe me, you don't."

"Yeah? Think again, *un*believer."

Mean Machine turned to his brothers. "Cut him down. If Pa says this'n is a Believer, why I reckon he is."

Fergie laughed as Link-Link and Junior Head-Dead scrambled up the post to cut him free.

"The Law doesn't make mistakes, Dredd, right? But I'm free and you're *toast*. Go figure, man!"

"Wrong. I'm toast, Ferguson. You're *meat*."

"What's that supposed to mean?"

"These are the Angels, dope-head. They're Cursed Earth scavengers. Scumbags. They're also cannibals."

Fergie stared. "Hey, no way. Don't go telling me shit like that, Dredd. Don't even *joke* about it, man." He turned to Mean Machine. "Right, pal? Tell him, brother."

"Hagga-lulla!" Pa Angel shouted.

"Snuk-snuk-snuk!" said Junior Head-Dead.

TWENTY-THREE

"This is terrific, you know? I mean, meeting you guys, a bunch of *other* Believers out here in the middle of nowhere, now what's the chance of that? Is that God's will or what?"

"G-g-g-glory!" Link-Link said.

"Snuk-snuk!" said Junior Head-Dead.

Fergie winked, and did a little bantam-weight shuffle. He tapped Junior lightly on the head. His hand came away with flecks of scorched hair. When the others weren't looking, he wiped it on his pants.

"I can do a Eee-Tee-Ay," Link-Link said. "I g-got real good navigash'nul skills. I got cord'nuts in my head."

"Right," Fergie said. "See a Medik next time you're in town. Fix you right up."

Link-Link and Junior were leading him down a narrow passage through the ruined building. Link-Link carried a burning torch. Fergie wondered where they were going, but didn't want to ask. What he wanted to do was get far enough away from the big spook himself and that lunatic with the muckin' machete for an arm, get his bearings straight, lose these freakos and get the hell out of town.

He felt bad about Dredd. Not bad enough to stick around, for sure, and hey, Dredd had gotten him into this squirrel nest, you couldn't forget about that. Better

Herman Ferguson on the loose than hanging there with what's-his-name and his oversized shiv, and the old guy with the speech defect. These two groons were bad enough, but *those* guys . . .

"So," Fergie said, "we're going where, out for some air or what? A quick tour's fine with me, I don't have to be back or anything. Man, it is great out here, you know? Away from the stinkin' city lights. God is good! Glory to His name!"

"G-Glory!" Link-Link said.

"Snuk-snuk!" said Junior Head-Dead.

Fergie looked at Link. "No kidding, fella, you get to a doc sometime, they could fix up that little problem you got with the nose. I mean, no offense, you don't mind me bringing up the nose, right? Like, the leatherwork's attractive and all . . ." He squinted at Junior's ears. "You people work with heavy machinery a lot? I was thinking, you know, industrial accidents, something like that? They got good safety gear, you take the right precautions this—huh?"

Link-Link had stopped. He held the torch up to Fergie and stared.

"Wh-what you talkin' about, f-fixing what?"

"Just talking, okay?" Fergie didn't like the guy's look. Like someone had stepped on his foot.

Link-Link looked confused. "Can't n-nobody *fix* nothin' except Pa. Pa's re-ordinated and—"

"Yeah, yeah, I heard."

Link-Link grinned. "Pa says if I w-walk in God's misery and pain, I can git the Holy Gouging when I'm fifteen. Mean Machine'll git it next year, an' I'm after that!"

Fergie's throat went dry. All the meals he'd missed stirred a queasy soup in his belly. "You're saying . . . nah, you're not sayin' that, like what I think you're saying . . ."

"Pa's got it *all*," Link-Link said. "The whole

B-B-Blessed Mutilation of God! Ears and eyes and nose
sewed up, and his m-mouth, too. He's the only Angel's
got that."

Link-Link rolled his eyes, thrust out his arms and
turned a circle twice.

"Lo, he hast s-sewed up his every wicked ori-fuss
against the evil of the world. He h-has shut out sin and
cast Satan aside. He hast b-b-become a pure abomy-
nation of the Lord!"

Oh, shit, I am out of here . . .

"Look, I got some private hygiene stuff, and you fellas
have plenty to do. If you can just point me outside—"

Link-Link kicked Fergie solidly in the rear. Fergie
grabbed air and bit a mouthful of floor.

"Hey, hold on there! What the hell, guys?"

Link-Link straddled Fergie's back, crushing all the air
out of his lungs. Junior wound a piece of rusty wire
around his hands, then looped the other end about his
feet. Link took one shoulder and Junior took the other.
Together, they dragged Fergie on his belly down the hall.

"Wait a minute," Fergie said, "I'm a Believer. I'm a—
I'm a Maggot of God, just like you!"

"That's why we l-love you, brother," Link-Link said.

"You got a weird way of showing it, brother."

"Like you better'n *him,*" Link said. "Lot's better'n that
one . . . Don't we, Junior?"

"Snuk!"

"Who? Who are we talking about here? Dredd? Is
that who, Dredd?"

Link made a face. "He's a agg-nasty or something. Ch-
chock fulla sin!"

Link and Junior let go. Link flipped him over on his
back. Fergie looked straight at a bed of hot coals. He
looked at the heavy iron spit, and he looked at the thing
that was crackling there, crackling red and black, juices
hissing down into the fire. It took him a second, a second
and a half, then the image took a clear and very definite

shape in his head. It kept kicking out then kicking back in and it wouldn't let go. It wouldn't let go no matter what he did.

Fergie threw up. He didn't have a thing in his stomach but his stomach didn't care.

"Them Unbelievers," Link said, "just d-don't *taste* right, you know? It's impure f-f-f-flesh is what it is."

"Snuk-snuk!"

Fergie closed his eyes. "Now this is a gag, right? What I want you to do is tell me this is a gag. Dredd said that you guys—what you—I know he didn't mean that you were—"

Junior kicked Fergie in the mouth. He grabbed his hair and pulled him closer to the fire. He drooled on Fergie's head.

Link found a knife somewhere in his rags, reached out and sliced off something from the spit.

"Lo, the Unbeliever's f-f-flesh is unclean, Lord, but a p-p-person's got to eat."

"I was lying," Fergie yelled, "I don't believe in *any*-thing, I mean, I don't even believe enough to be an *Un*-believer, what do you think of that? I mean, that is something you don't want to mess with, man. I also got a skin condition. I got athlete's foot, guys!"

"Glory!" Link said.

"Snuk!" Junior Head-Dead said.

". . . biled ob be, troppin' chu vrom duh skie endo by hans . . ."

"Pa says the Lord's sure been good, says it's a sign is what it is. Says the Lord has smiled on him, droppin' you from the sky into his hands."

"Why don't you tell Pa to get the mush out of his mouth?" Dredd said. "You think God understands that crap? Even if He's listening, He is sure as hell not listening to Daddy Dust-Bunny there."

"Waaaaaaaka-waaaaaka!" Mean Machine's eyes turned

black with rage. His knife-arm swept out in a wicked arc. Dredd felt something like a breath of Arctic air across his chest. He forced himself not to look down. He knew he would see a line of red, a cut no deeper than Mean Machine wanted it to be. He did what he liked with that thing, and he did it with surgical skill.

"You bringin' wrath and retry-bution down on yourself, Dredd." Mean Machine shook his head as if he wished there were some way he could help. Pa Angel didn't move. He was a scarecrow with darkness as a face.

"The Lord is fearsome in His gaze," Mean Machine said. "He will smite you down and grind you under His heels. Your flesh will tremble with the terror of His ways . . ."

"You ever been in a rumble in Red Quad, pal? You don't know shit about the terror of his ways."

"Eeee-nuph!"

The Reverend Billy Joe Angel raised one filthy hand above his head, then lowered it slowly until it stabbed at Dredd.

"Vinits hib, sud. Vinits hib dow!"

Mean Machine glowed. "I'll finish him, Pa. I surely will."

"Dree, poi. You kun coe ub to dree."

"Three? I can go up to . . . You mean it, Pa? Oh, Glory, I'm gonna do a *Three!*"

Mean Machine tapped the top of his mechanical head. His mouth fell open. His eyes turned to glass. His whole body shook; his arms and his legs jerked straight out like a droid on happy-oil. The copper squares on his face turned blue then red. He squealed like tires on a white-hot road, lowered his head and came straight at Dredd.

Dredd tried to twist aside but the crazy was moving too fast. His head hit Dredd in the gut. Dredd bellowed and gasped for air. The pain nearly took him. He shook his head to keep from passing out. The cords around his wrists had snapped tight at Mean Machine's blow, tearing at the muscles in his shoulders and his chest.

Dredd knew that was it. He couldn't take it again. The freako would break something vital and he'd bleed to death inside.

Dredd forced his head up off his chest. He made himself smile through the pain.

"That's it? That's the whole bit? This is what you *do?*"

Mean Machine blinked. He stared at Dredd and then showed him a sly little grin. He was dumb, but he wasn't as dense as Dredd had hoped. He knew the damage he'd done, knew what would happen when he came at Dredd again.

"That was my *practice* run," Mean Machine said. "I got you sighted in good now."

"Quit talking and do it, then," Dredd said. "You're starting to piss me off."

It is not unusual that the facts concerning an historical event are often overshadowed by a more lurid, wholly distorted account. One could cite a number of cases where—at least temporarily—truth gave way to a more colorful version of a particular occurrence.

A good example is the true cause of the world-wide chaos of the middle- and late-twentieth century. War, famine, disease, and racial unrest were attributed by historians of the time to the clash of political movements such as democracy, communism, and the like. As every schoolchild knows today, the fact of the matter—dismissed as folly at the time—is that every event of any importance between the years 1908–1998 was carefully planned and executed by members of a single, tightly-knit family in the former European nation of Luxembourg.

While the name of this family has remained secret to this day, the name of their cabal is well known. It was called Der Zischen, which can be roughly translated as The Fizz. The reason behind the name becomes clear when it is understood that Der Zischen controlled the leaders of all nations, began and ended international conflicts at their will, and controlled the earth's natural resources—all the while hiding behind the corporate structure of the world's two leading carbonated beverages.

Only a handful of people were aware of this conspiracy at the time. Yet The Fizz managed to keep the entire world under its thumb for ninety years.

Closer to our own time are the myths that have sprung up about the inhabitants of the Cursed Earth.

In the years of the famous Judge Dredd (circa 2139), videos produced and distributed through illegal channels often pictured the people of Cursed Earth as political dissidents, victims of "injustice," or even "mental defectives" turned away from the Mega-Cities. Those scattered bands of people such as Culls, Booters, Krazies, Dusteaters, Cutters, Zippers, and other groups mistakenly labeled as Outcasters, were in fact never victims of Society, but the very people who sought to bring about the destruction of the Mega-Cities themselves.

Who were the real inhabitants of Cursed Earth, and where did they come from? We can eliminate those persons loosely defined as "mentally or physically disabled." Every Citizen of the Mega-Cities has always been entitled to free health care, including necessary genetic correction procedures to assure the elimination of those traits undesirable to contemporary Society.

It is true that even in the mid-twenty-second century medical personnel would still come across the occasional psychopathic individual or persons afflicted with a minor personality disorder. Such Citizens were quickly identified and given immediate, and effective, care.

The inhabitants of Cursed Earth were neither outcasts nor defectives of any kind. They were, rather, Citizens who expressed a keen desire to pursue a more solitary life outside the Cities—people who felt they would be better suited to an alternate lifestyle in a semi-hostile environment. Upon written request, such persons were processed, innoculated, and given free transportation to the Citygates.

While it is difficult to present an accurate picture of the many diverse groups who lived in that vast and challenging land that spans the continent from east to west, social studies indicate that while these groups experienced some problems adapting to areas offering little water, no arable soil, and ruinous weather, many persons learned to live reasonably pleasant, productive lives.

—History of the Mega-Cities
*James Olmeyer, III
Chapter XIX: "Alternate
Life-Styles"
2191*

TWENTY-FOUR

Hershey had many fond memories of her days at the Academy—Unarmed Combat, Street Tactics, and the harrowing but always exciting Lawmaster Endurance Course. The one class she'd always dreaded was CCT—Cadet Computer Training. She wasn't *bad* at it; she had finished in the top eighty percent.

It was the computer room itself that gave her the creeps. There was something about the place. It was too alien, too cold, too antiseptically *clean* for Hershey's taste. The harsh, sterile atmosphere seemed hostile to human life. The constant, almost imperceptible buzz of a billion electronic bees told her, *You don't belong here . . . we do . . .*

Hershey knew it was a ridiculous, wholly irrational feeling, and she had the good sense not to share such thoughts with anyone else.

It's not any better than it was. Over a year on the street and I still detest this damn place!

Tiny lights winked at her from the walls, like animal eyes in the night. Tiny sounds chittered in the floor.

"Judge, you all right? You okay?"

Hershey nearly jumped out of her skin. "Of course I'm all right, Olmeyer, why wouldn't I be all right? You know of any reason, Cadet, why I wouldn't be *all right?*"

Olmeyer stepped back, withering under her glare.

What did I do? What did I do? It was always something, and most of the time he didn't know what. Sometimes he didn't even have to say anything. Sometimes he could offend just being in the same room.

"I'm—no, sir, uh, Judge. No reason at all. I'm certain everything's fine, Judge."

"Good," Hershey said. "I'm pleased to hear it, Cadet. Shall we get on with it, now?"

"My station's over there. Over near the end."

Hershey muttered under her breath. She followed Olmeyer across the long room, past the cramped and numbered student cubicles. Hers had been number thirty-seven. A number she'd never forget.

"I don't know why it has to be so damn *cold,*" Hershey complained. "You could store meat in here. It could *snow.*"

"The machines like it cold," Olmeyer said. "They prefer the—"

"Machines do not *like* anything, Olmeyer." Her look cut him down a good foot. "Computers do not have the capacity to like or dislike. They *function* better under certain conditions and certain temperatures. This does not mean they *like* it that way."

Olmeyer started to speak, then wisely kept his mouth shut. Judge Hershey wouldn't want to hear that he felt his computer was friendlier and more responsible than most of the people he knew. She *certainly* wouldn't want to hear that he'd programmed his station to speak in her voice when he wanted it to, to speak certain . . . personal phrases when they were alone. What Hershey would do if she knew that was grind him into a greasy spot on the floor.

Olmeyer took a seat at his station, pulled up an extra chair for Hershey from the cubicle next door. The screen came alive as he sat, coded to his presence.

Hershey nodded at the trick. "Very impressive, Cadet."

"It's not—I just . . . It's a simple heat sensor is what it is. It's coded to body weight, fat content, iris pattern, stuff like that."

He cut himself short again. She was here, she was right next to him. He didn't want to do anything dumb, he wanted to *keep* her there.

"I appreciate what you're doing," Hershey said. "I want you to know that, Cadet."

"I'm glad to help, Judge, I—"

Hershey stopped him with a gesture. "I want to tell you again. This is a personal request. This is not official Judge business."

"Judge Hershey . . ." He looked straight at her, one of the few times he'd managed to do that without turning to jelly. "It's for Judge Dredd. You told me that. There's no way you could keep me from helping if I can."

"Yes, well . . ." Hershey cleared her throat. "I appreciate that, Cadet."

She reached in the slim metal case she carried and handed Olmeyer one of the framed viewies of Dredd she had taken from Dredd's locker.

Olmeyer looked at it, then looked at Hershey.

"I want it identified," she said.

"It's Dredd. I don't know the other guy."

"I don't want *you* to ID it. I want Central to tell me."

Olmeyer nodded. He took the picture and slipped it onto a plate at the base of his computer. With a slight hiss, the viewie disappeared into the machine.

"Central, access Graphics Data Base."

"*Accessed . . .*"

"Give me an ID, please."

"*Dredd, Joseph. Formerly Judge Dredd. Now serving a life sentence at Aspen Prison . . .*"

"Keeps up to date, doesn't it?" Hershey said beneath her breath.

"I want both IDs, Central," Olmeyer said. "Give me the other one, please."

"Scanning for identity . . . Unknown male . . . approximately two hundred centimeters tall . . . weight: ninety-five kilos . . . skin-tone: three-ten-nine-eight-seven-six . . . Further identification characteristics are—"

The screen flickered. The data vanished, replaced by the official eagle and shield of the Judges.

"This terminal has been disconnected from the main system for a systems check. You no longer have access to the system. Thank you."

The viewie popped out of the slot.

"Uh-oh." Olmeyer leaned back in his chair and frowned at the screen.

"What was that all about?" Hershey said. "That didn't sound like Central."

"It wasn't. That's a standard taped interrupt message that means 'butt out, we don't want you in here.' "

"Why? What did we do to set it off?"

"No way of telling." Olmeyer stretched his fingers and pulled his chair up closer to the screen.

"Is that it?" Hershey said. "We're through, we're locked out?"

Olmeyer looked pained. "With all due respect, Judge, *nobody* locks out Olmeyer. Nobody. They shut the door, I climb in the window. They nail up the windows, I go in through the floor—"

"I think I've got it, Cadet."

"Huh!" Olmeyer's fingers blurred across the keys. "Keep me out. Are you people kidding? There—Graphics Analysis coming up . . ."

The screen blinked. A picture of Dredd as a baby swam into view. Dredd and his parents. The same picture Hershey had found in his locker.

"Olmeyer, you've analyzed the *wrong* picture," she told him. "It's the other one, you droog!"

"I—I did?"

"Of course you did. I want the one of Dredd and the man with him at graduation."

"Yeah, right." Olmeyer studied the screen a long moment. "If that's the wrong picture, Judge, why does the computer keep telling me it's a fake?"

"What?"

Olmeyer jabbed a finger at the screen. "See all the numbers running along the bottom of the image? That's Graphic Analysis. It's telling me in its own language everything that's wrong with the picture. And so far, there isn't much that Graphic thinks is *right.*"

Olmeyer shook his head and punched a dozen keys. "It's chock-full of anomalies. Really clever ones, too. Someone must have used a GCI terminal *and* a scan quadrupler to come up with this. Man, that's state of the art twenty years ago."

Hershey squeezed Olmeyer's arm. "What are you saying, it's not—it isn't real?"

"Watch. Keep your eyes on the screen. I'll drop out all the imposters, all the artificial pixels."

Hershey watched, stunned, as the elements of the picture began to fade and disappear, one by one, vanishing into mist, each scan line erasing another part of the image until nearly everything was gone.

"My . . . *God,*" Hershey said.

Olmeyer spread his hands. "That's it. Sky, foreground, house, parents . . . it's all fake, Judge. Every line of it."

"Everything except—"

"Right," Olmeyer finished. "Everything except the baby. The baby's real. The rest of it is zero, zilch. It doesn't exist."

TWENTY-FIVE

"Quit talking and do it," Dredd said. "You're starting to piss me off."

Mean Machine threw back his head and laughed like a wolf in heat. He'd never seen a wolf, and he'd never seen anything in heat except Pa, and that was too scary to even think about.

"I *like* you," Mean Machine said. "I like you 'bout as good as that other'n, I surely do."

He turned to Pa Angel, standing close to the fire. "He's just a'spoofing, Pa. He's hurt bad. *Real* bad. I heard stuff crunkle inside. I figure I hit him real low in his private sinner parts he'll bring glory to the Lord like you never seen before."

The Reverend Billy Joe Angel turned his hooded face toward his son. He raised his wooden shaft and aimed in the direction of Dredd.

"Prink ib do kot, poi," he shouted. "Prink ib do kot!"

"I'll do it, Pa, I will. I'll bring him to God real good!" His yellow eyes flashed. "Is this a—a Four you think, Pa? You think it maybe is?"

"Vore!" Pa bellowed in a voice like rocks in a can.

"Four!" shouted Mean Machine. "Four! *Four! FOUR!*"

Mean Machine reached up to his shiny silver head and

dialed himself a Four. His mouth fell open. Blue fire crackled in his eyes. A low sound started in his gut, trembled up his body and out his throat in a ragged roar. He spread his arms wide, the good one and the bad, spread them out wide like a man who fully intended to fly. He swept in a dizzy circle around the fire, twisting and turning and shaking himself into a frenzy and a froth, a small tornado looking for a trailer park, looking for a kill. Then, with a howl that shook the ruined walls, he lowered his head and came straight for Dredd.

"Glory! *Glory! GLOOOOOR—EEE!*"

Dredd knew exactly how this maniac's charge had to end. He would hit with the impact of a truck, and all of Dredd's organs would spurt out of his ears. He tensed the muscles in his belly, in his thighs. Everything hurt. Every motion brought a new jolt of pain. Dredd opened his mouth and roared, lifted his body at the waist, snapped his legs straight out.

His boots met the top of Mean Machine's head. Mean Machine's speed kept him going for a second and a half. He stopped, then, shook all over, and staggered off in a ragged dizzy course. His head found the wall. He turned on his heels and stumbled off toward Dredd again. The deadly blade whirred above his head. Smoke came out of Mean Machine's nose. Dredd jerked his body aside, felt the blade hum by, wrapped his legs around the metal head.

Mean Machine howled. Dredd closed his eyes against the pain and lifted Mean Machine off the ground. Mean Machine's leg kicked air. The pole holding Dredd's hands snapped. He fell in a heap, came to his feet, and ripped the leather thongs from his wrists.

Mean Machine turned in a circle, got his bearings and came at Dredd again. Dredd lifted half the broken pole, swung it in an arc at Mean Machine's head. Mean Machine went down, shook himself, and came to his feet again.

"Okay," Dredd said, "I get the message, friend. You can take it in the head. Forget about the head."

Mean Machine jerked up straight, scanned the room and settled on Dredd.

"Don't *like* you no more. Liked you real good. Don't like you no more at all."

"We've got a problem, then," Dredd said. "You don't like me and I'm still fond of you."

He whirled the broken pole above his head. Mean Machine came at him. Dredd let go. The pole made half a turn in the air and struck Mean Machine solidly at the knees. Mean Machine yelled and went down. His eyes rolled back in his head.

Dredd moved in to finish him off. The earth exploded at his feet. Dirt and stone geysered into the air. Dredd threw himself to the ground, rolled, and came up on his knees. The Reverend Billy Joe Angel had an antique automatic weapon in his hand. He was screaming out a hymn, and blasting every corner of the room.

Dredd tried not to move. A blind man with a weapon like that was a hazard to everyone's health. A totally whacked-out squirrely-in-the-head blind man with a weapon was a case of walking death.

Mean Machine suddenly came to life. Smoke curled out of his head. His legs kicked the air like a beetle on his back.

Pa Angel swiveled on his knees, centered on the sound.

"Huh! Goht-chew! Goht-chew, Tread!"

Lead stitched a nasty fence around Mean Machine. Mean Machine yelled, and scooted for his life.

"Sh-shit, Pa, it's me, it ain't him! He's over that-away!"

Pa Angel cocked his head from side to side, raised his weapon and blasted a crooked line a foot above Dredd. Brick and plaster showered on his head.

"Enough of this," Dredd muttered to himself. He picked up half a brick, tossed it across the room.

"Yuuuuuh!" Pa Angel turned in a blur and blasted the brick to bits. Dredd went low and scurried along the wall, into the narrow hall. He decided he was losing it, that something was wrong with his head. Looking for Ferguson after what that moron had done. Maybe he'd get lucky—maybe they'd already quartered and barbecued the little crook. Dredd could scoop him up, mail the scraps to Aspen in a box.

He could smell Pa Angel's boys. They left an odor strong enough to cut up and stack.

Dredd stopped. There was another smell now. Different, but not much worse than the first. The smell of burning flesh. Dredd had smelled it a hundred times. Always as a casualty in the street, though, never as an item on the menu before.

He stepped out of the corridor and into the small room. The ceiling had collapsed, scattering plaster, marble, and rusted steel bars across the floor. On some of the marble, there were broken bits of names, flowers and leaves carved in stone.

Across the room, something that used to be a prisoner or a guard sizzled on a spit. Dredd drew in a breath. A few feet away, one of Pa Angel's loonies was basting Fergie's naked backside with half a broom. The other hummed a hymn. Fergie's hands and feet were bound to the spit. He squawked and rolled his eyes. Dredd thought he looked a little skinny for a really good meal, but the freakos didn't seem to care.

Dredd walked up behind Link-Link, picked him up by the collar and tossed him against the wall. Link-Link's head made a terrible sound. Junior Head-Dead turned and stared. He said, "Snuk-snuk-shuk!" He tried to get his motor skills working, drew a long-barreled pistol from his belt. His reaction time was six months slower than Dredd's. Dredd took the weapon from his hand, turned it around, pulled the trigger, and shot Junior in the head.

"Snuk-snuk yourself," Dredd said. He looked down at Ferguson.

"What I ought to do is leave you here, you groon. Did I tell you these crazies *ate* people? You didn't get that? That too hard for you?"

"Go muck yourself, Dredd. Have one on me."

"Right. First intelligent thing you've said all day."

Dredd stood watch while Fergie got into his clothes. Fergie whined and complained. Dredd studied Junior's weapon, looked at the cylinder and blew down the barrel. It might fire again or it might blow off his hand. He decided to keep it until something better came along.

Someone roared down the hall. Pa Angel, or Mean Machine, Dredd couldn't tell.

"Come on," he said, glancing at the thing on the spit, "I don't want to stand around here."

Fergie looked at him. "What are you going that way for? Man, I am headed the other way, I am not going back in there."

"I'm not through in there," Dredd said.

"Yeah? Well, I am. You go ahead. Write sometime."

Dredd looked at him. "What are you worried about? Lo, He shall stomp out evil, He shall smite the Unbelievers . . ."

"Okay, okay." Fergie shrugged. "Hey, you been right all your life? You ever goof up, do something didn't work out the right way?"

"Yes," Dredd said. "You. Shut up and stay behind me. Pick up a brick. When no appropriate weapons are available, utilize those materials at hand."

"Judges. 'How to Cover your Ass,' right?"

"Dredd. 'Survival Against All Odds.' I wrote the course."

"I had to ask."

"Normal behavior for lawbreaker scum. Asks a lot of questions. Never listens to anything anyone says."

"You write that, too?"

"No," Dredd said. *"You* did. You've been living it all your life. You and all your kind. That's why there's us."

"Us."

"Us. Judges. As long as there are people who think the world is their lunch, there has to be someone to show them they're wrong."

"Oh. Okay, I got it," Fergie said.

"Good. Now button it up and stay close. Don't fall behind."

Button it up seemed like a good idea, Fergie decided. Likely not the best time to remind Dredd he wasn't an "us" anymore—that officially, he was a lawbreaker scum. Just like Ferguson, Herman, ASP-900764. Probably not what Dredd would like to hear.

The tunnel was silent. No sound. Nothing. Fergie didn't care for that. Quiet got on his nerves. You hear something, you know what's going on. You don't, something isn't right. Noise is good. Noise is the way things ought to be.

Dredd hadn't bothered to tell him how he'd gotten loose. What the old freak and the lead-head might be up to now. Why tell a con, right? What's your common ordinary habitual offender need to know?

Fergie hefted his broken brick. Dredd was a couple of feet ahead. It might work out, it might not. Lay him out flat. Make a deal with the freaks. Get out of this place. Yeah, right. They'd really go for that. Especially after they found the mess Dredd had left in the other room.

At the end of the hallway, Dredd waved Fergie to a halt. The fire was nearly gone. The embers cast a feeble glow. Ancient white columns across the room looked like pallid ghosts.

Dredd waited, letting his eyes grow accustomed to the shadows, to the starlight from the shattered roof overhead. There. The two posts that had held the pole where they'd strung him up by his hands. Fallen by its base was

Pa Angel's automatic weapon. Good. The old man was out of ammo or he wouldn't have left it there.

The dying fire caught a dim point of light. Metal. Mean Machine's head. He was still laid out where Dredd had left him. With any luck, dead. That's one. One more . . .

Dredd held his breath. A scarecrow shadow, a bundle of rags. The Reverend Billy Joe Angel, sitting on the ground by his son.

Dredd turned and touched Fergie's arm, signaled him to stay where he was. Fergie nodded. Doing anything else had never crossed his mind.

Dredd took a cautious step into the room. He sniffed the air and kept his eye on the shadow across the room. Junior's long-barreled weapon was at his side. There were likely no other members of the Angel crew, or they would have showed up by now. Still, Judge training told him *thinking* the way was clear was not enough. Playing safe was how you stayed alive. Thinking safe was how you got dead.

He took another step. Come up behind the shadow. Take the old man out. Make sure metal-dome was dead. Look for any more weapons and—

He heard the rush of air, had a quarter of a second to duck, curse himself, and remember Chapter Nine of his own damn book: "When you think the area's secure, chances are it's not." Then Pa Angel's staff hit him squarely on the side of his head and he went down like a rock.

TWENTY-SIX

Dredd felt the ground coming up. Plenty of time to think. Hour, hour and a half. Time works different somehow. Wham. Drop. Fall on your face. Stationary target. Get the hell up. He clobbers you again and you're flat-ass dead . . .

Dredd pushed the darkness aside. Just enough to wake up motor control for a tiny little nudge to the right. Not bad. Good. He hit the dirt hard.

"Gaht-su, Tread! Got-su, you sinner sum-bish!"

Pa Angel's staff came down again. Missed. Half an inch is good as a mile.

Dredd reached out and grabbed a filthy foot. Nothing. The action took place in his head. His hand was paralyzed. Pa Angel kicked him in the knee. Dredd howled and rolled away. He thought about Herman Ferguson. Ferguson and his brick. What was he doing that was more important than this? *Your own fault, Dredd. Count on a criminal type you deserve whatever you get.*

From the corner of his eye, he saw the scarecrow loom up above him, the staff gripped in his scrawny hands, the weapon raised up behind his shoulders, ready for the deathblow, ready for the kill.

And in that instant, in a second, in a breath, he watched the dirty hood fall away, saw the scarred and razored flesh, saw the leather thongs tangled in strange configuration, in ritual array, lacing the horror's ruined face, covering the darkness where ears and nose and mouth and eyes of madness used to be.

The Reverend Billy Joe Angel bellowed out his rage and swept his weapon down, and Dredd knew he didn't have time, that this was the one where he wouldn't walk away, the one where a blind man had fooled him with a stick and a pile of smelly rags when he wasn't really there, and Dredd wished it might have happened any other way, nearly any way but that—

"HUUUUUK!" Something exploded in the ragman's belly and scattered him in several bloody parts.

Dredd pulled himself up, stared at the Judge Hunters dropping from the ceiling, blasting through the wall, following the drill the way they'd trained to do, fast and quick and clean. One, two, three . . . maybe more outside but only three in here.

Dredd threw himself at half a wall as gunfire stitched a pattern at his feet. A visored figure came right at him, firing an ugly weapon black as night. Dredd pulled Junior Head-Dead's revolver from his belt, squeezed the trigger and fired. Lead struck the visor, glanced off the armored plastic and whined off into the air. The Hunter paused a fraction of a second, thrown off his guard. Dredd came in low. The gun clattered to the ground. Dredd raised up, jerked the Hunter's helmet off his head, and slammed it across the man's jaw.

He heard the sound behind him, knew there were two. Picked up the Judge Hunter's gun, fired it in a circle an inch above the ground. The first man stopped, stared at his leg and went down. Dredd swung his weapon by the barrel, and smashed the Hunter's face. He glanced at the Hunter he'd shot in the foot. The man cursed him and started up again. Dredd kicked him soundly in the head.

Okay, three. Everybody down. He swept the weapon around the room to make sure.

Fergie walked out of the corridor, clutching half a brick in his hand.

"You're not going to finish 'em off? Why the hell not?"

Dredd looked at him. "Because I'm innocent, remember?"

Fergie shrugged. "Yeah, I remember. So? You think those groons give a damn about that?"

"Thanks for jumping in," Dredd said. "I appreciate the help."

"Hey, I was *ready,* you know? You were terrific, man. I said to myself, I said, 'Fergie, you can hop in the ring and finish these guys, but if you do, you're going to knock Dredd's timing off. You're gonna'—*shiiiit, Dredd!*"

Dredd swung around in a blur. The Hunter was up on his knees, finger on the trigger of his weapon. His head exploded in a shower of red. Dredd stared at the man in the doorway, a dark silhouette against the stars. The Remington hanging from his hand, the long duster coat . . .

"Fargo?" Dredd took a cautious step forward. Maybe he was tired, maybe it was somebody else.

Fargo showed him a weary grin. "Welcome to Cursed Earth, Joseph. Hell of a place we've created out here. I guess hell's the right word, all right."

Fargo glanced at the dead Hunter, then looked back at Dredd.

"I'd like to say I felt something for him. I'd like to, but I don't." He studied Fergie a moment, decided he was too tired to ask who Dredd's companion might be.

"I don't guess I'm who I was when I came out here. I don't think anyone *could* be. You have any water, Joseph? I ran out half a day ago."

"Yes, sir. Sit down. Please."

Dredd nodded at Fergie. Fergie searched the room, and came back with two glass jars of water. Fargo took a healthy swig, letting the liquid trickle down his chin.

"Tastes good." He leaned back, took off his hat and wiped his brow. He looked about the room and smiled.

"A little irony, I guess. You and me and the others winding up here."

"Sir?" Dredd raised a brow.

"Don't know where you are, do you? Those columns, that piece of carving up there . . . This is a courtroom, Joseph. Or used to be. That, part of a face, what's left of it. Up there?"

"Yes, sir." Dredd agreed, though he wasn't certain what he could or couldn't see.

"That's the blind lady. Justice. Before your time. Mostly before mine, too. She treated everyone the same. No favors, no secrets. A jury of ordinary people. Hard to believe *that* one, but it's true. They decided. Not us. We should never have taken the law out of their hands."

Dredd shook his head. "You had to. You brought order out of chaos."

"That we did. Solved a hell of a lot of problems. And *created* more than we knew how to handle."

He saw Dredd's confusion, and laid a hand on his arm. He seemed to hesitate, lost for a moment in thought.

"I never thought we'd be sitting here together. Or that I might have the chance to tell you what I could never tell you before. To be a Judge, to decide the fate of thousands of lives during your career, I think that's . . . too much power in one man's hands. Too much, Joseph. For me, you, any man."

He looked right at Dredd. Dredd read the doubt in the old man's eyes, the sorrow and regret, the pain of recalling a past that was written in the stone of lost years.

"I once tried to compensate for that," he said. "To strike some kind of balance, to eliminate the mistakes we might make, to put Justice beyond the possibility of error. We tried to . . . to create the perfect Judge. We called it Janus."

Dredd frowned. "I don't understand, sir. I've never heard that name before."

Fargo shook his head. "No, no you haven't. It was forty years ago, Joseph. To create the perfect Judge, DNA samples were taken from all members of the Council. The samples were analyzed and studied. One was chosen for the Janus project. Mine. It was then refined again and again. Altered to enhance the best qualities and screen out the worst. Weaknesses. Frailties. Any physical or mental characteristics that might obstruct the purpose of the project. We . . . we created you, Joseph."

Dredd's breath caught in his throat. *"Me?* Sir, that couldn't be. I—"

"Listen to me." Fargo shook his head. "Let me finish this."

"I had real parents. I wasn't made by any . . . *project!"*

"Yes, you were, Joseph."

"No!"

"Joseph . . ."

Dredd gripped Fargo's arm. "My parents were killed. When I was just a kid. They told me at the Academy. *You* told me!"

"It was a lie."

"I have a *picture* of my parents!"

"You have a fake, a lie." Fargo shook him off. *"We lied to both of you!"*

"Both of—both of who?"

Fargo wouldn't look at him. "There was another person created in that experiment. But something went wrong. Terribly wrong."

Dredd blinked in sudden understanding. "I have a *brother?"*

"Yes."

"And what went wrong with him? Is he dead, did he die?"

"He didn't die. You were best friends at the Academy.

Inseparable. Both of you star pupils. Then he . . . turned. Went bad. We didn't know until then. We created one perfect Judge, and another who genetically mutated into the perfect criminal." Fargo stopped. "And for his crimes . . . you judged him."

Dredd came to his feet, fists clenched at his sides. *"Rico?* You let me judge my own brother and never *told* me!"

"I couldn't, Joseph. You were like a son to me."

"A *son!*" Dredd's hand swept out and grabbed the water jar from Fargo, shattered it against the wall. The parched earth drank the precious fluid at once.

"Rico had to be killed," Fargo said. "To protect you. To protect the city."

"To protect *yourself,* you mean."

"Yes. That's true. God help me, I cannot deny that. I did it for myself, for all of us, for—"

"Wait, wait . . ."

It struck him, then, like a physical blow, real and so suddenly clear it nearly brought him to his knees.

"Rico. He's not dead." He stared at Fargo. "Rico's still alive."

Fargo looked at his hands. "No, he's not dead, Joseph. He's alive. I signed the order myself. He's in Aspen Prison. Special quarters there. I couldn't—I couldn't destroy him, whatever he was. He's part of me. Part of you."

Dredd struck his fist against the wall. "Damn it, *don't you see it?*" He gripped Fargo's shoulders. "I didn't kill Hammond. *He* did. It was his DNA that convicted me. *Our* DNA. It was Rico. I don't know where the hell he is right now, but he's not in Aspen Prison!"

"Oh, Joseph, Joseph . . ."

All the color drained from Fargo's face. He looked at his hands, as if he might make the whole thing go away.

"How, though? How could he . . ." He looked up at Dredd. "Griffin. It has to be. There's no one else. He's deceived us both. Sent us both to hell and brought Rico back."

"The Janus project."

"Yes. Of course." Fargo's eyes went cold. "He's going to do it. He's going to activate the project, open up that box of horrors again."

Dredd shook his head. "No. He won't. Griffin can't do anything without Rico. We get to Rico and we stop Griffin cold."

"Joseph—"

"Sir. I *will* stop him. There are ways to get into Mega-City, we both know that."

"It's not that easy. You don't *know,* Joseph."

"I know I can sit on my butt in this pesthole and die!" Dredd's voice clattered off the walls. "I know I will *not* do that, sir. He took my badge away from me. That's all I ever had, and I will get it back!"

Fargo slowly pulled himself to his feet. Dredd thought he looked every one of his years. Dust filled the lines of his face, a map of his long days of service, of giving himself to a cause he was no longer sure had been a just cause at all.

What of all those years now? Dredd wondered. *What had it come to, his faith in the system, in himself?*

Dredd had never imagined he could look at this man with any feelings except those of respect, devotion. Fargo had been like a father to him, the only father he'd ever known. Now, with the twisted irony of truth, he knew that Fargo *was* his father, in blood as well as name. And with that realization came the shadow of doubt, the confusion of love and hate—rage, sadness, despair.

Dredd felt the heat rise to his face, the heat of sudden shame. Emotion of any kind had always troubled him deeply, and now those emotions battled with one another, clashed like dark and angry stormclouds in his head. That terrible conflict paralyzed him with doubt. He wanted to turn away, be anywhere but here. He wanted to reject his father for what he'd done . . . to go to him, tell him he understood, that he, himself, felt the torment of the decision this man had been forced to make. Right or wrong, he had followed his heart, served in the best way he could . . .

And as he watched the old man in the long duster coat, watched him as he looked out at the cold night stars as if he sensed Dredd's thoughts, as if he knew that he, too, was being judged, judged by the son he had created, loved, and finally betrayed, as Dredd watched his father's tall silhouette, another shadow rose, stirred, brought itself up on its haunches, came out of the dark with the quickness, with the awesome blurring speed of a snake, striking before Dredd could move, before the message of danger could flash from his senses to his brain.

Mean Machine screamed, a high-pitched senseless babble of sound, a hymn of joy and death. Fargo sucked in a single breath. His arms and legs went rigid, his head snapped back, his hat slid across his face. Mean Machine's blade arm ripped through Fargo's back, lifting him off the ground.

Fergie sat far away from the ruins, alone out in the night. He didn't like it out there. It scared the hell out of him to be alone in the dark. But it didn't scare him half as much as staying back there. Not after what had happened, not after what he'd seen. Sitting out here with the scorpions and centipedes and the god-awful spiders bigger than his head was better than being back there. Better than being in that building with Dredd.

TWENTY-SEVEN

"*T*his is Duncan Harrow with the news . . .

"I'm sure most of you were watching less than twenty minutes ago when we interrupted our programming to bring you a bulletin on the explosion at Blue Quad Heights' Mega-City Bank. Reports have been confused and scattered, with conflicting stories of a daring daytime robbery, a utilities explosion and the crash of an inter-city shuttle. Judge squads and Mediks are on the scene. An area between Nine-hundred-fifty-seventh Street and Nixon Avenue has been sealed off tight. And while authorities are *not* answering questions, this reporter has obtained an interview with a source close to the disaster scene.

"Here, in an exclusive story, are the facts as we know them behind the explosion in the heart of Mega-City's exclusive Blue Quad Sector. At nine-thirty-five this morning, just thirty-eight minutes ago, an All-Judges call reported Citizen Unrest in Blue Twelve. According to our sources, a squad of seven Lawmaster-mounted Judges arrived on the scene at the Mega-City Bank. Minutes later, four more Street Judges reported in at the site. The Judges entered the bank in what is reported as a standard intervention wedge. Only seconds later, an explosion ripped through the building, sending flaming

debris into the street. While we don't wish to anticipate
official word on this incident, early reports indicate that
all eleven of the Judges are casualties, as well as an undetermined number of bank employees and Citizens. At
least four stories of the bank were destroyed, as well as a
number of public and commercial vehicles in the streets
nearby.

"Death tolls already mount into the hundreds, and
many severely- and critically-wounded persons have
been admitted to area hospitals . . .

"Ah, yes—here it is, our first video coverage of the
disaster from our News-Drone unit over the scene.
There are the . . . remains of the entrance to the bank.
You can see isolated fires still burning in the building.
There is a . . . a Judge Emergency Van, I believe, and I
believe there are at least a dozen vehicles, including a
ground shuttle, destroyed there in the street. That's all
the video we have at the moment, but there'll be more as
additional news units arrive.

"Let me say that since officials have *not* issued a statement, we have no indications at this time of the cause of
this explosion. We'll be going into the Hall of Justice
now, where Willi Cupp is standing by. Willi . . . ?"

TWENTY-EIGHT

"**D**uncan Harrow here with a special bulletin . . .

"Only moments ago, tragedy struck again in Mega-City. This time, unknown perpetrators struck at the heart of the social order. At two minutes after one this afternoon, an explosive device of undetermined strength detonated in the Street Judge locker room, deep inside the Hall of Justice itself. There are no casualty reports as yet, but an anonymous spokesman at the scene has reported that the death toll will almost certainly be high. The device exploded moments after the mid-day shift change, a time when the locker room is normally filled with personnel coming on duty, as well as those just finishing their tours.

"Though no official will comment at this time, there is little doubt that this tragedy and the earlier massacre of Judges and civilians at the Mega-City Bank are most certainly connected. Our news-drones are on the scene, and we'll bring you an update on this story as soon as possible."

TWENTY-NINE

*T*he six Lawmasters stopped in the street, just at the entrance of the darkened alley. The deep throb of muffled engines was the only sound except for the steady drip of water overhead. Senior Sergeant Landdale knew the city as well as any man could, and he didn't like this place at all. Downtown, as deep as you could go. If the underbelly of Mega-City was a cesspool, the stink started here.

"Dispatcher said a Six-Oh-Three, Sergeant. If there's an Armed Robbery in Progress here, they're being nice and quiet about it."

"Keep your eyes open and your mouth shut, Colter. You haven't seen the dog, don't go telling me what color it is."

"Yes, Sergeant." Colter felt the color rise to his cheeks. He didn't have to look at the other Judges. He knew they were grinning behind their visors. Senior Sergeant Judge Landdale was always putting him down with shit Colter didn't understand. "Don't start singing till they pass out the music" was last week's helpful hint. This week it was the damn dog.

"All right," Landdale said finally, "Bolo, take the point. Pierce, you back him up real close."

Landdale spoke softly into his visor-comm, telling the

dispatcher there was no sign of a Six-Oh-Three or anything else except a lot of bad smells, and they would henceforth investigate the said area in question, stand by.

The harsh headlights of the six Lawmasters had enough power to light up the cellars of hell, but they scarcely ate through twenty feet of the murky atmosphere of the alley. Landdale didn't care for that at all. He had stayed alive as a Street Judge for fifteen years by religiously following Landdale's Law: "If it's light, yell 'Halt!' then shoot and bring up the body bags. If it's dark, just shoot and check it out the next day." The only thing wrong with this practice was it *never* got light in this part of town. Never did and never would.

Bolo and Pierce were entering the alley, hugging opposite walls, Lawgivers off-safety, suit-lights on blind. The other members of the squad waited, holding their breaths. Suddenly, a high, whirring sound cut through the silence of the dark. Landdale and his men turned on their heels as one, fingers on the squeeze. The landcar wheezed to a stop, scant milliseconds before the Judges would've opened fire and turned it into a blossom of superheated gas.

Landdale put his rage on hold, stalked over to the squat vehicle, and yanked open the door.

"All right, groon-breath," he said, "haul it out of there. I want to see ten empty digits dancing in the air."

The man stepped out. He was a small man with a face as round as a pie.

"No need for alarm, Judge. I'm not armed. My name's—"

"I know who you are." Landdale lowered his weapon in disgust. "You're that sum-bitch on the video. What are you doing here, Harold? This is a potential crime scene."

"Harrow. Duncan Harrow with the news," Harrow corrected. "I run the scales, follow the little blips, the little lights. I look and listen in. That's how I get the news. I was down in Yellow Quad, got the Six-Oh-Three, possible Armed—"

"I know what it is, mister." Landdale glanced down the alley, then back to Harrow. "I got an interdiction in progress here. You get your ass back in that vehicle now. Turn it around and go quiet-like back the way you came in."

"Huh-uh. I don't have to do that. I'm a certified journalist. I have every right to be here."

Landdale raised his visor. His eyes were hard as flint. "I'll tell you what you got. You got every right I *tell* you you got. So far that isn't even *one*." He poked the muzzle of his Lawgiver between Harrow's eyes. "Now you turn this piece of crap around and git."

Harrow took a deep breath, ready to tell this uppity Street Judge who he knew in what high places, and decided that really wouldn't help. This was a man who'd been around a while, and likely had a broad understanding of resisting arrest.

"Yes, sir," Harrow said. "You got it, sir."

He wound up the window, turned the car in a quick circle, and disappeared down the block.

Landdale watched him go, muttering under his breath. He didn't like the video or anyone on it. They said whatever they wanted to, even something bad about a Judge. Landdale was sure it was video people behind that awful business with Fargo and Dredd. Things like that shouldn't happen. The Judges ought to take care of their own. And if something *did* happen, groons like that Harold guy shouldn't be allowed to stand in front of a camera and crow.

He thought about the groon. He thought about his hair. If he remembered, the guy didn't have any hair. He had hair on the video, he didn't have any hair now. Maybe that was a rule. You had to have some hair on top, you were on the video. You were off, you could do whatever you wanted. So why not wear it all the time?

Landdale wondered. Guys like that, who's to say what they might do?

"Nothing, *nada,*" Polo said into his visor-comm. "Zero plus two up here."

"That's a double," Pierce said. "I got junk and bad smells and that's all."

"Okay, squad, standard line-and-stagger, let's move it in," Landdale said.

The Judges began their sweep. They were pros, and they kept the chatter down to a word here and there to let Landdale know what was going on with every man. Nothing happened. The water dripped steadily from the city up above. The alley was thick with murky poison air.

"Up here, team," Bolo said suddenly. "I've got potential lifeforms, Sarge."

"Shit," Pierce put in, "how can you tell? It's bums, Sergeant. Scummos and vags. We've landed in Maggot City, guys."

Landdale walked up toward where Bolo and Pierce were shining their lights. Colter was up there, too, Rodger and Workman on Landdale's right.

Landdale shook his head at the pitiful sight. Judge Pierce was right. These miserable creatures were human, but only because you couldn't classify them as anything else, not without offending some other group like earthworms or slugs. They shuffled away, squealing in fright, turning their sallow faces from the light, ducking beneath their ragged hoods.

Landdale made a mental note to tell Dispatch what he thought of their Armed Robbery in Progress report. There was something in progress here, all right. Like lice.

"All right, get 'em out of here, move 'em out."

"Where, Sarge?"

"What?"

"Where you want us to put them?"

Landdale recognized the voice. Colter again. The guy was a pain, had to have an *answer* to everything. Landdale wondered if the droog would notice he was still a corporal when he retired, and maybe wonder why.

"I don't *care* where you put them," Landdale said. "They're here. Take them somewhere that *isn't* here. Bolo, you see another alley up there?"

"Got nothing but alleys up here, Sarge."

"Fine. Put 'em up there."

What is wrong with these people? Landdale thought. *I got to do everything? I got to tell them to wash their hands before dinner, I gotta—*

"Sarge—something *up* here. Pierce, Workman, cover me . . ."

"What is it, Two, what've you got?" Landdale caught the urgency in Bolo's voice, a man shifting into second gear.

"Don't know . . . Something wrong, over there. Give me some more light, Rodger. You—come out of there. *Now.* Put your hands up high and—*yaaaaaaak!*"

Bolo's voice went dead. Landdale heard static and then that was gone, too. Pierce or Workman or someone screamed. He couldn't tell who. A Lawgiver chattered, lighting up the dark. A visor light went out.

Landdale snapped off his beam and went low, keeping to the wall. No use calling on the comm. Bolo was dead, out of it for sure. Maybe the other guys, too. What happened up there?

Someone breathing hard . . . no, chest wound. Sucking air. Landdale took a cautious step forward. His boot found something soft. One of 'em, no way to tell who.

Don't stay here, get out, get help. No one's going to blame you for that . . .

"Sarge! Oh my *Gaaaah . . . !*"

"Shut up, can it, whoever that is!"

The spot went on, turning dark into light. Landdale's visor darkened, compensating for the blinding flare. Not a visor light. Too damn bright. Too—

He saw it, a fraction of a second before he fired, big

son of a bitch, copper and steel, muckin' feet as big as a car, shiny stuff blinking in his gut, awful red eyes . . .

Landdale squeezed his trigger and didn't stop. A beam of blue light sizzled along the wall above his head, slicing through brick like fat, hissing through Senior Sergeant Landdale from his visor to his crotch.

THIRTY

Ilsa lowered her hood and sniffed the air.

"It smells dreadful here. Really unpleasant, dear."

Rico smiled. "Well, that *is* the point, isn't it? Drama. Horror. Death. Really dreadful smells. A theatrical event."

"It's all of that," she said.

Rico glanced over his shoulder. The massive robot stood silent, light from the still glowing fires in the alley dancing on its mirrored hide.

"Come on, Fido. Be a good boy, and Daddy will get you a very nice bone."

THIRTY-ONE

"**T**his is Tommy Waco with the news . . .

"Bear with me, if you will, ladies and gentlemen. There are—there are times when it's difficult to do a journalist's job in the professional and objective manner in which that job should—and must—be performed.

"I'm certain that everyone who's watching me now is aware of the latest tragic event that has shocked and stunned Mega-City—the ambush and slaughter of five, possibly six Judges—we can't say exactly how many at this moment—an ambush that took place in the notorious downtown district, Black Quad Nine.

"There are few facts available at this time. What we do know is that the Judges were burned beyond recognition, along with several vagrants. Sources report that an illegal weapon was used in this brutal killing, but that information is not confirmed . . .

"Sorry, I'm still here, my friends. This is—difficult, as I said. This part of the story has *not* been on the news. Another person lost his life in that chaotic event in the Black Quad. A colleague, a friend, and a fine journalist. A man you, the viewers, have come to know and respect as a commentator on this station.

"Duncan Harrow died in that same alley tonight. Duncan's car was found parked several blocks from the alley in question. But Duncan's remains, along with his blackened video camera, were found several feet within the alley itself, near the scene of the disaster.

"It was like Duncan Harrow to put himself in harm's way in order to bring you the news. That's the kind of man—the kind of reporter—Duncan Harrow was. A man very like another journalist we sorely miss, Vardis Hammond.

"Maybe I'm going out on a limb now. Maybe it's no longer *safe* for a journalist to speak to you in this manner, but here it is. Vardis Hammond felt that much of the lawlessness in Mega-City could be laid at the feet of those very persons responsible for upholding the Law. I'm speaking of the High Council of Judges itself. If you're listening, members of this respected body, what's your answer? Is Mega-City out of control, at the mercy of criminal terrorists? As Citizens, we need to know where we stand in these dangerous times. As the self-appointed guardians of our Society, you have an obligation to *let* us know. You have an obligation to the living. And you have an obligation to those who have died for the cause of Law and Order. Citizen and Judge alike.

"This is Tommy Waco with the news. Back to you, Katie Chloe, for an on-the-scene report from the site of the tragic Black Quad massacre . . ."

THIRTY-TWO

*T*he only trouble with the Judge Hunters' sand cruiser was the sand. Fergie wondered how technology could build a Mega-City, and still make an air valve that ground a fine engine into mush.

"We're finished," Fergie said, pulling himself from under the machine. "Finished. Done. Dead."

"We're walking," Dredd said.

"We're what?"

Dredd didn't answer. He picked up Fargo's shotgun from the hood, turned away, and started east. Fergie squinted at the sun and gently touched his cracked and swollen lips.

"You're crazy, Dredd. It's about two million miles to Mega-City. We don't have any food. We don't have any water. I can't even spit anymore."

"It's *seventeen* miles, you moron. You can take a droid apart, you can't add? Those Hunters punched a trip-dial before they left home. It's a regulation."

"Might as well be a million miles," Fergie muttered to himself. "We're not going anywhere without water."

"Have a nice day," Dredd said.

He kept on walking. He didn't stop or turn around. Fergie watched him go. In a moment, he seemed to be walking on glass. His body wavered as the heat rose up from the earth. The horizon rippled like a cheap video.

He's nuts, Fergie told himself. *He's a Judge and he's nuts. Judges don't think like normal people, and Dredd's about seven times crazier than the rest of that bunch.*

Fergie couldn't see him anymore. All he could see was a quivering silver lake. The lake turned upside down and shimmered in the sky.

He's crazy, but he's not that crazy. He didn't walk out there to die. He left me here to die is what he did. He's got water . . . the bastard's got water and he's left old Fergie to die!

Fergie ran. He ran for a minute and a half. Then he dropped on his face and ate sand. Then he got up and ran again.

When Dredd came back and found him, he was on his hands and knees, chasing a centipede. He said the centipede had a canteen and wouldn't tell him where.

"You're a groon," Dredd said. "You want water, pick that thing up and eat it. Insects have moisture inside."

Fergie looked at him with red and hollow eyes. "Forget it. I'm not really thirsty. I'll wait until we find a nice bar."

"Good."

"You want my bug? You can have my bug."

"I don't want your bug."

"Maybe I'll keep it."

"Fine."

"Just in case, you know?" Fergie squashed the bug and put it in his pocket. Dredd would be sorry. Dredd would get thirsty and want his bug. Fergie would tell him, "Forget it, find your own bug, man." Fergie grinned. It made him feel good to think about that.

"I knew you were out of your mind. I didn't know how far, is all."

"You can stay here. Nobody says you have to go."

"That's right."

"That's what you want to do?"

"Absolutely. That is exactly what I want to do."

Dredd shook his head. "Just the answer I'd expect from the criminal mind. The habitual offender has no initiative, no will to survive."

"Hey, nix on that. I got a will to survive."

"Only if it's not any trouble. If you don't have to get off your butt you'll maybe give it a try."

Fergie mumbled to himself. He huddled on the parched ground, his knees folded under his chin. What the hell kind of world was this anyway? Five minutes before, the sun had been frying his head. Now, there was only a glow in the west and he was freezing to death.

Craning his neck, looking nearly straight up, he could see the broad stripe of gold, the dying sun's reflection on the great Mega-City wall. The band of light was climbing fast; the sun was already far below the curve of the Cursed Earth.

In a moment, the stripe narrowed and disappeared at the top of the wall, half a mile high. Now, as the darkness began to gather in, he could clearly see the glare of flame low on the wall, not twenty yards ahead. A brief puff of smoke appeared, then vanished in the air.

"It's a vent from one of the city's incinerators," Dredd had explained. "There's a burst twice a minute. That means we've got a thirty-second interval to get through the tube before it flames again."

"That means you are out of your mucking mind," Fergie said.

"You thirsty?"

"Yes."

"You got any water?"

"No."

Fergie thought a minute. "The guys that went through, they made it okay. They got in, right?"

"Wrong." Dredd shook his head. "They were droogs. Cursed Earthers. About as bright as Junior Head-Dead."

"You're saying, you're saying they didn't get in."

"They got fried. But that's because they didn't figure it right. There is no reason it can't be done."

Fergie looked at him. "I'm stupid, remember? I'm a habitual offender."

"Right. But you're smarter than Junior Head-Dead anytime. Come on, get up. Let's go."

"No way, man."

"What's wrong?"

"What's wrong?" Fergie stared. "Are you kidding? Wearing that pot on your head all these years has baked your brains, Dredd. You're going to get me killed. You're —oh, God, look at that!"

A fireball roared out of the vent, a tongue of flame thirty feet long. Fergie felt the heat on his face, smelled the charred remains of a million garbage cans.

Dredd waited until the flames died down, then walked up to the edge of the vent, keeping close to the wall. "Do what you want," he said. "I'm going in, I've got things to do. There's a maniac loose in Mega-City."

"There's another one loose out here," Fergie said. He looked at the darkening sky, pleading with whoever might reside up there.

"Great time I'm having. I'm out of Aspen, I got a new life ahead, right? Wrong. I'm crashing in a shuttle. Cannibals think I'm the catch of the day. Now I got fireballs up my ass. And I owe it all to you. Thanks, Dredd."

Dredd looked at him. "Me? You're blaming me?"

"Of course I'm blaming you. If you hadn't arrested me on false charges, I wouldn't be here in the first place."

"That's faulty logic. That's lawbreaker talk, that's—"

"Yeah, I know. It's the criminal mind." He glared at Dredd. "Well, that's it. I've had it." Fergie slid to the ground against the wall. "I'm sitting right here. Someone arrests me, fine."

"All right."

"Or until you apologize, Dredd."

Dredd looked at him. "Until I what?"

"Don't look at me like that. You heard what I said."

"You're mentally impaired."

"Okay."

"The Law doesn't apologize, Ferguson. Do I have to remind you of that?"

"So? You're not a Judge anymore. I gotta remind you of *that?*"

Dredd looked tired. "Ferguson, what difference does it make? What if I was sorry, which I'm not. This is going to change your life or what?"

Fergie brought himself to his feet. He looked at the dark horizon, he didn't look at Dredd. "I'll bet you've never said the words in your life. Not ever. You *owe* it to me, Dredd."

Dredd cocked his head and looked at Fergie as if he'd just dropped in from Mars.

"I'm supposed to say . . . exactly what?"

" 'I'm sorry.' That's it. That'll do fine."

"I'll review your case, Ferguson. I will take the circumstances into consideration."

The vent belched flame again, then retreated in a veil of foul smoke.

Fergie thought about that, then a smile spread across his face. "Review. *Review* is okay. Review is good. I'll accept that. That's a start, it's a—huh? *Dredd!*"

Dredd picked him up by the waist and tossed him into the chute.

"Go, Ferguson! Thirty seconds—run!"

"No!" Fergie turned and started back. Dredd was right behind him. He stiff-armed Fergie in the back and sent him sprawling down the chute.

"Twenty-eight . . . twenty-seven . . . twenty-six . . ." Fergie said.

"Stop counting, droog," Dredd shouted. "Move!"

"Twenty-two . . . twenty-one . . . twenty—where was I? Dredd, I'm going to fry!"

"Right. I'll make sure you don't." Dredd racked a shell into the chamber of Fargo's gun. Fergie looked over his shoulder, saw the weapon pointed at his head.

"Okay, okay, I'm *running!*"

Fergie heard a low rumble, then a tremor he could feel through his boots, a thunder so deep it shook the walls. Something flickered far ahead. Something bright and red. The sight nearly stopped his heart. The fireball, coming right at him . . . God, he couldn't be that slow, he still had time!

"Damn you, Dredd! You were wrong!"

"Maybe it wasn't thirty seconds," Dredd said behind him. "Maybe it was something else."

"Oh, *shiiiiiiit!*"

Dredd suddenly stopped. He reached out and grabbed Fergie's collar and jerked him to a halt. Fergie stared. Dredd shoved him against the wall. He braced himself and fired the Remington at the floor of the chute. He pumped the weapon again and again. Fergie felt blood in his ears. Through a veil of dirty smoke, he saw the twisted grate at Dredd's feet. Dredd kicked it with his boot. Kicked it again. The grate gave way with a clatter and vanished in the dark.

Dredd shouted in Fergie's ear. Fergie couldn't hear, but Dredd's gesture was perfectly clear. Fergie jumped into the dark hole. Half a second later, he saw the fireball roar overhead, felt the awful heat, smelled the hair burning on his head.

Fergie flailed his arms in the air. Hit something soft, plowed through it and didn't stop. Struck bottom on his knees, came up hacking and spitting black ash. Felt Dredd's boots hit his back and went down again.

A dim light, from somewhere to the right. Dredd rose from the dark, his face black with soot.

"I'm alive," Fergie said. "Hey, you are, too. How about that? We're both alive!"

"Right. I can see that."

"Dredd?"

"What?"

"Review's okay, like I said. I mean, I'll accept that. If you wanted to, you know, if you wanted to do any *more*, like actually apologize . . ."

"Forget it," Dredd said. "I must have been out of my head. Let's get out of here. I've got work to do."

"You admitted you got it wrong."

"I did what?"

"You said maybe it wasn't thirty seconds. You said it was maybe something else."

"So what?"

"So it wasn't thirty. It was maybe thirteen."

"It wasn't thirteen."

"You don't know, you don't know that. It might have been twelve."

"Shut up," Dredd said.

THIRTY-THREE

*H*e shut out the fury, turned it aside. Cast a blind eye to the carnage, to the chaos, to the oily smoke from the city's funeral pyres. A sky-lite bus had hit a barge head on, two-thousand feet above White Quad's famous Crystal Dome. The explosion rocked the heights of the city. Twisted shards of molten metal, plastic, glass, and body parts ripped through the Dome, tearing, shredding, bringing razor-death to the naked fun-seekers below.

He ran down the alleyway behind Two-thousand-twenty-third Street, Fergie close behind. There were screams from the street, the sound of breaking glass. A looter with dragons tattooed on his face raced by with a holo set.

Now and then he saw Judges. Some of them were holding back the crowds. Some of them were dead. He used all the courage at his command to keep from jumping in to help, to fight beside his friends. He knew he couldn't do it, that he had to stop Rico if he could. Besides, he was a fugitive. Even men who knew him might kill now.

That hurt. That hurt a lot. Almost as much as watching the people of the city tear his world apart.

Getting into the Hall of Justice wasn't hard. Every veteran Judge knew how. Fergie didn't want to come.

Stay outside, Dredd told him, go anywhere. Fergie kept quiet after that.

The Judge in the locker room turned, startled. It was clear that he recognized Dredd. Dredd hit him carefully, a point below his neck. The man sagged. Dredd eased him to the ground and began stripping off his uniform. It wouldn't quite fit, but that was fine.

"Oh, hell, why not?" Fergie rolled his eyes. "What else can they do to me? I'm dead already. They catch me, they can't kill me twice."

"Don't count on it," Dredd said.

THIRTY-FOUR

THE SETTING:

> The lighting is subdued in the Council Chamber. The massive marble carving of the eagle and badge of the Judges is almost lost in shadow. Perhaps this somber atmosphere reflects the mood of the Justices themselves. They know this is not a time for secrets or evasions, for half-truths and Council politics. This is a time of reckoning, of honest exchange, of sharing the strength, the wisdom, and the craft that brought them where they are. This is a time when they will perish or survive.

JUDGE ESPOSITO

This is the latest casualty report: Ninety-six Judges have been assassinated. I'm sure that's a conservative figure. Our lines of communication are severely disabled. Property loss, civilian deaths . . . we can't keep up with that.

JUDGE McGRUDER

Whoever's behind all this is familiar with our every procedure. They have our security measures . . . they even know our scrambler frequencies. *Nothing's* safe! They know everything we do!

JUDGE ESPOSITO

With only a handful of Judges on the street, riots are breaking out all over Mega-City. We don't even have emergency personnel anymore—we don't have anyone to send. The situation is critical!

[Judge Silver studies a sheaf of papers. He crushes them in his hand and lets them fall to the floor.]

JUDGE SILVER

It's more than critical. It's a *disaster!* We cannot *replace* these Judges. Even if we put the Cadets on the street— an action I cannot bring myself to think about—we would not be at full strength for years.

JUDGE McGRUDER

We don't *have* years, my friend. I doubt very much we have days. And mark my words, with nothing to control them they'll be up here, at *our* doors next. You can bet on that.

[The Judges glance at one another, then quickly look away. This is a horror that each of them has experienced, alone, in the safe and guarded havens of the Heights . . . the nightmare of the horde, the swarm, the Citizens of Mega-City free and un- leashed, the havenots of the overcrowded warrens down below, thinking of the wonders, of the dream, of the beautiful toys of the few they have only glimpsed on their videos . . . Silence. The Judges can hear the hiss of sterile air. Chief Justice Griffin looks at his hands, stands, and turns to the others.]

CHIEF JUSTICE GRIFFIN

There is a solution, you know. It's there. And perhaps this is exactly what it was designed for. Project Janus.

[The Council erupts in babble. The explosion of anger, astonishment, fear, and disbelief echoes about the vast room. Judge McGruder comes to her feet.]

JUDGE McGRUDER

Chief Justice Griffin. The mere *mention* of that name, that abomination, is intolerable—and grounds for impeachment!

JUDGE SILVER

No. It is unthinkable, sir. Out of the question. This Council tried to play God once before. It almost destroyed us then.

CHIEF JUSTICE GRIFFIN

And if this wholesale slaughter of Judges continues, then what, Judge Silver? We shall surely be destroyed if that occurs. What possible purpose would that serve? If we bring Janus into play it can—

JUDGE ESPOSITO

It can *what?* A new batch of *test-tube babies* won't solve this crisis, Chief Justice. We do not need reliable Judges twenty *years* from now. If we are going to survive, if this city is going to survive, we need help this minute, *today!*

(The lines of age and weariness are deeply etched into Judge Esposito's face. The skin is dark and blotched beneath his eyes. Last night he heard the sirens wailing far below. When he finally slept, he dreamed of men with tattooed faces, men with blood in their eyes . . .)

JUDGE SILVER

I quite agree. With all due respect, Chief Justice, we have a desperate emergency here, a problem of the moment. This is not the time to speak of measures whose ends likely none of us here will live to see. If, indeed, we dared to consider such an action.

CHIEF JUSTICE GRIFFIN

But I am not speaking of procedures that would take *years,* Judge. I would hope you'd give me more credit than that. No, you are right, all of you. We cannot wait. And, in truth, *we don't have to.* Science has come a long way since we initiated the Janus Project. Accelerated growth incubators are far more technologically advanced than they were at the time.

We could create adult subjects now, fully grown and trained at birth. We could replace the Judges we've lost in a week.

[The Judges are stunned. Judge Silver clasps his hands to keep them from shaking. Judge Mc-Gruder feels a quick stab of pain in her chest. The Mediks have told her this likely wouldn't happen again. But it has. Judge Esposito closes his eyes. He sees his nightmares walking in the full light of day. Judge McGruder is on her feet, staring at Chief Justice Griffin.]

JUDGE McGRUDER

Good God, man! Have you lost your senses, sir? Do you know what you're saying?!

(Chief Justice Griffin is perfectly calm, as cold as the black marble slab that looms above his head.)

CHIEF JUSTICE GRIFFIN

All I am asking, Judge McGruder, is that we unlock the Janus Files. That does *not,* in any way, compel us to take action. It merely gives us an option. Is there anything wrong with that, with exploring answers to our dilemma?

[Chief Justice Griffin waits. No one speaks. Each Judge, perhaps, is hoping that the other will say the word that will break this terrible spell.]

CHIEF JUSTICE GRIFFIN

Please. I only ask that we find out. Nothing more than that. If the Council decides I am totally in the wrong, that the Janus Project is definitely *not* the answer to this crisis, why, then I will of course accept that decision . . . and further, I will at once resign my position as Chief Justice of this Council.

[Again, the Judges look at one another in silence.]

JUDGE SILVER

I would . . . not be opposed to looking into the matter. I will certainly not commit myself further than that.

CHIEF JUSTICE GRIFFIN

I would not want you to, sir.

JUDGE McGRUDER

I will agree. Reluctantly, Chief Justice.

JUDGE ESPOSITO

I would like to go on record against even bringing this subject into the open. However, if the other members of the Council are in favor . . . I will not oppose you.

CHIEF JUSTICE GRIFFIN

Your objection is noted, Judge. And I go on record here as saying I greatly appreciate your candid opinions on this most important subject. That is what this Council is all about. Now. Would the members please acknowledge their voice codes for Central Computer?

McGruder, Eve. Council Judge. Authorize file, code name Janus.

Acknowledged.

Esposito, Carl. Council Judge. Authorize file, code name Janus.

Acknowledged.

Silver, Gerald. Council Judge. Authorize file, code name Janus.

Acknowledged.

CHIEF JUSTICE GRIFFIN

Report present status, Central.

CENTRAL

I have received unanimous authorization for access to the file code-named Janus. Removing Security Blocks now. Awaiting password command from presiding Chief Justice.

[Judge Magruder, closest to Griffin, draws in a quick breath. One hand goes to her breasts, an ancient and unconscious gesture of protection, a gesture of alarm. Chief Justice Griffin's eyes seem to glow, to generate a brighter, silver shard of light

that is not a reflection at all, but some illumination
from within.]

CHIEF JUSTICE GRIFFIN
Password command . . . origin.

CENTRAL
The Janus file is open.

THIRTY-FIVE

Griffin looked straight ahead.

He didn't dare look at his fellow Judges. They knew him too well, as he knew them. They would see, and they would know, and he was not quite ready for that. Not yet, not yet . . .

The holo blinked into life before the Council table, a perfect sphere, a small blue world turning slowly in the inner space of the Council Chamber.

"Central," Griffin said, "utilizing current technology, give me a time factor on the ability of the Janus Project to produce a fully-grown adult subject. Priority Reply."

At once, a solid field of zeros and ones began crawling across the sphere, like the onset of day, like the end of dark night, following the blue planet's curve from west to east, a dazzling field of green digits changing too swiftly for the ordinary eye.

"Given the current status of genetic engineering, an adult subject could be incubated and completed in eight-point-two-two-standard hours."

"My *God!*" Judge Esposito sat up straight. "Stop this, Chief Justice. Stop it now."

Griffin didn't look at him. "I believe you agreed to . . . consider the project, along with the others."

"I withdraw that agreement!"

"I . . . don't believe procedure allows for that," Judge Silver said.

Esposito glared. "I don't give a damn what procedure says." He jerked his head toward Griffin. "What he's doing is criminal. You're fools, both of you, if you let him continue with this."

"Carl . . ." McGruder leaned in and laid a hand on his arm. "Carl, it's a *presentation*. We agreed to that. It doesn't have to go any further."

Esposito started to speak. He looked at the others, shook his head and placed his hands on the flat surface of the desk. Griffin glanced at him, then turned to the shining sphere.

"In what quantity, Central? Give me a projected number of incubated and completed subjects."

"Laboratory Number One of the Janus Project is currently equipped with one hundred subjects. Under fully operational conditions, seven hundred subjects could be completed in seven days."

Silver stared at Griffin in disbelief. "That many? This is true? Why, we could replace our losses in one *day!*"

"Exactly," Griffin said. "We could regain adequate control of the city almost at once, clean out the riotous elements in every sector. Before the week is out, we could reinforce trouble spots at such a strength that these unruly dissidents would think twice about showing their faces in the streets again."

"These *unruly dissidents* you're talking about are people, Chief Justice." Esposito watched the blurr of data flashing across the sphere. "People. Not numbers."

McGruder shook her head. "He's right. We shouldn't even be considering this. It's . . . it's *inhuman,* the whole concept was inhuman from the beginning. It is madness, sir. It is *not* the Council's job to play God."

"Judge . . ." Griffin spread his hands and smiled. It was a weary, patient smile that reflected a teacher's concession to a backward child. "We sit in judgement of our fellow citizens because we must, because order is necessary for the continuation of a peaceable Society. If there was no need for such supervision, we could disband and go frolic in the park."

"Don't you patronize me, Chief Justice!" McGruder came to her feet. She glared at Griffin and jabbed her arm at the shimmering globe. "Central, restore the Security Blocks on the Janus Project. At once!"

Griffin smiled. "I'm afraid you can't simply *vote* all by yourself, Judge. We are a Council here. We act together." He looked at the others. "I find it most painful that I have to handle this myself, without your help and support. I am deeply hurt that none of you have the will, the strength, these dangerous times require.

"Central . . ." Griffin spoke without looking up. "Janus will remain unlocked. My command only. Authority: Override Mega-City Emergency One-Niner-Five."

Esposito came to his feet. "This is *treason*, sir!" His eyes were dark with rage. "You have gone too far, you have sealed your fate here, Chief Justice!"

"No," Griffin said quietly, "I'm afraid you've sealed yours. Rico—in here!"

He spoke without moving his eyes from Esposito. He felt a great sense of satisfaction, of completion, as the color drained from his face, as the meaning of the name he had spoken was reflected in the taut lines of fear about his lips, as he knew and understood what he had done, that it was finished, over, that there was nothing more for them now.

Rico walked into the great room. He wore the full-dress combat black of the Judges. He held the Lawgiver straight down at his side. He looked at the Council and smiled.

McGruder's face was drawn, frightened. "Damn you, Griffin. Damn you to hell for this!"

"That kind of talk is not constructive, Judge," Griffin said.

"Send-him-away! Stop this horror at once!"

"Judge." Griffin let out a breath. "I have to ask you to—"

McGruder's left hand dipped beneath the table. Rico seemed to make little effort at all. McGruder's head slammed into the massive slab at her back, spattering the marble red.

Silver cried out once. Esposito didn't move. His eyes were on Griffin as he died.

Rico smiled, studying his weapon as if he'd never seen it at all. "Who said politics is boring? I might run for office sometime."

A pall of acrid smoke hung over the room. Griffin sniffed the air and turned away from the carnage.

"I want you out of here. Now. I don't want anyone to see you *near* this place. Go out the way you came. Ilsa will be there."

"Ilsa is getting on my nerves."

"Get out of here, Rico. Do it now!"

Rico shrugged. He laid his weapon across his shoulder, gave Griffin a mock salute, and disappeared behind the marble slab.

Griffin walked quickly toward the doorway to the hall. Judge Hunters would hear the gunfire. They'd be on the run by now. If he hurried, there was still time to—

The big wooden doorway exploded, slammed to the ground. Griffin stepped back. Dredd stalked into the room, the weapon smoking in his hand. He looked at Griffin, then past him at the horror of the Council table.

"No . . . *Nooooo!*" Dredd tried to grasp the sight, tried to comprehend what had happened here. He raised his eyes slowly, aimed the Remington squarely at Griffin's head.

"You murdering bastard, you—" Dredd stopped, shook his head. "Rico. *He* did this. You wouldn't have the stomach for it, would you? Where is he? Where *is* he, Griffin!"

"Don't be foolish," Griffin said. "Rico's dead. He's been dead for years—"

"Talk to me. *Where is he?*"

"Dredd, listen to me, all right?" Griffin raised his hands and backed away. "Things are going to change, whether you like it or not. Nothing's going to stop this. Not you, not anyone."

"Janus. Is that what you're talking about?" Dredd turned his thumb straight down. "I won't let it happen. I will stop you any way I can."

"There's nothing you can do. Not now. Nothing that—"

A shout echoed through the corridor. Heavy boots pounded the granite floor. Dredd jerked around and faced Griffin.

Griffin smiled, grabbed his belly, doubled up and writhed on the floor.

"In here," he yelled. "Hurry, for God's sake!"

Dredd stared at the man, then suddenly understood. He cursed Griffin under his breath and ran, dodging into the small anteroom off the Council Chamber. Half a second later, Judge Hunters swarmed into the room, Lawgivers at the ready.

"Get him!" Griffin pointed shakily from the floor. "Damn it, go—he's murdered the whole Council!"

The Hunter squad turned and charged out of the room. An officer bent down over Griffin. Griffin recognized his face.

"We'll take care of you, sir. I'll get Mediks on the way—"

"Captain, never mind that. Get Dredd! *Kill him!*"

"Sir—"

"I'm not badly hurt. Do it now!"

"Yes, sir."

The officer hurried away. Griffin waited until his footsteps echoed down the hall. He stood and walked to the black table. He looked into McGruder's dead eyes. He touched her with his finger, then drew a red smear across his chest. Word would get out that he was wounded, that he wouldn't even let the Hunters stop to give him medical care. He smiled at the thought. He could picture them, at dinner, in their barracks. It was pleasant to imagine the things they might say.

THIRTY-SIX

Dredd tore through the anteroom, stopped to jack a shell into the chamber of the Remington pump. He could hear the Judge Hunters in the Council Chamber, Griffin's ragged shout.

He listened a moment, then stepped into the hall. Two Hunters turned and stared. Dredd squeezed the trigger twice. The blast thundered off the walls. Dredd ran without looking back. Someone yelled. Bullets whined off the stone floor.

Dredd rounded the corner and stopped, searched the dark hall.

"Ferguson! Damn it, where are you?"

Fergie peeked out of a closet. "What the hell did you do in there, Dredd? You got all the groons stirred up again. Everybody's after me, right?"

"Come on, get out of there." Dredd grabbed a handful of shirt and jerked Fergie into the hall. "Stay close. Don't stray off anywhere."

Fergie looked pained. "Where have I heard *that* before?"

The end of the corridor narrowed. There were doors on either side. Dredd moved quickly, opened the third door and shoved Fergie in.

"Where are we?" Fergie said. "What are we doing, Dredd?"

"Shut up," Dredd said.

The room was almost dark. Dredd knew he couldn't risk a light. A faint glow came from the skylight, reflecting the brightness of Mega-City outside. The light didn't matter. He knew every corner of this room in the dark. It was the Academy Training Center, and it was as familiar as his own bedroom.

He passed a table stacked with weapons and locks and stopped at the gleaming black machine. He felt a slight catch in his throat at the sight of brushed chrome and stainless steel, at the metal black as night.

"What is it, why are we stopping here?" Fergie looked nervously across the room. "We don't have *time* to be doing any shopping now, Dredd. We've got company dropping in."

"The Mark IV Lawmaster. State-of-the-art. Double sixty-fours, rapid-fire."

"Yeah, yeah, great."

"Get on."

"Do what?"

"Get on or stay behind. Your choice."

Dredd threw his leg over the broad leather saddle. He ran his fingers swiftly over the panel keys imbedded in the black steel dash. Red lights blinked in a line. Dredd punched the ignition. The lights turned green. The big engine came to life and roared.

"You coming or not?"

"Huh-uh, not me." Fergie backed off. "I don't think so, man. You enjoy yourself. Give me a call—"

The door to the room exploded in a burst of broken glass. Gunfire whined past Fergie's head.

"Let's *go*, what are we waiting for, haul it *out* of here!"

The engine climbed up the scale, wailing like a demon, howling like a lost soul. Fergie wondered briefly where Dredd intended to go. What was he going to do, charge for rides around the room? Would the Judge Hunters care, would they stand around and clap?

The floor shook. Something caught fire. Dredd slammed his palm down hard. The Lawmaster's black fenders whirred, folded up, and disappeared. Two ugly snouts appeared in their place.

"Side arms—FIRE!" Dredd said.

The Lawmaster buckled. White flames blossomed from the twin sixty-fours. The far wall exploded, loosing a geyser of glass, brick, and assorted debris. Fergie stared at the large, gaping hole, at the towers of Mega-City that suddenly appeared, at the diamond-bright lights as far as the eye could see.

"You're kidding, right?" Fergie gripped Dredd's arm. "You're not going to do that. Nobody in their right mind would do that . . ."

AERIAL MODE—AERIAL MODE—AERIAL MODE . . .

"What?" Fergie closed his eyes. "No way, man."

"Work-work-*work!*" Dredd said between his teeth. "Work, you son of a bitch!"

The Lawmaster's engine sputtered, howled. The big machine trembled, pitched forward with a gut-wrenching burst of speed and roared through the hole in the wall.

Fergie screamed.

Gunfire followed the Lawmaster into the night.

"Please-work-please-work-please-work . . ."

The broad wheels sucked up into the frame. The lights on the console went wild.

AERIAL MODE—AERIAL MODE—AERIAL MODE ON-LINE—AE-RIAL MODE ON-LINE . . .

The engine changed pitch. The Lawmaster banked gently in the air.

"All *right!*" Dredd shouted. He pounded on the dash.

"Yeah-yeah-*yeah!*" Fergie yelled.

The engine sputtered. Died. The Lawmaster fell like a stone.

AERIAL MODE MALFUNCTION—AERIAL MODE MALFUNCTION
—AERIAL MODE MAL—

"Do-it-do-it-do-it!"

The Lawmaster tumbled dizzily toward the ground. The towers of Mega-City flashed by in a sickening streak of lights. Fergie yelled in Dredd's ear. Dredd tore at the controls, punching every button he could find. Lights turned red-green-blue-yellow-white.

The wind spread Dredd's skin flat against his face, opened his nostrils, pressed his lips against his teeth . . .

MALFUNCTION . . .

MALFUNCTION . . .

MALFUNCTION . . .

MAL—

AERIAL MODE ON-LINE—AERIAL MODE ON-LINE . . .

The engine came back to life, the most beautiful sound Dredd had ever heard. Safety rockets exploded beneath the Lawmaster, lifting it on a stable column of super-heated air. Dredd twisted the control bar gently to the right. The Lawmaster jerked through four gears, and screwed itself in a dizzy circle through the night.

"What the hell are you doing!" Fergie wailed.

"Relax. I'm trying to get the feel of this thing."

"What, this is your first time? Don't tell me that, Dredd, I don't want to hear tha—uh-oh!"

"What?"

"Company. Hunters on our ass. Two of 'em—three."

"Great. Just great. Hang on."

Dredd squeezed the control bar and gritted his teeth. The Lawmaster protested, stood on its tail, and shrieked straight up. Dredd left his stomach a thousand feet below. The bottom of a skyway appeared up ahead, blotting out the night. Dredd yanked the big machine aside, saw the startled face of a taxi driver flash by.

Fergie was babbling in his ear. Dredd risked a look back. The Hunters were good. Right on his tail.

"Here, take it," he shouted. He ripped the Remington's strap from his shoulder and passed it back.

"What?"

"Cover our rear. Hold those bastards off."

"I can't do that."

"Why not?"

"I never shot a gun in my life!"

"What the hell kind of criminal are you, Ferguson?"

"I'm a *nice* criminal. I rob droids. I steal things. Just little things. I don't do guns, man, I never—"

"*Shoot,* damn it!"

Fergie closed his eyes and fired. The muzzle flashed and the stock slammed into his shoulder.

"I missed, I knew I'd miss . . ."

"Again!"

Fergie pulled the trigger. Nothing happened.

"It doesn't work anymore. I think the batteries are down."

"You've got to *pump* it, you moron," Dredd yelled. "Get a shell in the chamber."

"I knew that."

"Ferguson . . ."

Fergie fired. Something sparked on the lead Hunter's machine.

"I got him!" Fergie pounded Dredd's back. "You see that, I shot the son of bitch!"

"You hurt his feelings, maybe. You chipped his paint. What do you think these things are made of, paper plates? These are Lawmaster IVs."

"Wonderful," Fergie said, "so whose side are you on, ours or theirs?"

"You've got to hit something important."

"Like what?"

"Like a power coil or cooler duct. The power coil is partially exposed during standard Aerial Mode. A well-placed shot would likely disable or seriously damage the machine."

"That's a lecture, right?"

"It's a lecture. It's *my* lecture. Just do it, Ferguson. Hang on, now."

"Hang on, right. He says hang on, like I'll maybe—Dredd, look where you're going."

"I'm looking."

"You're *not* looking. If you're looking, you're not looking like a regular person looks. That's how I want you to look—Dredd, *shit!*"

Fergie held his breath. The thing loomed up ahead, a droid nearly twenty stories high. It's eyes blinked red. One hand held a giant candy bar. The hand thrust the candy bar in and out of the droid's mechanical mouth. The mouth chomped up and down. The droid grinned. It's eyes winked on and off. Purple letters floated in the air overhead: YOU DON'T HAVE TO BE REAL TO LOVE ZEEL!

"We're going to do it, we're going to hit, we're going to hit that thing!"

"I'm the driver," Dredd said. "I'm the driver, you're the shooter. Shoot, or I'll kick your ass off of here."

"I'm shooting, I'm *shooting!*"

Fergie twisted in his seat. The wind howled around his head. The three Hunters were close, spread in a narrow wedge. The two in the back weaved from side to side. Fergie didn't care for that. He liked the one that stood still. He brought the gun to his shoulder again, took a breath, and fired. He even remembered to pump. Four shots. Three missed a mile. The last glanced off the Judge Hunter's armor-glass visor and whined off to the side. The Hunter had been trained to ignore harmless missiles of any size. Every groon in Mega-City tossed bottles or bricks at Judges when they could.

The Hunter forgot. Before he could remember the drill, he'd pulled the Lawmaster down seven degrees. The machine hit the spire of a Mega-City condo and blossomed in a ball of white fire.

"I did it, I got him, I got him, I—*waaaah!*"

Fergie looked forward in time to see Dredd hurl the Lawmaster straight into the enormous mouth of the droid. He saw the red eyes streak by, the candy bar big as a family car . . .

He shut his eyes tight. Nothing hurt. Everything was fine. He'd learned something. It didn't hurt to die. Dying felt good. He opened his eyes. Mega-City was still there. A billion lights shimmered below.

"You *missed* it? You didn't miss it, nobody could miss it."

"I didn't miss it," Dredd said. "It's a holo. There's nothing to miss."

"It's a holo?" Fergie was astonished. "It's a real *good* holo."

"You've been out of town."

"Six months, yeah, but—"

Nineteen balls of yellow fire appeared directly in the Lawmaster's path, lined up neatly like a string of pretty lights. The sound reached them half a second later, a solid wall of air that sent them tumbling out of control toward the sea of lights below.

Dredd shouted something Fergie couldn't hear. He smelled the sharp and unmistakeable scent of electric fire. He'd smelled it a hundred times before. You break into a droid, something doesn't go right, everything starts to go wrong. Fine. Stuff like that, it always happened on the ground. It didn't happen five thousand feet up in the air.

The Lawmaster's engine coughed, died, and came to life again. Dredd struggled with the controls. He pounded on the dash. Fergie saw the street coming up fast. The street was full of people. People. Buses. Cars. Something didn't look right. Fergie looked again. People were killing people. Breaking into stores. It was a battlefield, a full-scale riot.

The Lawmaster limped above the crowd, dragging its tail and spilling an acrid cloud of smoke. Dredd heard the Hunters' cannons begin to chatter again. A missile screamed by his head. It exploded in the crowded street below. Flesh and metal fused, vaporized in the terrible heat. Screams went by in a blur, horror frozen for an instant, then gone.

Dredd steered the damaged craft to the right. Cannon fire stitched a brick wall ahead. Dredd muttered under his breath, and yanked the control bar all the way back.

Fergie felt his stomach lurch up into his throat. Flame scorched his hair. He turned, looked back, saw the Hunter explode against the wall a hundred feet below. Dredd's Lawmaster jerked into a tight one-eighty, heading back the way it had come.

Fergie was too scared to scream. He hated being upside down. The last Judge Hunter was below him, looking straight up. He twisted his machine in a killing turn, firing his cannons in the split second Dredd's Lawmaster was in his sights. Dredd's machine shuddered. Fergie felt something drop off. It sounded big and important, something they'd probably like to keep.

The Hunter suddenly loomed into sight next to Dredd, half a dozen feet away. The Hunter aimed his Lawmaster and fired. The first shot missed. The second plowed through the control panel, leaving an ugly molten scar. The Judge Hunter grinned, and pushed his visor up on the brow of his helmet.

"Steer," said Dredd.

"What?"

"Steer!"

"I don't know how to steer!"

"You don't know how to do shit, Ferguson. Learn real fast."

Dredd leaped from his seat. The Judge Hunter stared. Dredd grabbed his arm, forced it back. The Hunter yelled, fought for balance, flailed his arms and disappeared.

The Lawmaster dipped, swerving sharply to the left.

Dredd held on, grabbing for the controls. The machine pitched wildly across the sky. Dredd bullied it back on course, cutting a wide arc above the Mega-City towers.

Ferguson—the little crook's got to be somewhere . . . hasn't had time to disappear . . .

There. Dredd spotted him, five hundred feet below, spinning like a top. Smoke spewed from the machine as the Lawmaster headed straight for a concrete wall.

Dredd muttered under his breath and punched the control panel with his fist. Red letters screamed EMERG/ OVERRIDE. Turbos roared, boosting Dredd forward on a stream of blue fire. He matched his speed with the twisting machine, working out the numbers in his head. Four . . . three . . .

Fergie's eyes were closed. Dredd grabbed him by the collar, jerked him free, sent the Lawmaster straight up.

Out of the corner of his eye, he saw the smoking machine hit the wall in a ball of fire and oily black smoke.

Fergie opened his eyes. He held on fast, digging his hands into Dredd's back.

"Never again," he said. "Never driving with you again. You hear me? Not anytime. Never."

"You can get off anytime you want," Dredd said. "How about here? Here's okay with me."

"One more chance," Fergie said. "One more, that's it . . ."

The "romance" of history often overshadows the more accurate, though pedestrian, picture of the past. Even though a relatively few years have passed since the era of Judge Dredd, legend and myth have already begun to blur actual events.

Was there a Herman Ferguson? Many sources mention this name as associated with Judge Dredd. He plays a major role in J. Ward's famous holo opera, The Tragedy of Rico, and is mentioned in numerous fictional treatments of the time. M. Karen, in her Judge Dredd: a Definitive Study (Kasey & Keith, 2146), mentions a "Ferguson" or "Fergie" as if he had some official connection with both the criminal element and the Judges as well. As R. Breazeale mentions in The Dredd Mystique (Lubbock & Wink, 2160), "It scarcely seems likely that an ordinary lawbreaker would be tolerated in the company of one such as Joseph Dredd, who exemplifies the spirit of the Law as no other in the history of the Judges."

The most likely answer to this historical anomaly is the obvious one: Herman Ferguson was probably a character composed of a number of colorful individuals of the time. Many such characters, such as the Reverend Billy Joe Angel, Mean Machine, Link-Link, and Junior Head-Dead—who represent the "evil forces" of the time—are clearly fictional representations.

Though history is rich with real heroic figures, such as Judge Fargo, Judge Hershey, and the courageous Judge Carl Esposito, writers will likely continue to create the "Fergies," "Ilsas," and the like.

—History of the Mega-Cities
James Olmeyer, III
Chapter XXXI: "Truth and Fiction"
2191

*The author can certainly vouch for one particular "character" of the era, Cadet James Olmeyer, who was the author's paternal grandfather. As every reader will likely know, "Cadet" Olmeyer became Judge Olmeyer, Council Judge Olmeyer, and, finally, Chief Justice Olmeyer.

THIRTY-SEVEN

"*T*here's nothing to keep us from going to fully operational status," Griffin said. "There is no longer any Council, and the city is in chaos. There is only one authority left that any government personnel will listen to. Me."

"Yes. That narrows it down, doesn't it?" Rico raised a questioning brow. "What you *didn't* do was kill Dredd when you had the chance. That was not a good decision, Mr. Chief Justice."

Griffin had years of experience in keeping his feelings to himself. He might have murder in his heart—as he did at that moment—but he would never let it show.

"He'll keep the Street Judges occupied while we work on Janus," he said. "It's not a problem, my friend."

"I do hope not. I don't *like* problems. I like things to go smoothly and quickly. I like things to *flow.*"

Rico cocked his head slightly, without taking his eyes off Griffin. "Isn't that so, Ilsa? Rico likes things to flow."

Lisa laughed lightly. "I believe you have said so on occasion, yes."

She stood behind Rico, hands at her sides. Griffin thought her features had an almost alien beauty in the flickering blue light of the Janus lab. It seemed inconceivable, almost a sacrilege of a kind, that such perfection stood so close to Rico's giant robot, that relic of forgotten wars.

Yet, he decided, if Ilsa was indeed perfection, she was a cold perfection, much like the silver monster itself. Maybe they belonged together, along with Rico, who was perfection of a sort himself.

"I'll be back," Griffin said, glancing at his wrist. "Someone has to mollify those fool officials. They think the sky is falling down."

"And indeed it is," Rico said.

Griffin rose from his chair. "You don't need me for routine initiation. You know the drill. Central . . . prepare the Janus facility for full operations. My command . . ."

"Janus . . . operational."

"One more thing." Rico stepped into his path. "I believe you *promised* . . . ?"

"What?" Griffin paused, then understood. "Yes, of course. Central, appoint Judge Rico to the Council of Judges. Appointment to take effect at once."

Central paused for a full second. *"Unable to comply."*

"Why not?"

"Legal difficulties. Judge Rico is listed as officially executed nine years, three months, fifteen days ago."

"Your listing is obviously in error."

"Central does not make errors. Judge Rico was sentenced and executed."

Rico grinned. "Obviously, I got better."

Griffin gave him a chilling look. "Correction of records, Central. Authority is Chief Justice Griffin. Correction is as follows: Central is not mistaken. You were given incorrect data. Judge Rico is alive. Please correct and carry out my command."

"Data corrected . . . Judge Rico is alive . . . Judge Rico is approved as a Council member as of this date . . . Entered."

"Thank you." Rico bowed slightly from the waist. "I

accept, and I will carry out my duties to the best of my ability."

"I have things to do. Get hold of me if you have to." This time, Griffin made no effort to hide his irritation. He turned on his heels and stalked across the room.

Rico watched him go. Ilsa walked up beside him. In the silence, Rico could hear the soft fabric of her dress against her legs. She laid a hand gently on his arm.

"You shouldn't anger him like that. There is no reason for it."

"Yes there is."

"What?"

"I *like* to."

Ilsa frowned. "That's a childish thing to say. It doesn't become you. You don't have to—*Rico!*"

She drew in a breath, tried to pull away. His fingers pressed into the soft flesh of her arm until she closed her mouth against the pain.

Rico let her go. "You don't want to say things like that, dear. Griffin thinks I'm insensitive because of what I am. He's wrong. I have feelings. Don't I, Fido?"

The big robot made a rumbling noise at the mention of its name.

"All—all right. I'm sorry." Ilsa rubbed her arm. She looked at him, let him see her own strength, the fury and determination there. Told him with her eyes that there were places he couldn't reach, places he couldn't hurt.

"You and I should not be in conflict, Ilsa."

"No. We should not."

He touched her cheek. She didn't move, didn't take her eyes from his.

"Then we won't, will we?" Rico smiled. "We will work as a close, smoothly-running team. I do so like for things to run smoothly. I said that, didn't I?"

Ilsa didn't answer. Rico turned, and walked to the computer bank, gazed at the thousand blinking eyes.

"Status of Janus Project, Central."

"The DNA samples have been removed from frozen state. Operation is on-line. I am prepared to begin the cloning procedure upon command."

"Put that on hold, Central. Slight change of plans. I wish to purge the DNA samples you have on hand."

"What?" Ilsa stepped forward, reached out to touch him, then drew back her hand. "What are you doing, Rico? What is this?"

Rico didn't answer. "Proceed, Central."

"DNA samples . . . purged."

"Central, activate the DNA sampling console."

"Sampling console activated and ready."

Ilsa clenched her fists at her sides. The robot warrior whirred, swiveled its head an inch to the right.

My God, it knows . . . it can sense my sense my emotions, heartbeat—something!

She watched, too frightened now to move, as Rico walked to the dark metal wall. A panel opened with no sound at all. A ceramic shelf appeared. It was antiseptic white, slightly concave. Rico ripped his sleeve away and placed his bare arm in the hollow. A shiny tube whined out of the wall, split itself into eight gleaming needles, clawed for an instant at the air, then plunged its silver fingers into Rico's arm.

Narrow columns of red began to climb the spidery points. The red disappeared. The needles rose quickly, and sucked themselves into the wall. Rico smiled at the eight crimson droplets on his arm.

"DNA samples have been obtained."

"Done, and done again, I believe somebody said."

Ilsa shook her head. "This isn't right, Rico. It wasn't part of the plan. Griffin did *not* authorize you to—"

Rico turned on her, faster than a snake. *"Griffin* got to be my keeper because he put me behind bars. What's *your* excuse?"

"Analysis and replication . . . proceeding."

"I'm not trying to *make* you do anything, Rico. Don't

get excited. I'm just telling you you don't need to do this. Griffin's thought this thing out. He's had years, he knows what he's doing. He's going to turn Mega-City around, make things the way they *ought* to be . . ."

Rico threw back his head and laughed. "Griffin is a . . . a plumber, a file clerk. All he's doing is exploiting my genius, my intelligence and abilities. And *yours,* Ilsa. Yours as well. We're the giants here, Griffin is the dwarf. Isn't that clear to you, don't you *see* that?"

Ilsa closed her eyes. "My God. It was a mistake to keep you alive. He should never have done it this way."

Rico poked a finger between her breasts, hard enough to make her gasp.

"I don't have to ask what *you* voted for, do I now?"

"Don't be foolish. You know better than that."

"I know what you said at my trial. You wanted me to live then. You want me to live now." He touched the lobe of her ear, let his finger trail to her cheek. "Don't you, Ilsa? Because then, as well as now, your reason, that fine cold intellect of yours, told you one thing, and another part of you could not imagine me dying."

Ilsa forced a laugh. "You don't—you don't know that at all, Rico. You don't *know* what I'm thinking. You have no idea how I feel."

Rico touched her lips. Ilsa held her breath, stunned by the power, the force, the raw heat that seemed to draw them together. It was even more intense than the first time, when Griffin had brought him here, the first time she'd seen him in the nine years he had been hidden from the world in the depths of Aspen Prison.

And, when he finally drew her to him, his presence overwhelmed her, took her in a rush.

He bared his arm again, showed her the red spots of his blood where the silver spider had drunk its fill. He didn't have to ask her, to tell her, she knew what to do, what she ached to do, though she had never known this need before.

"You are an extraordinary woman, Ilsa. This is a moment only you and I could share. No one else, because there are no others like us in the world."

She brought his arm to her face, let the droplets brush her cheek, brought her lips to each small well of red.

"Yes . . ." she heard herself say. "Yes . . . yes . . ."

THIRTY-EIGHT

He stood in the narrow hallway, clutching the Remington, squeezing the stock until his fingers went white. He remembered every break-in he'd ever seen, a thousand doors he'd found twisted, violated, broken into splinters because they stood in the way of a terrible rage, of an anger shut out that wanted in. He remembered, too, the things he'd seen, the things he'd found behind those doors.

Hershey . . .

"Stay behind me," he told Fergie. "Whatever I do, I don't want you in the way."

"Hey, no problem," Fergie said. "You won't even know I'm here."

Dredd stepped quickly into the living room, bent at the knees, and swept the room with the Remington. He felt the tight constriction of his throat. The room was totally wrecked. Furniture was overturned, the upholstery slashed with a knife. Pictures had been torn off the wall. Broken glass littered the floor. At the far end of the room, a desk was broken in half, papers scattered about. Hershey's computer had been dashed against the wall. Dark scars on the wall said someone had picked up the machine and tossed it half a dozen times.

"You got a machine abuser here, is what you got,"

Fergie said. "I've seen it before. Guy doesn't like any-thing of the electronic persuasion, he's going to take a little extra time, hurt it all he can. It's something happens when that person's a kid. Maybe he sticks his finger in a socket, sees something scary on the screen—"

"Shut up," Dredd said. "Hold it down."

He left the living area and moved quickly down the hall. More broken glass. Blue shreds of paper that looked familiar to Dredd. He picked up a piece, held it to the light. It came from a Judge Training Manual: *Civil Disorder 201.*

"Can I say something? Can I talk?"

"What?"

"This is not what we ought to be doing, Dredd. We stick around up here, this is where the Hunters are going to expect you to be. Let's get *low,* man. Ol' Fergie'll take you Downtown, where I know how to *survive.*"

"Sewer rats."

"Pardon me?"

"You want me to hide out with the sewer rats, the lawbreakers, the scum."

"Oh, *excuse* me." Fergie raised his hands. "See, I keep forgetting myself, like *I'm* a sewer rat, one of the crimi-nally inclined, and you're not. I mean, just because every Judge Hunter in Mega-City wants your ass nailed up on the wall doesn't mean I shouldn't show proper respect at all times—"

"Can it."

"What?"

"I said *can it,* Ferguson. I'm busy, I don't have time for this."

Dredd stepped into the bedroom. Everything was torn apart, upside down. "You don't like the company, take off," he said. "Nobody's holding you down. Go find a sewer rat. Go find a—"

The boot hit him hard in the chest, driving him back against the wall. Hershey stepped from behind the closet door. She held the Lawgiver steady in both hands, the muzzle aimed between his eyes.

"Both of you, you know the drill! Up against the wall, spread 'em wide!"

Dredd stared at her. There was a dark smudge on her cheek, an angry cut above one eye.

"Hershey, I thought they'd—"

"Thought they'd what? *Killed* me? You thought so or hoped, Dredd?"

"Hold it a minute. Stop it. What happened here?"

"I'm a Judge. Someone wants to kill me. Someone almost did. They get you in the street, in your home, anywhere." She paused, and gave Dredd a chilling look. "Why don't you tell *me* what's happening? They're dying out there. A hundred and eight Judges in forty-eight hours. *What the hell is going on?*"

Dredd shook his head. "You think I'm part of this?"

"I don't know who or what you are anymore. I don't know anything."

"I would never hurt you, Hershey."

Hershey studied him a long moment, glanced at Fergie, then backed off across the room. Without lowering her weapon, she reached in her jacket and and tossed a viewie to Dredd.

"Tell me about this. Make me believe in you again— the way I did when I defended you. I did, Dredd. I honestly did, I-I couldn't imagine you doing anything that was against the Law. I couldn't, and then I found *this.*"

Dredd let out a breath. He took the viewie without looking at it. "The man beside me in this picture is my— brother. His name is Rico. He was the best Judge on the street. The smartest, the most dedicated. Then something happened to him, to his mind. He went insane, Hershey. He said the Judges should *rule,* not serve. He said that was our destiny in life, our place in history.

"He finally became more dangerous than any of the

criminals he'd put away. A lot of men died trying to stop him. I had to judge him . . ."

"That was the one," Hershey said quietly.

"Yes. That was the one."

"And you're telling me *he's* doing all this? All this killing?"

"Not by himself. He's working with Griffin."

"Griffin?" Hershey slowly lowered her weapon. All the strength seemed to drain from her body. "Oh, my God. It fits, doesn't it?" She looked at Dredd. "We've got to let the Council know. They've got to stop him before he—"

"It's too late for that. There isn't any Council. Rico murdered them all an hour ago. Griffin set it up. Griffin was there."

Hershey sat down. She laid her weapon on the floor. Dredd watched her. She was staring past him, looking at nothing at all. Fergie glanced at Dredd, then quietly left the room.

"I shouldn't have even thought you had anything to do with this," Hershey said. "I didn't know. All I could think about was the Tribunal, what happened there. I should have known when I found out you'd been drugged. I thought it was Fargo, that he didn't want you to try to stop him from taking the Long Walk for you . . ."

She caught Dredd's expression, stood, and reached out and touched his hand. "You didn't even know that, did you? What they'd done. Oh, Dredd!"

"It's all right," he told her. "You didn't have any way to know what the son of a bitch was doing. No one did."

"That's why the DNA convicted you. You and Rico are the same. Brothers. Did Fargo know? Was he . . . ?"

"He was a part of it. They all knew. Everyone on the Council."

Dredd turned away. "It's not exactly like Rico and I are brothers. Not like real brothers, *normal* brothers, Hershey. We're the same. Clones. We're inhuman. Defective. He just broke down first."

"No, oh, no, that's not true at all, Dredd! You're *not* the same!"

Dredd wouldn't face her. "You said it, Hershey. Remember? That I had no feelings, no emotions? Now you know why. I'm not *programmed* to feel. Like Rico."

"They didn't do that to you," she said softly. *"You* did, Dredd. You did it to yourself. You hurt. You hurt because you had to condemn your brother. You told yourself you would never let that happen to you again. You would never care for anyone, never let anyone get close. If you shut it all out, they couldn't touch you.

"Don't you see? They made you do it, but you did it to yourself."

Dredd faced her. He felt confused, mixed up inside. He understood what she was saying, but her words didn't seem to apply to him. They didn't and they did. It was like she was talking about someone else, someone like him.

Fergie poked his head into the room. "Sorry, guys. I messed around with that terminal, but I'm afraid it's torn up pretty bad. Hey, I fixed your microwave, though. Listen, is this a bad time?"

He looked at Hershey, then at Dredd. "The computer's back up to the idiot stage. That's the best I can do for right now. I've got enough working to go in and look around. I tried to find this Janus business. There's nothing. Nowhere."

Hershey looked puzzled. "Janus?"

"That's the code word for the project that brought Rico and me to life. I'm not surprised Ferguson can't find it. It would be buried under so many security barriers . . ."

Dredd stopped. "If Griffin's got Janus back on-line now, it's going to be using a lot of power. That thing's bigger than a toaster."

Fergie shook his head. "Tried that. No new energy allocations for anything that big. Even under an alias. Of course, that moron machine I patched together, I wouldn't trust it to count apples."

"No, they wouldn't risk putting something like that on the net, would they?" Hershey said. "But it's still got to use power, so they'd . . . They'd have to *steal* it, wouldn't they? From everything they could get their hands on."

Hershey turned to Fergie. "Check the sectors for recent black-outs. Any sudden power surges. Can you do that?"

Fergie looked pained. "*I* can handle anything you can dream up, Judge. Okay, atomic disintegration, I can't handle that. This mortally-wounded machine of yours, though . . . Hey, I can try, I don't know."

"Try," Dredd said.

"Right, right, I'm *doing* it."

"Wait a minute . . ." Hershey bit her lip and frowned. "The day of that fracas in Red Quad? I had to write up *every*thing that happened, because those groons blew up my Lawmaster. I called up all the data in that area within the time parameters—temperature, bio-air samples, *pollen* count, for God's sake. I remember there was a significant power surge about thirty blocks wide. A big one. It didn't mean a thing to me at the time."

Fergie whistled under his breath. "Something like that'd shut down the power grid in the whole sector. We ought to be able to pin down a lot more than you get on a first-level data report."

"What do you mean?" Dredd said.

"I mean it's like you shoot up with battery acid, right? I wouldn't do anything like that, that's stupid, you'd be flat-ass dead, but I know some droogs who would—"

"Ferguson!"

"Yeah, right. Okay. What I'm saying is, it doesn't just burn up everything in your body it touches, it leaves a *trail*. Nerve endings all crudded up, stuff like that. If you didn't know where the trouble started, you could pick up the trail about anywhere and trace it right back. To the point of origin, I mean."

Hershey looked at the ceiling. "You had to go through all that to get to the point?"

Fergie looked hurt. "Well, yeah."

"He's right, though," Dredd said. "Wherever all that power went, we can follow it. We can find it!"

"Maybe," Fergie said. "I don't know, man . . ."

"You said you can do anything. So do it."

Fergie looked at him. He had a good comeback but decided to keep it to himself. Dredd didn't have a real good sense of humor. If Fergie had learned anything at all, he'd learned that.

"I'll get the easy stuff first," Fergie said. He tapped the keys, frowned, looked at the screen. "Let's hope this thing's still got the brain cells to—yeah, all *right!*

"That's your basic power record for the date in question everywhere close to Red Quad. Those little peaks are minor over-loads. This one, the big daddy, is the power surge you're talking about, Judge. Now, let's see where it *came* from, okay?"

Fergie's fingers ran lightly over the keys. Hershey and Dredd stood over his shoulders.

"Okay, it's coming up now, breaking down the power load to—huh?"

Dredd squeezed his arm. "What the hell's that?"

"I don't *know* what it is. Sorry. What I meant to say was . . ." He leaned in and squinted at the screen. Grid buildings rose up from the ground, shimmered for an instant, then vanished out of sight. Others popped up to take their place. Geometric mountain ranges blinked up and down, the beat of the city's heart.

"I told you this computer's glitched out," Fergie said. "What it's doing is taking us the long way around. It's tracing back that sector of the city for, what? A hundred, maybe two hundred years. About a year every half a second."

"Fascinating," Dredd said. "When do we get to now?"

"There's nothing I can do. It'll run itself down and we'll get to the source of our power drain."

"It's coming," Hershey said. "That's almost Red Quad today."

"Couple of seconds . . . Okay, we're home. Block War day." Fergie nodded at the screen. Intricate capillaries of energy webbed the sector, merging at one central point, a glowing amber ball.

"It's underground," Dredd said. "No big surprise."

"Way underground," Fergie added. "Nothing goes that deep, man. Nothing I ever heard of."

"Wait. What's that? That thing right there." Dredd jabbed a finger at the screen.

"After-image," Fergie said. "I could clean it up if everything was working right."

"No. No you couldn't," Hershey said. "It's there, where it's supposed to be. See that profile? That's the Liberty Lady. What's left of her. The city relocated it, what, seventy-five years ago?"

Fergie slapped a fist into his palm. "I've *seen* her. They built one of those death traps across from Heavenly Haven. Built it right around that Lady of yours, swallowed it up again."

Hershey looked at Dredd. "They built the Janus Project directly beneath it. Under the Liberty Lady."

"Yeah," Dredd said. "Where else?"

THIRTY-NINE

*T*he crisp smell of ozone was in the air. Griffin could almost feel the energy, the awesome surge of raw power that throbbed beneath his feet. That much power was frightening to imagine. New life, the pulse of Creation itself . . .

They were together, Ilsa and Rico, at the far end of the lab. They turned as he entered. The thousand eyes of the computer cast dancing shards of color about the room. The big robot stood silently behind Rico, only its ruby glow visible in the shadows.

"Dredd got away from the Hunters," Griffin told them. "Took some good men with him, too. Bastard's got nine lives."

"Not to worry," Rico said. "Little brother won't get in our way."

Griffin stared at him. Rico looked bored with the whole thing, a man thinking about an afternoon nap. *Damn you! When this is over . . . when you're not useful anymore . . .*

"Well, I'm glad you're so confident," he said aloud. "I'm pleased to hear we have no problems at all, Rico."

"Not with Dredd, we don't." Rico made a note on a comm-board and passed it to Ilsa. "He's going to be *seriously* outnumbered quite soon. Current figures please, Central?"

"Current figures, Council Judge Rico . . . The new DNA sample has been multiplexed as ordered . . . Gametes are dividing."

"New—" Griffin turned on Rico. *"New* samples? What the hell's going on here, Rico? I didn't order any new samples."

"No, but I did." Rico grinned at Griffin's expression. "That DNA in there was thirty years old. Sooner or later, you *have* to clean out the fridge."

Ilsa laughed, the sound of silver bells. Griffin watched as she leaned in against him, watched her slide her hand down the length of his arm. He knew at once. Knew what had happened between them. It had all gone wrong. It was Rico who had seduced the woman, not the other way around, not the way he'd planned.

"You dare to do something like that? That sample was created with the greatest of care for the—" Griffin stopped, the cold chill of realization constricting the muscles in his throat. "What—what did you replace it with, Rico?"

"Uh-oh," Ilsa said. She buried her laughter in Rico's sleeve.

"Oh, my God, no. You didn't!"

"Please!" Rico looked hurt. "You should be congratulating me, Mr. Chief Justice. I'm going to be a father."

"You don't know what you're doing," Griffin told him. "The sample has to be pure of defects or the accelerator will form mutations. That's what happened before!"

Rico laughed aloud. *"That's* why Dredd's so ugly."

"No!" Griffin stepped into his path, his fists clenched at his sides. "It's *you*, for God's sake, Rico. You were defective—your *copies* will be even more defective!"

Rico's eyes blazed. "You're lying, Griffin. All you are about is *control. Your* control. But the Janus Judges won't be the puppets you want. They'll be *my* brothers.

Who do you think they're going to listen to? You, or me?"

Griffin closed his eyes a moment. "Ilsa, you're with him on this? You can't be. You know better, you know what he *is.*"

"I don't think you've ever understood the full potential of this . . . opportunity, love." She let her fingers rest on Rico's chest. "This project needs vision. Not politics."

"No, this can't happen." Griffin shook his head. "It *can't.*"

"I'm afraid there's not much you can do about it, Chief Jus—"

Griffin took a quick step to one side, braced his feet and whipped a small pistol from his tunic.

"No, not again," he said. *"No more like you!"*

The robot's arm came out of nowhere, wrapped a flexible steel tendril around Griffin's arm. The weapon clattered to the floor.

"Get it . . . off of me, Rico!" Griffin's eyes were wide with fear. *"Get . . . it . . . off!"*

The robot snaked another arm around Griffin's arm and lifted him off the floor. Griffin tugged at the tight bands of steel, kicked his legs in the air.

"Rico, for God's sake . . . please!"

Rico shook his head sadly. "You never understood me, did you, Griffin? I'm alive, I'm real. I'm not something you made to carry out the trash."

"Central . . . override!" Griffin strained against the robot's grip. "Help meeee!"

"Request is denied, Chief Justice. The ABC War Robot is not linked to my main processor."

"You need to keep up with the times," Rico said. "Look away for just a tiny minute, technology passes you by."

He watched the man dangling helplessly above, looked

at his eyes, at the terror in his face. He felt a sense of completion, a great sense of peace.

"Fido, tear off Chief Justice Griffin's arms and legs, please. Save the head for last."

FORTY

*T*hey left the Lawmasters behind a rubble-strewn wall
half a block away. Dredd wasn't sure what kind of
sensors Griffin might have above-ground, but he saw no
reason to take any chances now.

Hershey caught up with him, peered over his shoulders into the near-darkened street. Dredd held a scanner
in his hand, watching the line of green static dance across
the tiny screen.

"Dead ahead," Hershey said. "Right?"

"Down there." Dredd thumbed shells into the Remington, racked the slide to bring number one into the
chamber.

"Looks like you guys have got everything under control," Fergie said. "I'll watch the Lawmasters. Nobody's
going to get past me."

"I might need you down there," Dredd said. "To help
shut down the Janus system."

"I knew you were going to say that. I knew it."

Dredd looked up. The street looked much the same.
The debris from the block war had been scraped up and
hauled away, but no one had bothered to fix the lights. In
the glow from the faraway heights of Mega-City, he
could see the broken profile of the Liberty Lady's face,
embedded in the ancient brick wall. One sad and empty

eye, part of a cheek, a piece of a heavy brow. Higher in
the wall, the suggestion of a hand, a rusted torch. Dredd
looked away, studied the scanner, and led his group inside.

The building had been closed for repairs, then forgotten. It was hard to guess how many years ago. Dredd
walked through the empty hallways, following the scanner's electric glow. A concrete stairway led to a cellar
below. Water dripped from old ceramic pipes. Something
squealed ahead, scuttled off into the dark.

Fergie stopped. "What's that?"

"We're down in the lower levels," Dredd told him.
"What's the problem? You said you had friends down
here."

Fergie didn't answer. He kept close to Dredd. He wondered what the creatures ate down here. Where would
they find any food? He decided not to think about that,
decided that he might not like it if he knew.

Dredd stopped. Ahead was a concrete wall. "The scanner says the source of the power surge is straight ahead."
He nodded at the solid wall. "Right there."

"My Lawgiver might blast through it," Hershey said.
"But I doubt it. If it did, everyone in Red Quad would
hear it."

"Forget it. Got to be some other way."

Fergie let out a breath. "People, just move aside, will
you?" He shook his head at Dredd. "I'll bet you locked
yourself in the bathroom when you were a kid, right?"

Fergie pressed his palms against the wall in a dozen
places, walked down the entire width, and started over
again.

"It's an old-fashioned pressure lock. Fifty, sixty years
ago. The Hush-O-Door. Big rage back then. Known in
the trade as 'The Burglar's Delight.' Nobody's been
dumb enough to use one since."

He bent down and touched the wall again. "Dealer
sold you the software. You set the gimmick up, picked

your own contact point. Most groons put it two, three inches above the floor. Like a good break-and-enter man would be too lazy to squat a little, right?"

Fergie pressed three fingers against the wall. Nothing. Moved a foot to the right. The third time, he moved down a foot and a half. Pressed against the cold concrete. A seam appeared, the width of a door. Fergie gave it a gentle shove. The slab of concrete hissed aside.

"Very impressive," Hershey said.

"Not bad," said Dredd.

"Thanks," Fergie said, "I'm underwhelmed by your support." The door slid shut behind him. "If anyone's interested, that thing hasn't been used in a hell of a long time. Whoever's coming in and out of this Janus deal has another way than this."

"Good," Dredd said. "Maybe they won't expect us."

"I'll drink to that. Soon as we find a bar."

"Scanner?" said Hershey.

"That way," said Dredd.

The passage went another hundred yards, twisting in every direction, the floor slanting steadily down. Dredd noticed the absence of rats and guessed the reason why. He didn't need the scanner now. He could feel the deep tremor of power. The rats didn't like that at all. Dredd didn't blame them. He hefted the Remington and nodded at Hershey. Hershey raised the Lawgiver above her head, telling him she got the warning and understood.

"Air." Fergie sniffed. "Fresher than where we've been. Processed air."

Dredd nodded. The corridor took a sharp turn to the left up ahead. "Douse the light," he said. "Stay near."

He moved past the corner. Hershey followed.

"We're close," she said softly. "I can feel the electricity in my hair. We'd better—*DREDD!*"

A blur of metal, cold and silver-bright. It whipped around Hershey's waist, jerked her off her feet. The Lawgiver fell from her hands. Dredd brought his Remington up to fire, The robot was faster. An automatic weapon chattered in its free hand, stitching a deadly path. Fergie stood frozen, staring wide-eyed at the monster overhead.

"Down!" Dredd yelled. He started toward Fergie, knew he was a millisecond late. Fergie cried out, grabbed his chest, spun around twice and slammed into the concrete wall.

Dredd didn't stop, couldn't risk a look back. He bent low and stalked toward the big robot, blasting with the Remington, racking one shell into the chamber after the next, knowing he wasn't even denting the metal warrior's hide, that he didn't dare fire at the brute's face or its steel and copper gut. He might put a hole in the son of a bitch's vital parts, but he might hit Hershey instead.

A bullet plowed a shallow furrow through the flesh of Dredd's upper arm. The pain rocked him on his heels. He sucked in a breath, fired again and again.

Useless . . . not hitting anything . . . not even making the bastard mad . . .

Hershey screamed, kicking out against the robot's grip. The warrior took a step toward Dredd, its massive foot sending a minor tremor through the earth. The other foot creaked, whirred, came down hard. Gray dust showered from the ceiling. Dredd threw himself aside, saw a flash of metal struts, hydraulics and coils, winking red lights, tucked behind the foot's steel plates.

The robot turned, its gleaming arms whirring as it fired a volley at Dredd. Dredd felt flecks of stone slice his cheek. He rolled, came to his feet, held the Remington at his waist and blasted at the narrow slit in the robot's metal joint.

A blue electric flash, a wisp of black smoke. Dredd fired again, saw the bright sizzle, heard the high-pitched whine as steel tendons snapped. A silver tube whipped free, writhed like a snake, and pumped dark and foul-smelling lubricants into the air.

The robot shuddered. Its brain said FORWARD MODE. One foot made it off the ground. The other didn't budge. The robot roared like a prehistoric beast, teetered, then hit the floor like a quake. FORWARD MODE was still intact. The robot pounded its good foot against the ground, a jackhammer gone berserk.

Hershey was still in the robot's grip. Dredd ran to her. Maybe he could find a handy tool somewhere, use the Remington to pry her free . . .

He heard the sigh of air, turned, saw the door slide open behind him. Rico. Rico and a woman. Both held weapons in their hands. He recognized the woman at once. Ilsa Hayden from Rico's trial. What was *she* doing here?

"That'll be enough," Rico said. "Just put the weapon down."

"No way. I shot this thing. I'm going to eat it."

"That's amusing, I'm sure." Rico turned to the robot. "Fido, you clumsy bastard, if you don't mind *functioning* a while, break Judge Hershey's neck, please, on the count of three. One . . . two . . ."

"Hershey? You all right?"

"I'm—yes, I'm all right, Dredd."

Dredd let the Remington fall from his hand.

Rico laughed. "How human of you. You've become a romantic, *brother.*" He motioned with his weapon. "Inside now. Fido, if the lady moves, crush her."

Ilsa walked past Dredd. She glanced down at Fergie, rolled him over with her foot, shrugged, and turned away. When she bent to pick up Dredd's weapon, she looked directly into Fergie's eyes.

"Nice. A bit crude, but nice."

"Watch her," Rico said. "She's a real tease, Dredd."

"Where's your boss?" Dredd said. "He let you out of your cage for the day?"

Rico shook his finger at Dredd. "If you're trying to get

on my good side, it won't do you any good. I don't *have* one."

"Where's Griffin?"

"Chief Justice Griffin has retired, so to speak. In his absence, I have assumed his responsibilities."

"You mean you've killed him."

Rico looked pained. "Me? Of course not. He had an accident with Fido. Doggie is not entirely housebroken, I'm afraid."

Ilsa raised her weapon, closed one eye, and let the muzzle drop to the level of Dredd's chest. "Rico said for you to move, dear. I think you should do what he says."

Dredd didn't answer. He walked toward the door where Rico and Ilsa had entered.

"He looks like you," Ilsa said.

"He is a *lot* like me. Naturally."

"I'm nothing like you," Dredd said.

Rico turned on him. "Wrong, brother." His eyes were slugs of lead. "The only difference between us is that you destroyed your life to embrace the Law. I destroyed the Law to embrace life." He grinned at Ilsa. "That's rather good, don't you think? I need to write that down."

He swept out his palm in a graceful motion, bowing slightly to Dredd. "After you, please. Step into the future, brother. This is how tomorrow looks. This is the way Rico's world is going to be!"

Dredd stepped inside. Rico spread his arms wide. Half a million razor-points of light burned in the darkness overhead. Dredd felt the tingle of static in the air, the deep hum of energy below. He drew in a breath. A hundred columns of luminescent brightness rose up from the floor, glittering capsules, pods of azure blue, shimmering tubes of life. They stood erect in the clear blue fluid, clones, mutants, beings unborn and already alive. Dredd stared at a watery face—sharp planes, rigid neck. It opened its silver eyes and looked back.

Rico laughed. "This is the *nursery*, brother. Don't you

recognize it? This is where you were born." He caught Dredd's expression. "Don't look at him with such distaste, Joseph. That isn't just me in there. It's *you.*"

Dredd felt the agony, the pain, and knew it wouldn't go away. Rico had guessed his thought, seen the revulsion, the horror there. And Dredd knew he was right. It was true. Looking at the clone was like looking in a mirror at himself.

FORTY-ONE

Rico walked away from Dredd, turned, the shimmering pods at his back.

"Look at them, Joseph, your brothers. In a few hours they'll be born. An endless supply of perfection. Now we have a choice: to create a race of robots like Fido out there or a race of free-thinking people and call them *humans.*"

"You're diseased," Dredd said. "You couldn't control yourself; what makes you think you can control them?"

Rico studied him a long moment, then looked away, up toward the swarm of glittering lights overhead.

"Why did you do it, Joseph? I've thought about it all these years. Why? Why did you judge me?"

"I didn't have a choice. You killed innocent people."

"Only as a means to an end, brother. You're forgetting that."

"That's a lie you tell yourself. It was a massacre. Murder. You can't call it anything else. You betrayed the Law."

Rico laughed. "I was your *blood,* your *brother.* The only family you ever had. You sent me to my death and you talk to *me* about betrayal?" He jabbed his finger at Dredd. "You are the traitor, brother, not me! Do you

want to be a slave all your life, do what you're *told* to do,
Joseph? You have the choice now. Them . . . or me!"

"You haven't given me any choice. I have to stop you,
Rico. If you want to stop me, you'll have to kill me."

Rico looked sad, then let his expression slide into a
grin. "Well, I can certainly accomodate you, brother. But
there's no hurry, is there? Fido . . ." Rico looked past
Dredd, through the great door of the Janus lab. "Bring
Judge Hershey in here, then tear the bitch's arms and
legs off."

Dredd didn't move. "Don't do it, Rico."

"Or you'll what, Joseph? Arrest me?" Rico's eyes
blazed. "Take this one too, Fido. Crush them. Let's make
some Judge soup!"

"Rico . . ." Ilsa stepped toward him.

"Stay away from me. Do as I say, Ilsa."

Rico's voice was calm, almost a gentle whisper. It
scared the hell out of Ilsa.

The giant robot clanged through the doorway, scrap-
ing its metal hide. It dragged its bad foot. One red eye
looked off a good twenty degrees.

Dredd saw Hershey in its grip. Hershey looked down.
He tried to read her eyes. Something . . . not the way it
ought to be.

"Take him," Rico said. "Do it now."

The robot stopped, whirred. Its blunt head swiveled on
its hydraulic neck. A heavy foot stomped against the
floor. It turned, then, dropped Hershey from its grasp,
raised its hand and slammed Rico in the chest.

Rico cried out in surprise, staggered back, and fell. Ilsa
ran to him. The robot moved in a blur, plucked her off
the floor and threw her to the ground.

The robot turned on one heel, its broad back to
Dredd. Dredd stared. Fergie was hanging on the monster's metal back, his hands buried in an open slot.
Dredd caught a glimpse of the controls—blinking lights,
tangled coils of wire.

"Dredd, over here!"

Hershey tossed him the Remington. Dredd racked a shell in the chamber, turned and fired at Rico.

The weapon's blast echoed through the domed room. Rico darted for cover, grabbed his Lawgiver and squeezed off half a dozen shots at Dredd on the run. Dredd went to his knees, aimed at Rico and fired. Rico disappeared in the maze of blue pods.

From the corner of his eye, Dredd saw the robot lurch, run headlong into a solid wall.

"Fergie, what the hell are you doing!"

"I'm not doing—anything," Fergie cried out. "This—damn—thing—wants to drive by itself!"

The robot staggered, beat on the wall with its head. It stumbled, clattered dizzily across the room, reached up to slap the tormenter off its back.

"No way, you tin-headed freak!"

Fergie thrust his whole arm into the robot's back, jerked out a tangle of flashing wires. The robot went berserk. It's head turned completely around. Blue fire sparked from its eyes and ears. It bashed itself against the wall, ripping Fergie loose. Fergie yelled and hit the ground hard. The robot took two jerky steps and toppled on its face. Smoke billowed from its chest.

"Watch it, Dredd!" Hershey called from the shadows by the big door. "The woman's off to the right, by the wall somewhere. Rico's back there."

Dredd saw her, bent low near the tall accelerator. She nodded toward the forest of blue fluorescent pods.

Hiding with your brothers . . . yours, not mine.

Dredd kept low, moving quickly behind the fallen robot. Fergie was on his back. He looked up and offered Dredd a weary smile.

"You okay, Ferguson? Take it easy, now."

"I'm—I don't think I'm too good . . ."

"You're going to be fine, all right?" Dredd looked at

his face, at the blood soaking the front of his shirt. Ferguson was right: he wasn't too good at all.

"You—never got to say it, Dredd."

"Never got to say what?"

"Hey, you know, man."

"Yeah, I do." Dredd drew in a breath. "I . . . I made a mistake. I'm sorry I misjudged you, Ferguson."

"And you'll never arrest me again."

"I'll—okay, I'll never arrest you again."

Fergie grinned. "All right, man."

"Take it easy."

"I'll do that, Dredd. What I think I'll do, I think I'll just—sorta . . ."

Fergie closed his eyes.

Dredd grabbed his shoulders. "Ferguson? *FERGUSON, YOU TALK TO ME, DAMN YOU!*"

Dredd let him go. He clenched his fists until blood came to his palms, felt the fury begin deep in his belly, felt the fire race through his veins.

"RIIIIIICO!"

He screamed out the name, grabbed the Remington, came to his feet and ran toward the blue pods.

"Come out of there. Come out of there, Rico!"

He was driven by a rage he could scarcely contain, an anger that blinded him to caution and reason, a hatred that could only focus on Rico's face, Rico's laughter, Rico's silver eyes.

He stalked through the eerie blue light, through the maze of glowing pods. Rico's spawn surrounded him, a company of ghosts, their coral lips open, their flesh unearthly white. A man, slim and unborn. He lifted pale arms above his colorless flesh, and seemed to mock him with a smile.

"Rico!"

Dredd squeezed off two shots. A crystal pod shattered, the clone blew apart in a blossom of pink and white.

"Rico, I'm coming for you. I'm coming . . ."

A hail of gunfire came at him from the dark. Dredd turned, went to his knees, firing back in a wicked arc. Incubators shattered, spilling slippery flesh to the floor. One of Dredd's shots hit a tall accelerator, a black-and-silver column at the heart of the Janus lab. Lightning crackled along the tower, snaked to the top, then exploded in a blinding fireball, showering the pods with comets of molten steel.

The incubators cracked. A flood of thick amniotic fluid hissed in the terrible heat.

Dredd saw him, then, as the computer burst into flame. Rico ran. Dredd fired, blowing a hole in the console, blinding a thousand red eyes.

The fire would keep Rico busy a minute, a minute and a half. Dredd broke into the open, keeping low, heading straight for Rico's hiding place. Rico caught him there, raised up and raked his path with automatic fire. Dredd cursed and scrambled for cover, lead tearing the heel off his boot.

Where the hell was Hershey? She had gone after Ilsa hours—no, only minutes ago. Time was playing its tricks again.

Another incubator exploded. Blue fire webbed the walls, sizzled the concrete floor. Dredd saw the flames beginning to burst from the equipment on the far side of the lab. *Getting hot in here. Going to get a hell of a lot worse . . .*

Rico laughed, a high-pitched, grating sound that set Dredd's nerves on edge.

"Central, hatch the first set of clones," Rico shouted. "On my command—now!"

"Rico, don't do that."

"The cloning process is not finished, Chief Justice Rico. The clones will be only sixty-three percent complete."

"I don't care if they're *pretty* or not. I want the damn clones now!"

Central's voice droned in answer, but Dredd didn't hear. Something exploded down below with the roar of a blast furnace, spewing a ball of yellow fire up through the floor. The place was going up; it couldn't last long.

Hershey, where the hell are you!

Hershey knew the woman was there, somewhere in the maze of piping, the bundled strands of cable and wire. She cursed her luck, letting Ilsa slip away from her into the damn maintenance area at the back of the lab. Not her best move of the day, she decided. Rico and Dredd were ripping the Janus lab apart. She could already feel the heat, see the flames licking at the pods. When that firestorm got back here, with umpty-zillion volts of power droning above her head—that, and pipes full of oxygen, nitrogen, God knew what . . .

Ilsa moved. Hershey heard her, then saw a slim shadow scramble by only two yards away. Hershey came to her feet, then threw herself into the dark. Ilsa cried out, twisted, and swung a heavy wrench at Hershey's head. Hershey drew back, winced as the wrench caught her shoulder, sending a numbing pain down the length of her arm.

Ilsa laughed. "Judge bitch! Keep away from me!"

"I wouldn't get near you on a bet," Hershey told her, "but duty calls, friend!"

Hershey feinted to the left. Ilsa swung her weapon again. Hershey jerked aside, balled her fist and hit Ilsa solidly in the belly.

Ilsa gasped, stumbled, reached out, and caught herself. Hershey caught the beginning of a smile on the woman's face, tried to pull herself away, knew there wasn't any time.

" 'Bye, honey," Ilsa said. She kicked out hard, a vicious blow with plenty of power behind it.

Hershey nearly went under. She felt something break,

fell back. She turned on her heels and saw the incubator coming, covered her face with her hands.

Crystal shattered, raining on her back in a rush of bilious fluid. The thing flopped out, slick as a fish, its head lying inches from Hershey's. Hershey stared, felt the hairs creep up the back of her neck. The thing made a strangled noise in its throat, tried to pull itself erect on boneless flipper arms. It came at Hershey on its wet, bare muscle, pulsing veins clinging to bare bone. It looked up at Hershey. A bubble came out of its mouth. It sighed once, dropped with a sickening sound.

Hershey got to her feet, felt the sharp bite of pain on her ribs. She looked around for Ilsa. Ilsa was gone. Black smoke was creeping across the floor. Hershey was sure she couldn't go back the way she'd come. And there was nothing but dead and smelly mutants up ahead.

Damn it, there is absolutely nothing about this in the Regs, not even anything close.

FORTY-TWO

*T*he flames licked at the heart of the pods, sending shadows leaping against the far walls. Dredd wrapped a shred of his shirt around his nose and mouth, but the smoke was too thick; nothing short of getting the hell out of there would help.

He couldn't see Rico at all. The forest of incubators had turned into the center of Hell. Fire shattered the crystal tubes, mutants writhed and twisted in pain, caught in the terrible moment of horror between birth and fiery death. Dredd turned away. He didn't need any more of this. The image was etched forever in his mind.

Rico caught him, his mind drifting for a second, his thoughts where a Judge's thoughts had no right to be. The manual made it clear: *Daydreaming* is spelled D-E-A-D.

Rico hit him with a broken steel bar. The blow caught him just below the knee. Dredd went down. Rico raised his weapon for the final, killing blow. Dredd rolled, caught Rico's leg with one hand, jerked him off his feet. Rico laughed, kicked him in the head. Dredd shook off the pain, grabbed Rico and held on. Rico grunted, tore his way free and pounded Dredd in the face. Dredd took the punishing blows, felt his mouth fill with blood. Dredd kicked him in the crotch. Rico took the blow on his thigh, pushed Dredd away, backed off. Dredd was sure Rico had fractured his leg. He watched Rico scramble along the floor, grab his Lawgiver.

"Shit," Dredd said.

Rico laughed, gave the weapon a loud command. "Grenade!"

"All lethal rounds exhausted . . . Select . . ."

"Standard fire!"

"All lethal rounds exhausted . . . Select . . ."

"Smoke bomb, damn you!"

Dredd saw the muzzle flash, saw the round coming at him in a blur. It sizzled, then blossomed into a ball of liquid fire.

Rico howled. "Central, turn off the overhead lighting —now!"

The room went dark. Flames lit the curved walls of the room. Dredd struggled to his feet, fighting the heat that tried to gnaw through his chest. He turned on his back, gagged on the oily black smoke.

"Central," he yelled, "turn on the damn lights!"

"Request denied. You are an escaped convict, Joseph Dredd. Surrender to authorities at once."

Dredd swore, tore at his armor, finally ripped it free and tossed it across the room. Another pod exploded, sending mutant parts high into the air. Something fell close by. It had a half-sized head. The head looked just like his own.

"Central . . . Central, look, I'll give myself up, okay? I'll surrender to Chief Justice Rico . . . Locate, please."

"Chief Justice Rico has entered Lift Nine-Nine-Oh . . . through the A door to your right."

Dredd pulled himself up. Lift? What lift? It had to be the other way in, the real way to the Janus lab.

Dredd tried to find his Remington. The heat drove him back. The A door took him down a long and narrow corridor. It finally came to an end at a metal door. An ordinary button. A glowing arrow pointing up.

Dredd punched the button. The door slid back, shut again quickly, locking him in. He could feel the lift moving fast, rushing him from the depths. Where? Where did the thing go? It didn't much matter. It was here, or stay down there.

He smelled Rico. Smelled his sweat. On the floor, smeared on the wall, Rico's blood. He thought about Ferguson, dead back there. He'd done his part and then some. More than anyone could ask. Hershey . . . she had to be all right. He should have stayed, found her, but there was nothing left down there . . . nothing but the dead.

The door slid open. Dredd sucked in fresh air. Lightning flashed in the distance, crackling through the towers of Mega-City. Rain beat down upon his head. Soot ran down and stung his eyes.

Rico stood just beyond him. His face was red with blood.

"Waiting for you, brother. Thought you'd never come."

"I'm here," Dredd said.

Rico shook his head. He aimed the Lawgiver at Dredd's chest. Thunder rolled through the blackened skies. Dredd guessed they were fifty, sixty stories high, the roof of Heavenly Haven, above the streets of Red Quad, where it had all begun.

"This is how you repay me, brother, for telling you the truth? How can you go against me, Joseph? I'm the only person in the world, in your *life,* who never lied to you."

"You broke the Law. I did what I had to do—"

"Oh, no, brother . . ." Rico's terrible grin twisted his features. "No, we won't go through *that* business again. You will not limp away telling me about the *Law!"*

Rico closed his eyes, opened them again. Rain pelted

off his face. He raised the Lawgiver, let its muzzle rest on Dredd's head.

"Joseph Dredd, do you stand ready to answer for your crimes?"

"Rico—"

"Dredd!" Rico shook his weapon in Dredd's face. "I hereby judge you, Joseph Dredd. To the charge of betraying your best friend . . . *Guilty.* To the charge of betraying your own flesh . . . *Guilty.* And finally, to the charge of being human, when we could have been . . . *gods! Guilty!"*

Rico's eyes went wide. "The sentence is . . . *death!"*
Rico squeezed the trigger.
Click.
"All lethal rounds exhausted . . . Select . . ."
"No!"

Dredd let out a breath. Rico had forgotten. The madness had overwhelmed him, clouded his reason, shattered his mind like the crystal columns below.

"Damn you, fire!" Rico's hands shook. He stared at the Lawgiver, as if the weapon, too, had betrayed him.

"All lethal rounds exhausted . . . Select . . ."
"Fire—FIRE!"

Dredd moved. His right hand struck out, a short sweep to Rico's jaw. He forced the fingers of his left hand over the weapon's grip, clamping down on Rico's hand.

Rico looked at him. "Joseph . . . ?"

"DNA accepted," the gun-voice whirred. *"Select . . ."*
"Signal flare!" said Dredd.

Dredd fought against Rico's grip, wrenched the weapon up, away from them both. The night turned red. The flare singed Rico's face and rocketed into the night.

Rico cried out, stumbling blindly away from Dredd. One foot found the edge of the roof, the other stepped into empty space.

"Rico!"

Rico flailed his arms, fell away. Dredd lunged for him,

caught him by the wrist. Rico hung there, blinked up at Dredd with blind eyes.

"You saved me, Joseph? Why did you do that?"

The rain whipped down in a fury, the cold drops hard as stones.

"I'll get you out of here. Hang on. You don't have to die, Rico."

Rico smiled. "All right, Joseph. I won't."

He brought his free hand up quickly, grabbed Dredd's wrist and forced his hand free.

"Life sentence, Joseph. Works fine for me."

Rico slid free.

"No!"

Dredd watched him turn slowly, his arms spread wide, watched him grow smaller, disappear in the dark veil of rain. His face was still there.

His face. My face . . .

He knew he was alone once more . . . hollow, nothing inside. Rico had taken it all away once, now he had taken it again.

Dredd was aware of the presence, the feeling of another person near. He looked up, saw Ilsa Hayden, the rain-soaked dress clinging to her slender form, the dark hair plastered against her cheeks. She held the Remington an inch from his head, showed him a gentle smile, drew her lips together, let them part like a lover's tender kiss.

Ilsa's head disappeared. A red mist hung in the air for a moment, then swept away in the driving rain. Ilsa's body folded, slid to the edge of the roof, and followed Rico down.

Dredd turned. Hershey stood in the lift, a Lawgiver clutched in her hand. Behind her, Fergie sagged against the wall. His face was pale. A strip of Hershey's uniform was wrapped tightly around his chest.

Dredd looked at Hershey. He shook his head at Fergie.

"You're alive," Dredd said simply.

"What did you think I'd do, *die* or something? Right when you and me were just getting to be good friends?"

"We are not friends, Ferguson. We know each other, we . . . Okay, we're *acquaintances.* I'll go as far as that."

"Right. Close enough. How about that—other stuff?"

"I said it once. Don't ask me again."

"Honestly, Dredd . . ." Hershey said.

"All right. I'm dropping all charges. Do whatever you want. You're free."

Fergie laughed. Laughing hurt, but what the hell?

"I knew that," he said. "What are friends for?"

FORTY-THREE

They were waiting in the street.

Hundreds of them—Street Judges, Cadets, Judge Hunters. Dredd couldn't guess where they'd come from, how they'd gotten the news so quickly.

The street was jammed with Lawmasters, blue, white, and green lights flashing into the night. The storm had moved off to the south, leaving the air clean and clear. Dredd walked out of the doorway and into the street. Hershey stood beside him, Fergie held up between them. Mediks hurried over to take him, easing him gently to a stretcher. He had passed out in the lift, but there was still a smile on his face.

An okay smile, Dredd thought. *The guy was maybe all right, maybe just a*—He caught himself, tried to think about anything else.

The two Judge Hunters walked toward him, stiff, proud, their faces devoid of any emotion at all.

Dredd drew in a breath.

"Easy," Hershey said.

The two Hunters parted. A third man stepped between them. He was taller than the other two, a dark-haired man in his forties. Dredd recognized him at once. He wore the white braid of Chief Judge Hunter across his chest.

The man stopped in front of Dredd. "I'm Judge Lackard." He nodded curtly at Hershey. "You're Joseph Dredd . . . ?"

"Yes, sir. Am I under arrest or what?"

Lackard looked at him a long moment. "That won't be necessary. We . . . Central broadcast the Janus plans in the clear. After Griffin's death. Everyone knows what happened in there. We, ah, owe you a debt of gratitude, Judge Dredd."

Not Joseph Dredd this time. Judge Dredd . . .

Dredd looked out at the crowd, the men and women he respected, the Law, the only life he knew.

"We have to reorganize the Council," Lackard said. "We'd like you to consider the position of Chief Justice."

"Thank you. I'm honored." Dredd nodded to his right. "I recommend Judge Hershey, sir."

The Judge Hunter nodded. "Would you consider it, Judge Hershey?"

Hershey looked astonished. "I—are you sure?"

"Don't be dumb, Hershey," Dredd said. "It's a good career move."

"Let me think about it, sir," Hershey said.

Dredd looked pained. "Don't think, Hershey. *Do* it. Haven't I taught you anything?"

Dredd turned and walked away. He spotted a Lawmaster standing ready and headed for it. Hershey followed him, stepped in his path.

"That's it, huh? A near-death experience and no good-bye."

"Hershey."

"What?"

"Good-bye."

Hershey grinned. "You're hopeless, Dredd. Totally hopeless." She touched the back of his neck, drew him close and kissed him full on the mouth, before he could pull away.

"That's a Code Two-One-Two," Dredd said. "Illegal Physical Contact with a Judge."

"No. That's a One-Three-Seven. *You,* impersonating a groon, Dredd. You're *human.* You don't have to fake it, friend."

Dredd threw his leg over the saddle of the Lawmaster. He looked at Hershey and grinned. "Typical behavior, Hershey. I knew you'd say that."

"Yeah? You think you know everything, Dredd. You don't. There's a hell of a lot of stuff you don't know."

Dredd thought about that. Decided she was right. He gripped the control bar of the Lawmaster, let the engine whine up to a roar, a thunder of raw power that trembled off the walls of Red Quad, and drowned every sound in Dredd's world . . .

In Judge Hershey's second year as Chief Justice, the Lady Liberty—or Statue of Liberty as it was known in the Way Back When—was ordered completely restored, and placed in a prominent position in the plaza across from the Hall of Justice.

While the Council felt this statue did not entirely reflect Mega-City's current standards of Justice, it was the majority opinion—under the leadership of Chief Justice Hershey—that the presence of the Lady Liberty underscored the need for reforms in several areas of criminal and civil law.

—History of the Mega-Cities
James Olmeyer, III
Chapter XLI: "The
Hershey Years"
2191

Alcatraz. The prison fortress off the coast of San Francisco. No man had gotten out alive before his time was up, until a 20-year-old petty thief named Willie Moore broke out.

Recaptured, then thrown into a pitch-black hellhole for three agonizing years, Willie is driven to near-madness—and finally to a brutal killing. Now, up on first-degree murder charges, he must wrestle with his nightmares and forge an alliance with Henry Davidson, the embattled lawyer who will risk losing his career and the woman he loves in a desperate bid to save Willie from the gas chamber.

Together, Willie and Henry will dare the most impossible act of all: get Willie off on a savage crime that the system drove him to commit—and put Alcatraz itself on trial.

MURDER IN THE FIRST

DAN GORDON

NOW A MAJOR MOTION PICTURE STARRING CHRISTIAN SLATER, KEVIN BACON, AND GARY OLDMAN

MURDER IN THE FIRST
Dan Gordon
_____ 95532-4 $4.99 U.S./$5.99 CAN.

Publishers Book and Audio Mailing Service
P.O. Box 120159, Staten Island, NY 10312-0004
Please send me the book(s) I have checked above. I am enclosing $ _____ (please add $1.50 for the first book, and $.50 for each additional book to cover postage and handling. Send check or money order only—no CODs) or charge my VISA, MASTERCARD, DISCOVER or AMERICAN EXPRESS card.

Card number _____

Expiration date _____ Signature _____

Name _____

Address _____

City _____ State/Zip_____

Please allow six weeks for delivery. Prices subject to change without notice. Payment in U.S. funds only. New York residents add applicable sales tax.

FIRST 3/95